Books by Robert Vaughan

HAWKE: DANCE WITH THE DEMON
HAWKE: RIDE WITH THE DEVIL

ROBERT VAUGHAN

HAWKE
RIDE
WITH THE
DEVIL

HarperTorch
An Imprint of HarperCollinsPublishers

❦

HARPERTORCH
An Imprint of HarperCollins*Publishers*
10 East 53rd Street
New York, New York 10022-5299

Copyright © 2004 by Robert Vaughan
ISBN: 0-06-072577-X

First HarperTorch paperback printing: November 2004

HarperCollins®, HarperTorch™, and ❦™ are trademarks of Harper-Collins Publishers Inc.

Printed in the United States of America

Visit HarperTorch on the World Wide Web at www.harpercollins.com

10 9 8 7 6 5 4 3 2 1

This book is dedicated to
James and Cille Cornett

HAWKE
RIDE
WITH THE
DEVIL

Prologue

~~~~~~~~~~

September 21, 1863

THE CONSTANT BOMBARDMENT OF THE UNION Army's heavy mortars prevented the exhausted men from getting any sleep during the night. The noise was continuous, from the solid thump of the mortars being fired to the scream of shells in flight to the crash of bombs bursting just overhead, bathing the area in a flash of light and sending out whistling shards of hot, jagged metal to kill and maim.

It was easy to follow the deadly transit of the missiles because of the sputtering red sparks that emanated from the fuses. The one-hundred-pound bombs described a high arc through the cold black sky before slamming down to explode among the weary Confederate soldiers.

The bombardment continued without letup until the eastern sky grew gray. Only with the coming of dawn did the bombardment end.

Then, as day broke, a low-lying haze rose over the open field that separated the Confederate position from the breastworks the Union soldiers had thrown up two nights earlier. The haze was partly due to a fog that the early morning sun coaxed from the frosted ground, as well as the gun smoke that continued to hover over the field where a two-day battle had taken place on the Chickamauga.

As the sun grew higher, the ground fog burned away and the smoke gradually began to dissipate. When the darkness, fog, and smoke had lifted, the horror of the battle was clearly revealed. The meadow between where Sergeant Mason Hawke was standing and the Yankee breastworks at the edge of the woods some half mile distant was covered with bodies. They were the easily identifiable blue uniforms of the Union soldiers, the natty gray of the Virginians, the Georgians' butternut, and finally the mixed bag of clothing worn by the Western Confederate soldiers. In addition to the dead and dying, there were hundreds of vultures, some circling overhead, others already on the ground, attending to their gruesome work.

Though the final numbers weren't in, the casualty estimates were running as high as six thousand killed and 25,000 wounded.

On this, the third morning, many of the wounded were still on the battlefield, having spent a long, cold night lying among the dead. With the dawn, these poor souls could be seen feebly waving their arms—those who could move—in an effort to signal their comrades to come for them. The result, when one looked over the battlefield, was an almost rhythmic movement, as wheat in the wind.

There was a sound as well; not the crash and roar of battle, but a low moan, often punctuated with sharp cries of pain and the plaintive cries for water.

On this day of the autumnal equinox, the sun would rise and set at exactly six o'clock. But it was nearly nine o'clock before everyone realized that the Union Army had abandoned the field, and not until then did full-scale rescue operations get underway. Hundreds of Confederate soldiers moved through the carnage, conducting triage in the field and putting on their stretchers only those they thought might benefit from medical attention.

Sergeant Mason Hawke was one of the soldiers recovering the wounded, and as he moved through the carnage, he saw one of his boyhood acquaintances. The young man's abdomen was red-brown from encrusted blood. At first Mason thought he was dead, but he saw a small movement, stopped and knelt beside his old friend.

"That one's dead, Sergeant Hawke, we'd best leave him be for now," one of the stretcher bearers said.

"He's not dead. I saw him move."

"Well if he ain't dead yet, he soon will be. Let's find someone in better shape."

"Take this one," Hawke said.

"Sarge, we're supposed to take only those—"

"I said take this one!" Hawke ordered sternly.

"All right, Sarge, if you say so. But if he's dead by the time we get him back to the aid station, you're goin' to have to explain to the cap'n why we got him."

Hawke watched them pick the man up and put him on the stretcher. His friend opened his eyes then and, looking up, saw him.

"I'll be damned," he said. "It would be you, wouldn't it?"

"You're going to be fine," Hawke said, but his words were unheard because the wounded soldier, having forced himself to stay awake throughout the long night, was by then unconscious.

Hawke watched as the stretcher bearers carried his boyhood friend back to the aid station, then he turned back to look out over the valley of the dead.

He closed his eyes. Only three years ago he had been in Europe, visiting such glamorous locations as London, Paris,

Rome, Vienna, and Berlin. That a man could experience such a contrast between that and this in so short a time seemed inconceivable.

He didn't know how many more battles he would have to face or how many more men he would have to kill before it all ended. He did know, however, that he could never go back to the genteel life that had taken him on the grand tour of Europe. That Mason Hawke now lay with the dead, not only here at Chickamauga, but at battlefields such as Antietam, Fredricksburg, and Gettysburg.

The music that he once offered to the world was now buried deep within his soul.

Chapter 1

Several years later

"HAWKE!"

The word was more of an angry bark than a name. It rolled off the speaker's lips like an obscenity.

"That is who you are, ain't it? You're the one they call Mason Hawke?"

The tall, slender man standing at the bar looked into the mirror. The big man who had addressed him had a matted beard and wore a shirt that looked as if it hadn't been changed in a month or so. His unkempt appearance contrasted sharply with Hawke's own clean-shaven countenance.

Hawke wore a white ruffled shirt poked down into fawn-colored trousers, a blue jacket, and a crimson cravat. His mode of dress set him apart from most of the others he encountered in his wanderings, and in fact Hawke made a conscious effort to dress well and to keep himself clean and well-groomed. It was his last link to a world he had abandoned so long ago.

"Yeah," the man said. "That's who you are, all right. I was told to look for the fanciest dressed son of a bitch in the saloon, and there you are, standing there like a whorehouse dandy."

With the man's challenging words, nearly everyone else in the saloon started moving, to get out of the way of whatever was about to occur. An intense poker game was left in progress, with the cards facedown in front of the players, the stack of money undisturbed in the middle of the table. The bottles and glasses were taken from all the occupied tables, and now men and a few women stood in rows along the front and back walls of the saloon, drinking beer and whiskey while intently watching the deadly theater unfolding before them.

But Hawke noticed that not everyone had joined those who rushed to get out of harm's way. Two men, as unkempt as the one who had accosted him, remained at opposite ends of the bar. They stood drinking their whiskeys while maintaining a studied indifference to what was going on. That assumed disinterest alerted Hawke. Before he turned around, he studied each of them in the mirror and saw that the two were not only armed, but that the pistols were loose in their holsters and kicked out for quick and easy access.

"Are you goin' to turn around and face me like a man?" Hawke's challenger called. "Or are you going to stand there like the coward you are, with your back to me?"

Slowly and deliberately, Hawke finished his drink, put his glass on the bar, then turned.

"Evidently, my friend, you have a burr under your saddle," he said easily.

"You killed my brother," the big man said angrily.

"Did I?" Hawke replied. "Well, if I did, he probably needed killing."

"You don't even know who I'm talking about, do you?"

"I'm afraid not. Who are you?" Hawke asked.

"My name is Purvis Tucker. That name mean anything to you?"

Hawke nodded. "Yes. I imagine you would be talking about Asa Tucker."

Three months earlier, Hawke had shot and killed Asa Tucker. It had happened unexpectedly. He'd been working in a saloon in Plano at the time and was taking the day's cash receipts to the bank for deposit. Tucker, who had plans to steal the money, was waiting for him in an alley. When Hawke approached the bank, Tucker stepped out into the street, already shooting. Hawke had no choice but to shoot back. Asa missed; Hawke didn't.

"I reckon you know why I'm here now," Tucker said, his voice a guttural growl.

"Let me see," Hawke said as he faced the man. A cold smile spread across his face. "My guess would be that you want to visit your brother. Well, I'll be glad to make the arrangements for you."

The anger in Tucker's face was replaced by a look of confusion. "What? What are you talking about, go visit my brother?"

"Why, I'm talking about sending you to hell too, of course," Hawke replied easily. "You and these two ugly bastards standing at either end of the bar," he added.

"Billy, he knows!" one of the men shouted. Stepping away from the bar, his hand dipped toward his pistol.

Hawke fired three times, his shots coming in such rapid succession that it was almost like one sustained roar. He took down the one who was going for his gun first, then the man at the other end of the bar.

Tucker, not ready to make his play yet, was caught by surprise when the fight was joined. Forced by events, he had just cleared his holster and was bringing his gun to bear when Hawke turned and fired. The heavy bullet from Hawke's .44 sent Tucker backward. He fell onto the poker table, breaking through it and scattering cards and money.

A quarter rolled halfway across the floor, spun a few times, then fell. Gun smoke drifted through the room—the smoke of three discharges from a single gun, because Hawke was the only one who had managed to get off a shot. With the room now silent, Hawke checked out the three men who had braced him.

The one who drew first was in an odd, kneeling position, one of his legs hung up in the brass railing at the foot of the bar. He was slumped forward, his cocked but unfired gun still in his hand.

The man at the other end of the bar—the one called Billy—was belly down, his head submerged in the brown liquid of the spittoon. His gun was lying on the floor beside his outstretched hand. The hammer hadn't even been pulled back.

Tucker was on his back between the two halves of the broken table, his open eyes already glazing over. The playing cards were scattered all around him, and one of them, the ace of spades, was faceup on his chest, just under the dark red bullet hole in his heart.

Before putting his pistol away, Hawke made a quick survey of the rest of the saloon to determine if anyone else might pose a threat.

Those who had moved to either side of the room were still there, looking on in a combination of shock and morbid curiosity. Upstairs, on the balcony of the second floor that overlooked the main salon, a couple of the whores and their customers had come to the railing to see what was going on. One of the whores had put on a dressing gown, but the other was standing there naked. It wasn't until someone pointed her out that the others in the saloon noticed her.

"Damn, Cindy Lou! Is that how you come to a shooting?" someone shouted, and Cindy Lou, perhaps just noticing that she was naked, let out a little yelp of alarm and turned to hurry back to her room, chased by the laughter of those below.

The sheriff and a deputy chose that precise moment to come into the saloon. The two lawmen were greeted with the sight of three dead men on the floor, while everyone in the saloon was laughing uproariously.

"What the hell! Three men get shot and you folks think it's funny?" the sheriff asked.

"You don't understand, Sheriff," the bartender replied. "It was Cindy Lou, she was naked."

The sheriff looked at the bartender as if he and everyone else in the room had gone insane.

"Ah, you had to be here," the bartender said with a dismissive wave of his hand.

"Has anyone checked? Are all three dead?" the sheriff asked. With his foot, he lifted Billy's head out of the spittoon, then rolled him over. Billy's face was covered with juice and pieces of expectorated tobacco.

By now Hawke had returned his pistol to his holster and had his back to the bar, leaning against it and resting on his elbows.

"They're dead," he said.

"Did you do this, Mr. Hawke?" the sheriff asked.

"Yes," Hawke replied.

"Are you telling me you shot all three of 'em?"

"Yes."

"What the hell did you shoot 'em for?"

"Because they were trying to shoot me."

The sheriff went around to each of the dead men and, picking up their guns, sniffed the barrels.

"It don't appear to me that any of these guns was fired," he said.

"They wasn't," the bartender said.

The sheriff looked up at Hawke. "None of these guns was fired, but you say they was trying to shoot you?"

"He's tellin' you like it is, Sheriff. He didn't have no choice," the bartender explained. "These here men drew on him first."

"That's right, Sheriff!" at least half a dozen others

shouted in support of the bartender's testimony. "They drew on him first, then he shot 'em. Damndest thing I ever seen."

The sheriff stroked his chin for a moment, then nodded.

"Mr. Hawke, you know, don't you, that I'm goin' to have to take you in for a hearing?" he asked. "It's for your own good. If what these folks are sayin' is true, the judge will rule that there's no charges and all this will be behind you."

"All right," Hawke said.

The sheriff looked at him for a moment. "From the way you handled these three, I don't reckon I can take your gun from you unless you're willin' to give it to me. But I wish you would."

Using his thumb and forefinger, Hawke pulled his pistol from his holster and handed it to the sheriff.

"When will we have this hearing?" Hawke asked.

"Not until tomorrow morning."

"Do I have to stay in jail tonight?"

"It would be better if you did."

"Sheriff, can I say something?" the bartender asked.

"Charley, I've known you for a long time," the sheriff replied. "And I've never known you not to say whatever it is that you have on your mind. So go ahead. What is it?"

"Well, you heard everyone say that it wasn't Mr. Hawke's fault. Can't you just release him to me? We've got a big crowd in here tonight and I'll be needin' him to play the piano. Fact is, after a shootin' like this, a little piano music might just calm things down."

The sheriff stroked his chin for a moment, then nodded and handed the pistol back to Hawke. "All right," he said. "But I expect you to be down at the courthouse by eight o'clock in the morning."

"I'll be there," Hawke said, slipping the pistol back into his holster. He looked over at the bartender. "Thanks, Charley."

"You want to thank me, get back to work," Charley said. He pointed to the piano in the back of the room. "Play something."

Two days later, in another part of Texas, more than half the citizens of Salcedo had come out to the cottonwood tree just east of town to watch the hanging. They stood around in morbid curiosity as Titus Culpepper saw to the final details.

"Has anybody got the execution order?" Culpepper asked.

"We don't need no execution order," someone said. "Just hang the son of a bitch."

"This is not a lynching, Vox," Culpepper said, speaking harshly. "This is a legal, court-ordered execution, and I plan to see that it is not only carried out, but carried out correctly. Now, does anyone have the execution order?"

"I've got it right here, Colonel," one of the other deputies said, riding over to hand a sheet of paper to Culpepper.

"Thank you, Deputy Bates," Culpepper said as he took the paper from him.

Culpepper, Vox, Bates, and all of the other deputies were mounted. So was the condemned man, who was now sitting on his horse with his hands tied behind his back.

By Culpepper's order, no one else from the town could be mounted, so more than one hundred people had walked the half mile to the hanging tree to watch.

Clearing his throat, Culpepper began reading from the judge's order for execution.

" 'Edward Delaney, having been found guilty of horse stealing and other crimes, this court sentences you to be hanged by the neck until you are dead.' "

The rope had already·been thrown over a convenient horizontal branch of the tree, and now the noose hung but inches from Delaney's head.

"Do you have any last words?" Culpepper asked.

Delaney stared at Culpepper.

"I don't have nothin' to say to these folks," he said. "I forgive them, because they are innocent people who don't know what they are doin'."

"Well, that's might righteous of you, forgiving us like that," Culpepper said sarcastically.

"I said I forgive them, not you. To you, I do have something to say."

"Well, I expect you better say what you've got to say, then," Culpepper said as he placed the noose around Delaney's neck. "Because you've got about thirty seconds left to live."

"I know what you done durin' the war, Culpepper. I didn't find out until it was too late to do anything about it, but I know it was you. And I'll be waiting for you in hell."

"Really?" Culpepper said. He chuckled. "Well, when you get there, kick the devil in the ass for me, will you?"

Without waiting for a reply, Culpepper slapped the rump of Delaney's mount.

The horse bolted forward and the rope tightened, pulling Delaney from the saddle. The tree limb sagged a bit under Delaney's weight, but the fall did not break his neck. Delaney was slowly strangling, and he kicked his legs and made gagging sounds as he swung back and forth, describing a wide arc. His eyes were open and bulging, his tongue ran out, and his face turned dark red, then blue.

Many of the people in the crowd, unable to look at his suffering, turned their faces away. A few, shocked by the unexpected dreadfulness of what they were watching, began to throw up. The mounted deputies, though, to a man, watched with barely concealed glee. Finally Delaney's struggles stopped and he grew still, save for the continuing but now gentle pendulum swing of his body.

By the time the townspeople started back into town, Delaney's body was hanging perfectly still.

Chapter 2

SMALL BROWN PUFFS HUNG IN THE AIR JUST BE-
hind the rider as the horse's hooves stirred up dust from the
low, sun-baked grass. From the perspective of an eagle circling overhead, the solitary rider was moving slowly but in-
exorably across a long, unbroken plain.

The morning sun was to his back.

Mason Hawke was tired. It was a saddle-sore, sleeping-
on-the-ground, bone-deep, butt-weary kind of tired, brought
on by dusty trails, people he couldn't remember, and towns
he wanted to forget.

Like Puxico.

It had been five days since his hearing in Puxico. After
listening to four witnesses attest to Hawke's innocence, and
with a dozen more ready to testify to the same thing, the
judge released Mason Hawke without charges. Hawke had
not been asked to leave town, but decided, on his own, that it
would be better for him to move on.

Charley had asked him to come back to work for him,
playing the piano, but Hawke turned him down. People who
played the piano in saloons tended to fade into the background, like a potted plant or a painting on the wall. Hawke

liked that anonymity, but after the incident with Tucker and the two men who turned out to be his cousins, continued anonymity in the town of Puxico was impossible.

Hawke did not hunt for trouble, but trouble had a way of finding him. One incident seemed so often to lead to another, and another, becoming a chain of events that would inevitably draw him into yet one more confrontation. Whenever that happened, Hawke would leave that town and press on to see what was around the bend, over the next hill, or just beyond the horizon.

Now, ahead of him, like irregular clumps in the land, a handful of ripsawed, windblown, sun-dried buildings rose from the prairie. The little town offered Hawke the prospect of sleeping in a real bed for the night and eating food that wasn't camp-cooked. He could have something to drink besides alkali water and trail coffee. Hawke thought that he might even find a woman he could enjoy having a conversation with.

He stood in the stirrups for a moment, just to stretch away his saddle ache, then urged his horse on. That was when he saw the vultures.

They were circling too warily, too cautiously, for it to be a small animal. Only one thing could cause this kind of display.

Hawke had seen them gather like this many times before, over the battlefields of Antietam, Gettysburg, and Chickamauga. He'd seen them since the war as well, during his wanderings through the West. Slapping his legs against the side of his horse, he hurried it on for the next mile until he saw what was attracting the carrion's attention. Hanging from the branch of a cottonwood tree was the body of a man, twisting slowly at the end of the rope. A sign was pinned to his chest.

THIS IS WHAT HAPPENS TO
OUTLAWS IN SALCEDO.
DRIFTER, MOVE ON. WE DON'T WANT YOU IN

OUR TOWN.
LEAVE THIS BODY HANGING.

Hawke pulled the paper off the dead man's chest. It was signed, "Salcedo Regulators Brigade."

Looking back up at the body, Hawke stared at it for a long moment. He had seen many bodies in his time; stabbed, shot, ripped apart by cannon fire, even some who had burned to death. People sometimes talked about dying peacefully, but Hawke had seen little of that.

There were few deaths more gruesome than hanging, and the expression of terror and pain remaining in the face of the corpse was evidence of that. The victim's eyes were open and bulging, his lips were pursed, his tongue protruding, his neck stretched, and his head twisted to one side. He was wearing a shirt without a collar, frayed cuffs, and missing a button.

"Well, I'll tell you what, friend," Hawke said aloud. "I don't give a damn what the sign says, I don't intend to let you hang here."

Pulling his knife, Hawke stood in his stirrups, then reached up to cut through the rope just above the man's neck. As he cut the man free, he maneuvered the body so it fell across the front saddle of his horse. Rigor mortis had already set in, making it difficult to get him draped over the saddle, but he managed to do it.

A small, hand-painted sign on the outer edge of the town read:

SALCEDO
OBEY OUR LAWS

No railroad served the town, and its single street was dotted liberally with horse apples. The first building Hawke saw was the Roman Catholic church. It was large and substantial, constructed of earth-colored stucco with a red clay-tile roof.

He had no way of knowing it, but this church had occupied the same spot for nearly a hundred years before the town itself came into existence. The church anchored the east side of a street that ran some one hundred yards to the west, where the street was anchored by St. Paul's Episcopal Church, a white frame building with a red door, a green shake roof, and a towering steeple.

At either end of the street, as well as in the middle, planks were laid from one side to the other to allow people to cross when the street was filled with mud.

The buildings of the little town were as washed out and flyblown up close as they had been from some distance. The first structure Hawke rode by was a blacksmith's shop.

SARGE'S BLACKSMITH SHOP
IRONWORK DONE
TREE STUMPS BLASTED

It was at the east end of town, and a tall and muscular black man was bent over an anvil, the ringing of his hammer audible above all else.

From the blacksmith's, one side of the street contained a butcher shop, a general store, a bakery, six small houses, then a leather goods shop next door to an apothecary. A set of outside stairs climbed the left side of the drugstore to a small stoop that stuck out from the second floor. A painted hand on a sign, with a finger pointing up, read:

CHARLES URBAN, M.D.

The city marshal's office and jail was next to the apothecary, then came the bank, a hardware store, and several houses, before that side of the street ended with the Episcopal church at the other end of town.

On the north side of the street, proceeding from the blacksmith's, there was a gunsmith, a newspaper office—the *Salcedo Advocate*—a café called Dumplings, then several houses, followed by a seamstress shop, the Ranchers' Hotel, a stage depot, the Golden Calf saloon, several more houses, and a small one-room school.

Citizens of the town stopped when they saw the body draped across Hawke's saddle, then started following him. Staying on either side of the street, they gave him plenty of room but, out of curiosity, kept pace with him as he rode into the town.

"Hey, he's got Delaney," someone said.

"That's Ed Delaney," another said.

"Delaney!"

The hollow clopping sound of his horse's hooves echoed back from the buildings. More people came out of those same buildings, and the crowd began to grow large.

"Lookie there," he heard someone say. "The rope is still around Delaney's neck."

One of the crowd ventured much closer than the others, coming off the wooden sidewalk to step out into the street for a closer look at Delaney. Hawke stopped then and looked right at him.

"Where's the undertaker, mister?" he asked.

For a moment the man was as startled as if Delaney himself had spoken to him. He stared at Hawke.

"The undertaker?" Hawke asked again.

"Uh, that would be Gene Welch," the man replied, pointing. "His place is behind the hardware store, which is just up there, on the left. You can't miss him."

"Thanks."

Hawke continued to ride down the street until he reached the building the man had pointed out. The sign out front read:

SIKES' HARDWARE:
NAILS, LUMBER, TOOLS

Underneath was a smaller sign:

GENE WELCH, UNDERTAKER
IN BACK

Hawke didn't have to go around back, though. A man wearing a long black coat and a high silk hat was standing on the porch of the hardware store. Obviously, word had already reached him that someone was coming into town with a body.

"You'd be the undertaker? Hawke asked.

The man nodded, but said nothing.

"I have a job for you," Hawke said. He gave Delaney a little push, and the body fell off the horse. When it hit the ground, the crowd, now close to one hundred people, gasped in unison. Many jumped back, as if they expected the body to explode.

"Whoa, Delaney's getting' a little ripe," someone said, and a few others giggled nervously.

"Mister, did you cut that body down?" the undertaker asked.

"I did," Hawke said.

"We, uh, weren't supposed to cut it down."

"You didn't cut it down. I did," Hawke said. "Now, are you going to give him a decent burial, or do I have to bury him myself?"

"What's he to you, mister?" one of the men in the crowd asked. He had a shock of unruly hair, a red, pockmarked face, and buck teeth.

"He's a man that needs burying," Hawke said.

"You read the sign, didn't you? If you don't want to answer to the Salcedo Regulators Brigade, you'll take him back and put him where you found him," the bucktoothed man said.

"No need for that, Vox," another man in the crowd said. "I think the point has been made."

"All right, Colonel. If you say so," Vox replied.

"Mr. Welch," the one Vox had called colonel said. "You may bury Mr. Delaney now. I'll pay the expenses."

"Very good, Colonel, I'll take care of it," Welch replied. "Thank you."

Hawke was sure he had heard that voice before, and when the man appeared out of the crowd, he recognized him.

"Mason Hawke," the man said. "It's been a long time."

"Titus Culpepper," Hawke replied, nodding toward him. "Indeed it has been a long time."

"All right, folks," Culpepper called to the others. "The excitement is all over. You folks tend to your business now, and let Mr. Welch tend to his."

"Yes, sir, Colonel Culpepper, thank you," Welch said. He looked toward a couple of men in the front row of the crowd. "You men, help me get Delaney back to my embalming table."

"Hawke, come on down to the Golden Calf with me. Let me buy you a drink," Titus Culpepper offered.

"Don't mind if I do," Hawke replied.

The Golden Calf was unremarkable in every respect. Just inside the bat-wing doors, a dozen round tables occupied the wide-plank floor, each one surrounded by half a dozen chairs. They showed the scars, burn marks, and spill stains of an establishment that stayed busy, as evidenced by the fact that twenty or more customers were now occupying the tables or standing at the bar.

On one side of the room, a wood-burning stove, cold at the moment, was redolent with the smell of last winter's fires. And on the other side, from front to back, was a bar constructed of unpainted wood. It had a brass foot rail at the bottom and brass rings attached about every ten feet, from which hung hand towels for the customers. There was a mirror behind the bar, and in front of it, glass shelves containing bottles of liquor, their numbers doubled by the reflection. Above the mirror was a painting of a golden calf, the saloon's namesake. At the rear of the saloon was an upright piano, the cover pulled down over the keys.

"The beer isn't bad here," Culpepper said. "The whiskey is good only if you really need something stronger. It's green as grass and flavored with rusty nails," he added with a laugh.

Hawke laughed with him. "Listen, after several weeks of trail dust, a beer would be like the finest wine right now."

"As I recall, you did have a taste for fine wine. Your father had a pretty good wine cellar, I believe."

"The best in Georgia," Hawke said.

"Two beers, Paddy," Culpepper ordered.

"Yes, sir, Colonel, two beers coming up," the bartender said, and a moment later hurried over with two mugs, the amber liquid crowned by high-rising heads of foam.

"Mr. O'Neil, here, isn't just a bartender," Culpepper explained. "No sir, he's one of Salcedo's leading businessmen. He owns this place, don't you, Paddy?"

"Or it owns me," Paddy replied with a chuckle as he sat the glasses before the two men.

Culpepper blew off some of the foam. "Here's to you," he said, holding his mug out.

Hawke held his mug out as well, then took a swallow.

"So, Hawke, how long has it been?" Culpepper asked.

"I don't know. Chickamauga, perhaps?" Hawke replied, wiping some of the foam from his lip. "You were wounded at Chickamauga as I recall."

Culpepper nodded. "Yeah," he said. "I guess you could call it a wound." His voice sounded bitter.

"I lost track of you after that. What happened to you? Where did you go?"

"Once I got out of that butcher shop they called a hospital, I took my discharge and went west. That's when I joined up with Quantrill and Bloody Bill Anderson. They were the real fighters. If Jeff Davis had put one of them in command instead of Lee, the South would have won the war. I should have joined them a lot earlier."

"Yes, well, I'm glad you didn't leave before Gettysburg. As I recall, you saved my life there."

"I was just paying you back for what you did at Shiloh."

"I had to. You owed me two dollars," Hawke said.

Culpepper laughed. "Yeah, I did, didn't I? By the way, did I ever pay you?"

"Yes, in Confederate money."

Culpepper laughed again. "Well, I was just being patriotic. Hey, whatever happened to that girl you used to sniff around all the time? What was her name? Tamara Snellgrove? She was a pretty thing, as I recall."

The smile left Hawke's face and his features tightened. He took another swallow before he answered.

"She took a fever and died."

"That's a shame," Culpepper said. "You were . . . wait, as I recall, you were going to marry her, weren't you?"

"Yeah," Hawke said without elaboration.

"I'm sorry to hear about that. So, what are you doing out here? I figured you'd be back in Georgia, running Goldcrest. I mean, after all, it is the biggest plantation in the county."

"It was the biggest," Hawke said. "But no more. Taxes took it. After Pa and my brother were killed in the war, my ma just gave up living and died of heartbreak. It stood fallow for two years, piling up debts." He was quiet for a moment. "At least none of them lived long enough to see me lose land that had been in the family for over a hundred years."

"You can't take that too hard, Hawke. My family lost Trailbreak. A lot of county people lost everything," Culpepper said. "Hell, that's why I didn't even go back home. I haven't seen Georgia since I left for the war."

"You were smart. I shouldn't have gone back," Hawke said.

"So, you have become one of the wanderers, have you?" Culpepper asked. "One of the dispossessed. Well, join the crowd, my friend. Just join the crowd."

"You seem to have found your place. I notice it's 'Colonel Culpepper' here and 'Yes, sir' there. What are you, the mayor?"

"No, not the mayor. I'm just the head of the Salcedo Regulator Brigade."

"I figured it was something like that. That slab-toothed, pox-faced son of a bitch called you colonel. And you seemed to be calling the shots."

Culpepper laughed out loud and slapped the tabletop in good humor. "Slab-toothed, pox-faced son of a bitch," he said. "A rather good description of Rufus Vox, I must say."

"So, when did you make colonel? Last time I saw you, you were a sergeant."

"The Confederate army had its promotion schedule and I have mine," Culpepper said, smiling. "When I formed the Salcedo Regulators Brigade, I just appointed myself colonel."

"Well, why not?" Hawke answered. "It worked for Napoleon when he appointed himself Emperor. What exactly is this regulators' brigade, anyway?"

"Some might call us vigilantes," Culpepper said. "But I

prefer to think of us as a group of concerned citizens who are enforcing the law."

"What about the sheriff, or marshal? Wouldn't enforcing the law be his job?"

Hawke's position at the table afforded him a good view of the piano. There were cobwebs over the closed keylid, and that told him that the saloon had no regular piano player. He wondered how long it had been since the piano was last used.

"It would be the sheriff or marshal's job if we had a sheriff or a marshal. But we do not. The Dawson brothers killed our town marshal about a year ago. We hired two more marshals, but the Dawson brothers made things too hot for them as well, so they ran out on us."

"Who are the Dawson brothers?"

Culpepper chuckled. "Better you should ask who were the Dawson brothers. Frank and Earl Dawson were two of the lowest, no-count sons of bitches you ever saw in your life. They made Salcedo their headquarters while they robbed and murdered innocent citizens for miles around. But just because Salcedo was their headquarters didn't mean the town got a pass. No, sir, they ran roughshod over the citizens here too."

"You are talking about them in the past tense."

"That's because they are past tense. They, and six of their men, are lying buried in the town cemetery right now."

"From the tone of the conversation, may I assume that was the work of the Regulators?"

"You're damn right it was. It reached the point where we just decided we'd had enough. So I went before the town council and offered to lead a group of brave and dedicated men on a mission to rid our town of the Dawsons. That was how the Salcedo Regulators Brigade began."

"If the Dawsons are gone, don't you think you could hire a city marshal now? Why is the brigade still here?"

"We'll hire a new marshal in due time," Culpepper said. "But I don't like to leave any job half done. And we still have some work to do here. One example is Ed Delaney, the fella you cut down."

"What did Delaney do?"

"What didn't the son of a bitch do?" Culpepper replied. "Steal, murder, you name it. He was one of those men who couldn't settle down after the war. I'm sure you've seen them before, restless wretches. He wasn't quite as bad as the Dawsons, but believe me, he was well on his way."

"I'm curious as to why you left his body hanging."

"Look at it from our position, Hawke. We had just come through a period of having our town ruled by outlaws, and Delaney was hell-bent to take their place. We wanted to send a message to anyone else who might have ideas of taking over where the Dawsons left off, so I got permission from the court to leave the body hanging."

"From the court?"

"Of course from the court. Delaney was legally tried, convicted, and sentenced to hang." Culpepper chuckled. "Come on, you didn't think we lynched him, did you?"

"I gave it a passing thought," Hawke said. "It's sort of unusual to find someone who has been legally hanged dangling from a tree for two or three days."

"I reckon it is rather unusual at that. Like I said, things around here have been unusual for quite a while now. But we're working hard to put things right again."

"How many do you have in your brigade?"

"Calling it a brigade may be a little overblown. There are actually only nine of us, counting me," Culpepper said.

"But still, nine of you? For a town this small, I wouldn't think you would need anything close to that many."

"If the war taught me anything, Hawke, it taught me the value of force and power," Culpepper replied. "With this many of us, nobody dares to give us any trouble. As I said, our job isn't finished yet, but we are getting there. And I'm proud to say that people can walk the street at night without fear of being robbed or murdered."

Turning in his seat, Culpepper called over to the bar. "Paddy, are we better off now, or before we got rid of the Dawsons?"

"There's no question about it, Colonel Culpepper," Paddy replied. "Salcedo's been a lot more peaceful since you started the Regulators."

"Sounds like your good work is appreciated," Hawke said.

"Well, I'm real glad you see it that way, Hawke," Culpepper said. Finishing his beer, he stood and extended his hand. "It was good seeing you again, but if you'll excuse me, I have to go make out the roster for the watch tonight."

Shortly after Culpepper left, Paddy came over to the table to get his empty mug.

"Say, wait a minute," Hawke said. "I just realized that Titus didn't pay for the beer. Do you keep a tab on him? Or do I have to pay for him?"

"You don't have to pay," Paddy replied. "Nobody from the Regulators pays for their beer."

"Why not?"

"Call it a courtesy."

Hawke laughed. "Well, if he doesn't pay, then it wasn't all that hard for him to buy me a beer, was it?"

Paddy laughed with him. "No, I guess not."

Chapter 3

AFTER HE LEFT THE SALOON, COLONEL TITUS
Culpepper walked down the street to the office of the *Salcedo Advocate*, which billed itself as "the Voice of Salcedo."

Cyrus Green, the mayor of Salcedo, was also the editor
and publisher of the newspaper. He was a work in progress
as far as being a newspaperman was concerned, looking for
a voice that could create enough controversy to hold the interest of the reading public, while not being so contentious
that he lost readers.

When one of his articles had angered the Dawson brothers, they came into his newspaper office, beat him up, scattered his type, and turned over his press.

A battered Cyrus Green put his newspaper back together
again, just in time to praise the formation of the Salcedo
Regulators Brigade.

> Almost one hundred years ago our forefathers
> took action to throw off the yoke of British op-
> pression, and a new nation was born.
>
> Less than a decade ago, brave men of our
> own generation took up arms to redress griev-
> ous assaults by the North upon our southern

way of life, and though we lost the war, we preserved our dignity.

Now, with the formation of the Salcedo Regulators Brigade, the citizens of Salcedo have the opportunity to emulate our forefathers and brave
southern compatriots by ridding our town of the
villainous presence of Frank and Earl Dawson.

He knew that if the Dawsons were to take offense, there
was nothing they could do about it. They were too busy trying to escape the Salcedo Regulators Brigade.

In addition to publishing the newspaper, Cyrus did job
printing, which was what brought Titus Culpepper to the
newspaper office directly from his visit with Mason Hawke.

Cyrus had seen Culpepper walking up the street, so he
met him at the front counter with a printers' proof of the job
he was doing for him.

"Hello, Mayor," Culpepper said. "I was just wondering if
you have—"

"Right here," Cyrus answered, interrupting. "How does
this look to you, Colonel?" Cyrus held out a poster for
Culpepper's examination.

VOTE FOR

TITUS CULPEPPER

FOR CONGRESS

A FIGHTER FOR JUSTICE

The text, in black, was set inside two concentric boxes,
one red and one blue. The effect was a patriotic red, white,
and blue.

"It looks very good to me," Culpepper said. "You've done
a fine job, Mayor."

"Thanks. Oh, and if you would like, I could take a photograph of you and send it to Austin, where they've got a good woodcut artist. Then we could print the posters with your picture."

"No, this'll do fine, just fine," Culpepper said. He laughed. "Besides, if you put my picture on them, people might think they are wanted posters."

Cyrus laughed with him. "How many do you want, Colonel?"

"Print up enough to plaster the whole district with them," he said. He put a penny on the counter and picked up a newspaper. "Is this your latest issue?"

"Yes, sir, just took it off the press an hour ago," he said.

Culpepper nodded, put the paper under his arm, then left.

Cyrus watched Culpepper through the front window of his office. Culpepper stopped to talk to a sign painter who was working in front of what had been the marshal's office. And though the painter wasn't completely finished with the sign, there was enough of it to be read.

SALCEDO REGULATORS BRIGADE
HEADQUARTERS
COLONEL TITUS CULPEPPER, CMNDG

Cyrus Green had been a big supporter of the Regulators. He'd drummed up public support through his newspaper articles, and as mayor he introduced the ordinance to the town council that authorized the recognition and funding of the Regulators.

Like many others from the town, Cyrus Green knew war. But his personal war experiences had a unique perspective, and though he saw more action than anyone else in town, he had not been a soldier. During the war, he was a correspondent for the *Richmond Dispatch*, and in that capacity was present at several of the most important battles. He shared the dangers and the hardships of the common soldier while writing the stories that brought the war home to thousands of readers.

"I would like to commend your journalist, Cyrus Green," one reader wrote in a letter to the *Dispatch*. "His command of the language and use of words puts the reader on the battlefield with such intimacy that one can smell the powder and hear the roar of the guns. Bravo for his skills, and may he continue to provide us with his brilliant and insightful contributions."

After the war, when he was presented with the chance to buy a hand press from the widow of a newspaper publisher who had been killed in the fighting, Cyrus seized the opportunity to produce his own paper. Salcedo was the fourth town in which he had attempted to start a paper, and it was not until he got there that his dream began to show promise of success.

The fact that he had won the last mayoral election by an overwhelming margin was evidence of the degree of acceptance he had achieved since moving to the town.

At the Golden Calf saloon, Hawke had walked over to the piano and was now examining it. Pulling the bench out, he sat down and opened the cover, then wiped away the gathering of cobwebs. He moved his finger up the keyboard, hitting all the white and black keys in order. To his surprise, the piano was in amazingly good tune.

"Well, hell, mister, don't just sit there," one of the other saloon patrons said. "Either scratch your ass or play the piano, whichever one you're the best at."

The other patrons laughed.

For a long moment Hawke didn't move. As he sat there, the smoke, the smell of bodies and beer, the noise, the heat, and the stained walls all faded into the background. For him, the little saloon in a tiny, flyblown town in West Texas became the Place de l'Opera in Paris in 1861.

"You have set all Europe on its ear, Monsieur Hawke," Monsieur Garneau said. "You are the musical genius of the year."

"The audiences have been very gracious," Hawke replied as he buttoned his formal jacket.

On stage, the concert master raised a megaphone to his lips and made an announcement.

"Dames et messieurs, Place de l'Opera fièrement présents Monsieur Mason Hawke."

The audience erupted into thunderous applause, and Mason Hawke, the most sought after pianist of the season, strolled quickly out onto the stage. Flipping his tails out of the way, he sat down to the keyboard and began playing to the enraptured Parisian audience.

In the Golden Calf saloon of Salcedo, Texas, the patrons were amazed to hear the intricate weaving of chords, melody, and countermelody of Wolfgang Amadeus Mozart's Piano Concerto Number 12 in A major rather than the hesitant and frequent off-key renditions of some familiar cowboy tune.

As Hawke played, he was transported to another place and another time, totally oblivious to the effect he was having on the saloon and its patrons. They sat in stunned silence, listening. Passersby came in from the street and stood quietly, just to hear to the music. Even women, who would never come into the saloon, were drawn by the beautiful sounds coming from the keyboard of the old, scarred, upright piano.

Hawke played every movement, every bar, every note of the composition, holding the now large saloon crowd spellbound by the beauty of the music and the power of his playing. Finally, twelve minutes after starting the piece, he finished it in a crashing crescendo.

The audience cheered and applauded. Not until then did Hawke bring himself back from that distant, ephemeral paradise that such musical interludes allowed him to visit. No longer was he Mason Hawke, the *jeune pianiste brillant d'Europe*. He was, once again, Mason Hawke, the displaced wanderer, sitting at a scarred upright piano in a beer-soaked, smoke-filled saloon in a town that he had never heard of until recently.

Standing, he turned and acknowledged the cheers and applause of the crowd.

"Paddy, give this man a beer, on me!" one of the patrons said.

"Do you know what you are doing there, Doc? You're not one who's known for buyin' many drinks," someone said.

"I admit to a degree of parsimoniousness," Doc replied. "But who can put a price tag on what we just heard?"

The one the others called Doc was the same man who had invited Hawke to play.

"Urban is the name, my friend," Doc said. "I'm a doctor, so folks call me Doc. And who might you be?"

"Hawke," he said. "And I thank you for the drink." Hawke walked over to the bar, where Paddy gave him another beer.

"I don't suppose you would like a job playing the piano, would you, Mr. Hawke?" Paddy asked.

"I would love a job playing the piano," Hawke replied.

"Can't pay much. Two dollars a week. But you can put a bowl on the piano and keep all the tips you get. Also there's a room upstairs where you can stay, and you can eat free here, what food as we have."

"Sounds good to me," Hawke said.

"Only thing . . ." Paddy said.

Hawke smiled. He knew what was coming.

Paddy held his hand up and shook his finger admonishingly. "Don't play no more music like that."

"Why not?" Hawke asked. "Your customers seemed to like it."

"Yeah, that's just it," Paddy said. "They liked it too much. Perhaps you didn't take no notice, but there wasn't a one of them ordered a drink for the whole time you was playin'."

"I noticed it," Hawke admitted.

"Uh-huh. Well, if you're goin' to play piano for me, I expect you to play songs like 'Little Joe the Wrangler,' or 'Buffalo Gals,' or something like that."

"Whatever you say," Hawke said. "You're the boss. By the way, where do you suggest I board my horse?"

"Well, we got a livery just across the street, but he don't do much boardin'. He mostly takes care of the teams for the stage line and he rents horses, buckboards, and the like. If I was you, I'd try Sarge's Place," Paddy suggested.

"Sarge's Place?"

"The blacksmith shop down at the end of town."

"Yes, I saw it as I rode in," Hawke said.

"He does some boardin' at his stable out back," Paddy explained.

The anvil was ringing as Hawke approached the blacksmith shop. The smithy had a red-hot, iron wheel band gripped with a pair of tongs he held in his left hand. With the hammer in his right, he was beating the iron band into shape. Sparks were flying from the repeated hammer blows.

As Hawke dismounted, the blacksmith dipped the glowing band into a tub of water.

"Yes, sir, what can I do for you?" the smithy asked.

"Are you Sarge?"

"I just call my place that 'cause I was a farrier sergeant in the Ninth Cavalry," the smithy answered. His skin was relatively light for a black man; the color of creamed coffee. He wore a well-trimmed moustache. "My given name is Ken Wright."

"Well, Mr. Wright, I'd like to board my horse with you, if you don't mind."

"How long are you going to be here?"

"I don't know."

"Reason I ask is, it's cheaper if you board him by the week. I get ten cents a night, but fifty cents for a whole week."

"I'll board him by the week. Will you feed him for that?"

"Hay for free, but for another ten cents I'll give him oats twice a week."

"All right," Hawke said, handing the reins over, "give him the oats twice a week."

"You the one that brought in Mr. Delaney?" Ken asked.

"I am."

"I'll give your horse oats twice a week for no extra charge," he said.

"Really? I appreciate that. Was Delaney a friend?"

"We sparred some," Ken said.

"Sparred? What is that?"

"Mr. Delaney wanted to learn to box, so he come to me for lessons."

"You're a boxer?"

Wright pointed to a faded poster on the wall of his shed. The poster showed a picture of him in a fighter's pose, his fists held up before him.

BOXING MATCH

BETWEEN

YANKEE SULLIVAN

CHAMPION OF ENGLAND

AND

KEN WRIGHT

"THE BLACK TERROR"

"That's me," Wright said.

"How'd you do?"

"I knocked him out in the eleventh round," the blacksmith replied.

"Well, good for you."

"Not too good," Ken Wright said. "I was supposed to lose. Lots of folks had money bet saying I would lose. When I won, it upset the applecart some, so I had to skedaddle out of there. That's how come I wound up with the Buffalo Soldiers."

"But you aren't with the Buffalo Soldiers now."

"No, sir," Ken replied.

Ken offered no explanation as to why he was no longer with the Buffalo Soldiers, and Hawke didn't ask.

Hawke nodded toward the sign. "I see you're not only a blacksmith, but you blast out tree stumps. You work with powder, do you?"

"Not powder," Ken said. "I use dynamite. It's a lot easier."

"Yes, I've seen it used."

"You plan to leave your saddle here?" Ken asked.

"Yes, I believe I will, if you don't mind."

"No extra charge," Ken said. "I reckon you'll be wanting this, though." He removed the saddle bags and snaked the rifle from the saddle sleeve then handed them to Hawke.

"Yes, thanks."

As the big blacksmith took Hawke's horse toward the stable, Hawke returned to the saloon.

The Golden Calf was not the first saloon Hawke had worked in since the war, and he was sure it wouldn't be his last. He had no plans to settle there or anywhere, and if someone questioned him, he would tell them that these piano-playing jobs were just stops along the way.

"Along the way to where?" some would ask.

Hawke had the same answer for all of them. "Anywhere in general, nowhere in particular."

Hawke's father had been a United States congressman. He was also the owner of Goldcrest, one of the largest cotton plantations in Georgia. But the elder Hawke was a strong believer in primogeniture, which meant that the entire farm would go to Hawke's older brother, Gordon.

Hawke was not resentful of that fact. He had no desire to be a farmer; he was a musician, and a very good one. Going to Europe, he studied piano under the brilliant pianist, Franz Liszt, and was playing the European concert circuit to tremendous reviews when the War Between the States broke out.

Shortly after the outbreak of the war, Hawke received a letter from his father, informing him that he had resigned his seat in Congress and was forming a regiment to fight with the Georgia Militia:

> *I tell you this as a matter of information only. I make no request, nor do I expect you to join your brother and me in the war that is to come. It is my fervent hope and belief that your art has lifted you above such human foibles.*

Hawke went immediately to Lucien Garneau, his manager, and asked him to cancel the rest of the concert tour.

"But Monsieur Hawke, what goes on in America is no longer any of your concern," Garneau told him. "You are a citizen of the world now, your music, your God-given talent, belongs to the world. Even your father has said so."

"I cannot remain safely in Europe while my family and my state are facing the perils of war," Hawke replied.

Returning to America, Hawke joined his father's regiment. As it turned out, the very skills that made him a brilliant pianist—digital flexibility and excellent hand-and-eye coordination—also made him especially proficient with weapons.

He was first a cavalryman and then, because of his marksmanship, he was made a sharpshooter, killing enemy soldiers from long distances. He killed so many that he became deadened to it. That induced numbness was the only way he could survive the horror with his sanity intact.

Hawke's room was upstairs at the very back of the saloon. The bed had a tightly drawn rope for the springs, and a straw-filled mattress. There was a scarred armoire with a cream-colored pitcher and basin on top. He had one window that looked out over the alley, and when the breeze was right, he could smell the privy.

Sitting on the side of the bed, he removed his boots, then lay back with his hands interlaced behind his head.

Seeing Titus Culpepper this morning had been totally unexpected. It had been a long time since their paths had crossed, but that wasn't always the case. During the war their destinies and survival were very much interlinked.

Hawke saw a roach crawling up the wall.

Maryland, September 12, 1862

"I hate roaches," Culpepper said, squashing several of them with the butt of his rifle.

"If you don't quit using your rifle like that, you're going to blow your head off," Hawke said. "Not that it wouldn't be an improvement in your looks."

"So I've been told," Culpepper said. He moved up to the opening of the lookout station. "What do you see?" he asked.

"Take a look for yourself," Hawke said, pointing to the north.

What Hawke pointed to was the army of General McClellan, marching columns that extended back as far as the eye could see in the distance. Many of the troops had already arrived and were in double lines of battle, while those who were still advancing were taking up positions as soon as they arrived.

"Damn!" Culpepper said. "Have you ever seen so many Yankees?"

"No," Hawke said.

"They're going to come pouring through us like shit through a goose," Culpepper said.

"I don't think so," Hawke said. "The way they are exposed like that, I think we'll be able to hold them off until General Longstreet can come up."

"Yes, well, I'd better go back and tell the colonel that the Yankees are here," Culpepper said.

When Culpepper left, Hawke raised his telescope and, studying the battlefield, began making annotations on his map.

He had just finished marking the position of one of the Yankee regiments when, out of the corner of his eye, he saw Culpepper and three Yankee soldiers. Culpepper had his hands tied behind his back and was being led away by the Yankees.

Grabbing his rifle, Hawke left the lookout position, then hurried down the mountain trail, slipping in and out of the trees to avoid being seen. Finally he came to within fifty yards of Culpepper and the Yankees.

"Let's just kill the Rebel son of a bitch here," the Yankee sergeant said.

"Yeah, good idea," one of the privates responded. "Kill him and be done with it."

The Yankee sergeant was wearing a pistol, and he pulled it from his holster, then aimed at Culpepper's head. Hawke could see Culpepper grimace as the sergeant pulled the hammer back.

"Reb, if you got'ny prayers, well, I reckon you better start sayin' 'em right about now," the Yankee sergeant said with an evil chuckle.

Hawke aimed at the sergeant and fired, killing him before he could shoot Culpepper. The two privates were carrying rifles and, startled by the unexpected gunshot, they raised them but were unsure of where the shot had come from.

With his rifle empty, Hawke pulled his pistol and stepped out into the opening.

"You Yankee boys drop your weapons," he called to them. If he could get them back as prisoners, they might have some valuable information.

"Shoot 'im, Carl!" one of the privates shouted, and both swung their rifles toward Hawke. Hawke fired two quick rounds, killing both of them.

"Damn! What took you so long?" Culpepper asked.

"You're welcome," Hawke replied with a chuckle.

Hawke sometimes felt as if he had led four different lives. As a young man he had grown up on a large plantation, enjoying a life of wealth and privilege. In his early adulthood he was a serious musician playing in the storied theaters and opera houses of Europe. That was followed by the horrors of war. Since the war, he was a wanderer with no more connection to time or place than the dust devils he often encountered on the hot, prairie trails.

Meeting Culpepper this morning had caused him to reach back across time to experience each of those lives. It was almost as if the early Mason Hawke had broken into many pieces, like a shattered mirror. From time to time he would happen across one of those shards, and when he did, he would see a disjointed piece. But only if those broken pieces could be rejoined would he get a complete picture of who he was then and who he was now.

Getting up, he walked over to the armoire, poured water into the basin, and washed his face and hands in preparation for bed. He thought about the concept of rejoining all the pieces to see the complete picture.

He wasn't sure he wanted to do that.

Chapter 4

WHEN HAWKE WENT DOWN TO BREAKFAST THE next morning, the saloon, which had been so busy the night before, was empty except for one other customer, who was eating his own breakfast. Paddy was behind the bar polishing glasses, adjusting the liquor level in the bottles, getting ready for the day's commerce. He looked up when Hawke came in.

"We have scrambled eggs and biscuits this morning," Paddy said.

"Sounds good to me."

"I'll tell Mary to bring some to you," Paddy offered, stepping back into the kitchen.

The other customer chuckled. "Friend, disabuse yourself of any idea that just because he said 'this morning,' there is something unique about scrambled eggs and biscuits. That's what he has every morning."

The customer got up from his table, came over and extended his hand. "The name is Cyrus. Cyrus Green, your local representative of the noble institution of the press."

"He's also the mayor," Paddy called across the bar.

"The mayor? Well, I'm pleased to meet you, Mayor. The name is Mason Hawke," Hawke said, taking Cyrus's hand.

"So, in addition to being the mayor, you are also with the newspaper?"

"I am with, work for, and own the newspaper," Cyrus said. "And you, I take it, are the new piano player."

"Yes."

"Well, that's good. All towns gain when they are enriched by culture."

Hawke chuckled as his food was brought to the table. "It's quite a leap of faith, Mr. Cyrus, to refer to playing a piano in a saloon as culture. However, I will do what I can."

"From what I heard about your impromptu performance yesterday, it won't be that large a leap of faith," Cyrus said. "I only regret that I wasn't here to hear it."

"Well, I'll be here every day," Hawke said. "Drop by any-time."

"Thanks, I plan to," Cyrus said. "Now, if you will excuse me, I must repair to my newspaper office to continue the never-ending search for truth, justice, and the pursuit of journalistic excellence. Paddy, put my breakfast—"

"On your tab," Paddy said, interrupting Cyrus. "It's already there."

No more than a few minutes after Cyrus left, the undertaker came into the saloon, wearing his long black coat and high hat.

"Mr. Welch, I don't mind you coming into my place," Paddy called to him. "But I do wish you wouldn't wear your long black coat and your top hat in here. People will think you are in here on business, and it tends to spook 'em."

"I *am* in here on business," Welch answered resolutely.

"You ain't got no business in here unless somebody died. And there for damn sure ain't nobody died in here over the last twelve hours or I woulda known about it," Paddy said.

"I'm told that the gentleman who delivered the deceased to me is in here. Hawke, I think his name is."

With the white cloth he was using in hand, Paddy pointed

to the table nearest the piano. "You would be talking about our new piano player. That's him back there, havin' his breakfast."

"Piano player? I didn't know that," Welch said.

Welch reached Hawke's table, then touched the brim of his hat.

"Mr. Hawke, I am Gene Welch, at your service, sir."

"What can I do for you, Mr. Welch?" Hawke asked as he spread butter onto a biscuit.

"Well, sir, I don't know if you would be interested or not, but I'll be buryin' Mr. Delaney at ten o'clock this morning."

"Thanks," Hawke replied as he took a bite.

Expecting a little more reaction than that, Welch stood by the table a moment longer. Then, realizing that Hawke had given him all the answer he was going to, he cleared his throat.

"Yes, well, I just, uh, thought you might like to know," he said.

Leaving Hawke's table, Welch walked back to the batwing doors, and for a moment could be seen only in silhouette against the bright sunlight that streamed in from behind him. Then he pushed the doors open and stepped outside.

The burial ground was just south of town, on the side of a treeless hill. A brisk wind was blowing, carrying on its hot breath rolling clumps of tumbleweed. The tumbleweed darted and bounced through the cemetery, sometimes catching momentarily on one of the grave markers before working loose and moving on.

The markers were made of whitewashed wood. Some were crosses, some were tablets whose epitaphs told the story of the struggle faced by those who had tried to carve a life in such a hard place.

MARY, WIFE OF JOS. BEAN.
DIED OF THE CONSUMPTION.

A FLOWER IN GOD'S GARDEN,
WILTED BY LIFE'S STRUGGLE.

UNKNOWN MAN
FOUND SHOT DEAD ON THE PRARIE

FAITH MARTIN AND BABY.
THE LORD TOOK THEM BOTH
WHILE THE BABY WAS BEING BORN.

MILLIE PATTERSON
SHE WAS A WHORE,
DIED OF THE DOXY DISEASE.
BUT SHE WAS A GOOD WOMAN, LORD
AND WE'D LIKE YOU TO KNOW THAT.

Toward the back of the cemetery, Hawke saw the undertaker and the blacksmith take a pine box off the back of a buckboard and, using ropes, lower it into the already dug grave.

When Hawke reached the graveside, he saw a woman, wearing a black dress and a long, black veil, coming up the hill from town.

"Is that Delaney's wife?" Hawke asked.

Ken Wright shook his head. "Mr. Delaney didn't have no wife," he said. "That be Miss Delaney."

"His sister?" Hawke asked.

"Yes. Flaire Delaney," Welch added. "She runs a dress sewing shop."

The climb up the hill was steep, and Hawke, noticing the woman struggle a bit, hurried down to offer her his hand. She took it, and he helped her up the rest of the way.

"Thank you," she said. Her voice was soft and well-modulated, but because of the veil, Hawke couldn't see her face.

"Would you be wanting me to read a few words over your brother, Miss Delaney?" Welch asked.

"If you don't mind," Flaire replied.

Welch began reading.

" 'Man, that is born of a woman, hath but a short time to live, and is full of misery. He cometh up, and is cut down, like a flower; he fleeth as it were a shadow, and never continueth in one stay.' "

Bending down, Flaire picked up a handful of dirt and, as Welch continued reading, let it trickle out from her closed hand. It made a hollow sound as it fell on the closed coffin.

" 'For as much as it hath pleased Almighty God in his wise providence to take out of this world the soul of our deceased brother, Edward Delaney, we therefore commit his body to the ground; earth to earth, ashes to ashes, dust to dust; looking for the general Resurrection in that last day, and the life of the world to come, though our Lord Jesus Christ, at whose second coming in glorious majesty to judge the world the earth and the sea shall give up their dead; and the corruptible bodies of those who sleep in him shall be changed, and made like unto his own glorious body; according to the mighty working whereby he is able to subdue all things unto himself.' "

Welch closed the book, then got a shovel from the buckboard. Ken Wright got the other, and for the next few minutes there was no sound except for the moan of the wind, the chunk of shovels biting into the pile of recently turned earth, and the thump of the falling dirt as it closed the grave.

When they were finished, they put the shovels in back of the buckboard. Hawke had stayed until the grave was closed only because Flaire Delaney had stayed and he thought it might be rude to leave before she did.

Flaire did not weep during the burial, nor did she utter another word after responding to Welch when he asked if she wanted him to read over her brother's grave.

"Miss Delaney, would you like a ride back into town?" Welch asked.

"Yes, thank you," she said.

Hawke helped her climb onto the seat to sit with Welch. Then he hopped up onto the back of the buckboard and, with his legs dangling over the rear, sat alongside the blacksmith as Welch drove them back into town. Until then, Hawke had not been fully cognizant of just how big Ken Wright was. He was a very muscular man, and even though his brindled hair was graying with age, Hawke figured he would not be a person anyone would want to tangle with.

Back in town, Rufus Vox stood at the window of the marshal's office, eating a chicken drumstick as he watched the burial through the back window. Culpepper sat at what would normally be the marshal's desk, reading a newspaper from Austin. It was two days old, having gone by train to Marva, which was twenty-five miles north of Salcedo. Marva was the nearest railroad stop. From there, the mail, including the newspaper, was brought to Salcedo by stagecoach.

"Looks like they's only three of 'em come to the buryin'," Vox said. "The blacksmith, Delaney's sister, and that fella that cut him down, whatever his name is. Only you can't really count the blacksmith on account of Welch hired him to dig the grave."

"His name is Hawke," Culpepper said without looking up from his paper.

"Hawke, yeah, I seen yesterday that you two knowed each other."

Culpepper didn't answer.

Vox turned away from the window and, finished with his

drumstick, tossed it into the trash can. "So, how come you know him? Was you two in the army together or somethin'?"

"Yes," Culpepper said. He didn't offer any more explanation.

Wes Bates came into the office then. Like Culpepper and Vox, he was wearing a star that identified him as one of the Regulators. The badge had no real standing, since the Regulators were not officially recognized by the city, county, or state. But the group's authority in the town was well known, and the badge conferred that on its wearer.

Bates walked over to the coffeepot and, using his hat as a heat pad, poured himself a cup.

"They're up there in the cemetery right now, buryin' Delaney," he said.

"Yeah, I been watchin' 'em through the back window," Vox replied.

"Colonel, I was talkin' to the other Regulators, and we all agree that we need to do somethin' about this here piano player," Bates said as he took a drink of coffee, slurping it through extended lips to cool it.

"What piano player?" Vox asked, his face mirroring his confusion. "Who are you talkin' about?"

"I'm talking about Hawke," Bates said. "He took hisself a job of playin' the piano, over at the Golden Calf."

"Piano player?" Vox said again, laughing this time. "You mean to tell me we all stood around with our thumbs up our ass and let a *piano player* make fools of us?"

"Yeah," Bates said. "That's what it looks like to me. That's why me and some of the other boys was talkin' about it. The way we figure it, we need to do somethin' about him."

"And just who are these others you have been talking to?" Culpepper asked.

"All of 'em," Bates replied. "Gillis, Hooper, Jarvis, Moody, Spellman, and Cole. They all agree with me."

"Is that a fact?" Culpepper asked.

"Well, yes," Bates said. "I mean, don't you agree?"

"And just what do you propose to do?" Culpepper asked.

"I don't know," Bates replied. "But we ought to do something, teach him he can't defy an order from the Regulators."

"Leave it be," Culpepper said.

"But don't you think—"

"I said leave it be," Culpepper said again.

"Hawk and the colonel is friends," Vox explained. "They go back a long ways together."

"Oh," Bates said. "Oh, well, I didn't know that. I'll tell the others you and him is friends. That'll explain it."

"Explain what?"

"Why you let him get away with what he done."

"I don't need anything explained," Culpepper said. "I'll do whatever I want to do when I want to do it, and I don't need the approval of you or anyone else."

"No, of course you don't, Colonel. I didn't mean nothin' like that."

Culpepper folded the paper, put it aside, then walked over to look through the window toward the cemetery.

"Looks like they're done. They're climbing onto the buckboard."

About a third of the way down the street toward the saloon, the buckboard stopped. Realizing that Flaire would be getting off, Hawke hurried around to help her down. Then Flaire lifted her veil for the first time, so Hawke could see her face.

Her soft voice had not borne false witness to her looks, because her high cheekbones, green eyes, and light brown hair were combined in just the exact proportion to make her an exceptionally pretty woman.

"Mr. Hawke, would you like to come into my shop for a moment?" she invited.

She motioned toward the building behind her. On the window were the words, FLAIRE DELANEY, SEAMSTRESS.

"I'd be glad to," he said.

Clucking toward his horse, Welch pulled away, with Ken still sitting in the back.

Hawke stepped quickly over to the boardwalk to help Flaire up. At the front door of her establishment, Flaire reached down into the small, black portmanteau she was carrying, took out a key, and opened the door.

"Coffee?" she invited.

"Yes, that would be nice. Thank you."

A blue steel coffeepot was sitting on the stove, over a low-banked fire. Flaire poured two cups, then handed one to Hawke.

"I would like to have invited Mr. Wright in as well," she said. "But of course, if I did, it would be quite a scandal, him being black and all. But I would like to thank him in some way. He did so much for my brother while he was alive."

"Yes, I had a conversation with him yesterday. He said he was teaching your brother to box."

"More than that. He was teaching Eddie to be a man," Flaire said.

Hawke chuckled self-consciously. "It was a little late for that, wasn't it?"

"You would think so, wouldn't you? I mean, Eddie spent four years in the war. But in so many ways, he never grew up."

"Is that what got him into trouble? The fact that he wasn't grown up?"

Flaire paused for a moment before she responded. "He was . . . high-spirited," she said.

"What do you mean by high-spirited?"

"He drank a lot. He gambled. He wasn't very good at cards and sometimes got into fights. Most of which he lost," she added. She chuckled. "That's why he was taking boxing lessons from Ken Wright."

"I figured it must be something like that," Hawke said.

Flaire nodded. "Yes. By the way, I want to thank you for what you did for him."

Hawke shook his head. "Miss Delaney, I didn't do anything for him," he said. "All I did was cut him down and bring him in."

"In this town, that took a great deal of courage," she said. "And it is of great comfort to me to know that Eddie got a decent burial. I don't know how long that band of ruffians who call themselves the Salcedo Regulators Brigade would have left him hanging on that tree."

"You don't approve of the Regulators Brigade?"

"I do not, sir."

"Well, I can understand how you might have hard feelings toward them, seeing as what happened. But most of the people I've spoken to seem to be glad they're around. I take it they've done some good things, such as getting rid of the Dawsons."

"How is it a good thing to get rid of one band of outlaws only to replace them with another?" Flaire asked. "You knew him before, didn't you? Titus Culpepper, I mean."

"Yes, I knew him before. We grew up together back in Georgia. And we served together in the same regiment during the war."

"So you were friends even before the war?"

"I suppose you could say that. His family had a farm near ours. And his father once ran for Congress, against my father."

"Oh? Who won?"

"My father won. But some may say that was because he had the advantage of incumbency."

"Incumbency? You mean you are the son of a congressman?" Flaire asked. "I'm impressed."

"Don't be. It was my father's accomplishment, not mine."

"Still, one doesn't meet the son of a congressman every day. Is he still in Congress?"

"No, my father was killed at Fredericksburg. He resigned from Congress and formed a regiment to fight in the war."

"Oh. I'm sorry to hear that."

"A lot of good men, on both sides of the conflict, were killed in that war."

"You said you and Culpepper served in the same regiment. Your father's regiment?"

"Yes."

"Then you really are friends of long standing."

"There are some folks back home who might take exception at hearing someone call us old friends. Truth is, we fought a lot as kids. And we were always in competition with each other to see who could run the fastest, throw the farthest, catch the biggest fish, wrestle better, and shoot better, that sort of thing."

"And who was the best?" Flaire asked, looking at him over the rim of her cup.

Hawke paused for a moment, then smiled. "I can say without fear of contradiction that I could play the piano better."

"Yes. The whole town is talking about your concert yesterday. I'm sorry I missed it."

"Well, maybe I can play for you someday," Hawke suggested. He finished his cup and set it down. "And, speaking of playing, I suppose I had better get back to work if I don't want to get fired. Again, let me say that I'm sorry about your brother, Miss Delaney. And thanks for the coffee."

"You're welcome," Flaire said.

Chapter 5

FLAIRE MOVED TO THE FRONT WINDOW OF HER shop, and using the curtain as a shield, watched Hawke walk back toward the Golden Calf. Flaire had what her grandmother had called the "gift." It wasn't that she could actually look into a person's soul, but she was sometimes disarmingly perceptive.

She was convinced that, at heart, Mason Hawke was a good man. But he had done some things, some terrible things, that scarred his soul. And she knew that he would carry those scars to his grave.

"I wish you could find peace, Mr. Hawke," she said quietly. "But I know that you cannot. I know that you are doomed to wander for the rest of your life."

Leaving the front window, Flaire went into the living quarters in the back of her shop and began changing clothes. Social custom dictated that she should continue to wear black for at least thirty days. But wearing black would be bad for her business. People did not want to buy gala dresses from someone who was dressed in black.

Flaire could not keep her thoughts of Hawke and his troubled past out of her mind. She could empathize with the scars on Hawke's soul, because she had a few of her own.

Opening the door to the stove, she tossed some pieces of wood in, then watched as the little fingers of flame curled around them, licking at the kindling until the wood was totally invested.

She stared at the fire for a long moment, throwing her eyes out of focus, until she could see the three mounted men backlit by the burning barn. They were in silhouette, as if they were ghost riders from hell. Their faces could not be seen.

By now the animals in the barn were screaming in terror, the horses kicking at the sides of their stalls, underscoring the snapping and popping of the fire.

Shuddering, and pushing the unbidden, unwanted memories away, Flaire slammed the stove door shut, turned and walked away.

Because the Golden Calf was the only saloon in town, it was more than a drinking place. It was also a restaurant, meeting hall, and even a hotel of sorts, since there were rooms to rent upstairs.

The employees and habitués of the saloon were almost family, and over the next several days Hawke became acquainted with them.

Principal member of the Golden Calf family was Paddy O'Neil, the owner.

"I live here on the premises," Paddy said. "Sure 'n' there's only one thing better for an Irishman than to live in a saloon, and that's to own it."

Hawke laughed. "Tell me, Paddy, what is an Irishman doing out here? I thought all Irish were in Boston or New York."

"Aye, and there's a bit of truth to that, lad, for I was born not on the old sod, but in Boston. And 'tis no secret from the citizens of this fair town that I fought in the war on the side of the Union."

"Most here were Confederates, I imagine," Hawke said. "How do they take it that you wore blue?"

" 'Tis funny about that. Odd, I know, but I think they feel a closer connection to me, even though I did fight for the North, than they do with their fellow southerners who, for one reason or another, did not fight a'tall."

"Not so strange at that," Hawke replied. "I've noticed it myself. It's funny how northerners and southerners tried for four long, bloody years to kill each other. But since then, there seems to be sort of a brotherhood of war that includes men from both sides of the conflict, while excluding those who did not fight."

"True, though 'tis only those of us who fought who notice such things."

"So, how did you wind up in Salcedo?" Hawke asked.

"You are interested in the trials and travels of Paddy O'Neil, are you? Well, sir, after the war I returned to Boston, where I bought a small bar. But I got into politics there, and made the mistake of backing the wrong candidate."

"That was bad?"

"Oh my, lad, you've no idea how bad that can be. In a town like Boston the worst thing a body can do is get into politics and support the losing side. The new mayor started, right away, exacting his pound of flesh from those of us who didn't support him. My taxes became so high that there was no way I could stay in business. So, when I had enough of it I emptied the cash drawer and left in the middle of the night."

"That seems reasonable," Hawke said.

"More than reasonable, I would say it is downright prudent," another man said, stepping up to the bar at that moment. "My usual, Paddy."

Paddy prepared a drink of Bourbon and branch and handed it to the new man.

"Mr. Hawke, this is Dr. Charles Urban," Paddy said.

"Doc is one of my regular customers, right, Doc?"

"That's right," Doc said. He pointed to a table in the back corner of the room. "You may have observed the chessboard on the table back there."

"I did notice it, yes."

"The pieces there represent an ongoing game I have with our mayor. Please do not disturb any of the pieces, or Mr. Cyrus will accuse me of cheating."

Hawke chuckled. "I won't touch the board, I promise."

"The mayor and I thank you," Doc said. Then, as he took a drink of his beer, he looked back toward the bartender. "Paddy, please, continue with your story," he said. "I apologize for the interruption."

"Before I do, would you like another beer, Mr. Hawke?"

"Don't mind if I do," Hawke said.

Paddy drew another beer and put it front of Hawke before he went on.

"Well, sir, after cleaning out my cash drawer, I bought a train ticket to Baltimore. But I got off the train in New York and took another one heading west." He held up his finger to make a point. "That way, you see, I figured I would be able to throw off anyone who tried to find me."

"So you wound up here?"

"Heavens no," Doc Urban said with a chuckle. "No good story proceeds in a straight line. Continue, Paddy."

"I settled in Memphis first," Paddy said. "I was there for about a year, and it was there that I met Mary."

"Your wife?"

"In a manner of speaking," Paddy replied. "There was a small problem."

"What sort of problem?"

"Mary was already married."

"I see. That can be a problem."

"Her husband was an abusive drunk, in a town where the

husband is always right. And in Memphis, divorces are next to impossible to obtain," Paddy explained.

"I think I'm beginning to get the picture."

"I hope you are," Paddy said. "Because you see, once again I pulled up stakes in the middle of the night, only this time I didn't leave alone. This time I took the woman I loved away from a bad situation.

"Mary and I wound up here, working in the Golden Calf. I was the bartender and she was the cook. Then, six months after we arrived in Salcedo, Gib Crabtree, then the owner of the Golden Calf, was hit by a stray bullet when a couple members of the Dawson gang got drunk and started shooting up the town. Gib hung on for a few more days, then he died."

Paddy paused for a moment, then crossed himself.

"After that, I bought the saloon from his widow, Marge Crabtree, who went back to Mobile, and now Mary—who is still the cook—runs the place with me."

As twilight came on, Paddy lowered the wagon-wheel chandelier to light the flickering kerosene lanterns. The dim, golden light combined with the tobacco smoke that hovered just under the ceiling like a cloud, creating an environment that was surreal, as if time and place existed only there.

It was a particularly good night. The saloon was full without being overcrowded, and Hawke was at the piano, playing light and bouncy tunes that would encourage drinking and congeniality. It had the desired effect, and the Golden Calf was ringing with laughter, conversation, and the clink of glasses.

During the last few years, such surroundings had somehow become Hawke's heritage. He was redefined by the saloons, cowtowns, stables, dusty streets, and open prairies he encountered during his wanderings. He could not deny these things without denying his own existence, and now he wasn't sure that he even wanted to. He was here, in a foul-smelling saloon, in a West Texas town whose name he had never even heard until a few days ago. And at that moment he knew that he didn't want to be anywhere else.

Although Hawke would play any requested song without charge, it was a general practice for the customer to give a tip. From time to time Darci would bring a coin over and drop it into Hawke's tip bowl, along with the song request she was delivering from the customer.

Darci had a sweet naiveté about her that belied her occupation. And it didn't take Hawke long to learn that she was as good for his business as she was for Paddy's, because she would often coax one of the customers into requesting a song, just for her. In fact, she was so good for his business that Hawke entered into a business arrangement with her, with Darci getting ten percent of all his tips. The agreement was working very well for both of them.

Darci had dark hair and dark brown eyes. Her skin was smooth and olive-complexioned, and her provocative clothing and flirtatious nature cajoled the customers into buying more drinks.

It was also no secret that, after hours, Darci entertained men in her crib, which was a small one-room house across the alley behind the saloon. Whoring was an established and wholly accepted occupation, and nobody thought the less of her for it.

"I'm twenty-two years old," Darci said. "My mama was a whore in a fancy house down in New Orleans, and I was born there. Mama was half colored, which means I'm what they call a quadroon. I started into whorin' when I was fifteen. I never had plans to do anything but whore, and ain't never done anything else.

"But I figured that just 'cause I was whorin' didn't mean I'd have to stay in New Orleans for the rest of my life. So I come west to see what it's like out here."

Chapter 6

FLAIRE'S SLEEP WAS FITFUL. SHE WAS LYING NOT IN bed, but on the cold, hard ground. She was aware of the golden, flickering light of the burning barn, and she felt as if she should do something about it, but she didn't quite know what to do.

Her mother was lying on the ground beside her, and her face was turned toward Flaire. Flaire stared at her mother. Her mother's open but sightless eyes stared back.

When Flaire awoke, she sat on the side of her bed for a few moments, letting the dream drift away from her. From time to time over the last several years she'd had this same dream. There was no way to tell when it would occur, and no way to prevent it. Fortunately, because it was a dream, it generally faded very quickly after she woke up.

After a few moments the dream was gone, drifting away in fragments she could not hold together. And with the peace that brought her, she was able to get up and get dressed to start her day.

Flaire did not normally open her shop on Sunday, so she didn't expect to hear anyone knocking on the front door. Leaving her apartment, she walked through the shop area, shaded by the closed curtains, and peeked out to see who it was.

Mason Hawke was standing on her front stoop, smiling at her. She opened the door to him.

"Mr. Hawke," she said. "What a surprise."

"I hope I'm not disturbing you."

"No, not at all. What can I do for you?" She laughed. "I don't imagine you want a dress made."

Hawke laughed as well. "I'll pass on that," he said. "But I've rented a buckboard from the blacksmith, and I've had Mary—from the Golden Calf—prepare a lunch. I was hoping you might come for a ride."

"Are you asking me to go on a picnic with you?"

"Yes," Hawke said.

Flaire ran her hand through her hair. "Oh, dear, I look a mess," she said.

Hawke laughed.

"What is so funny?"

"If you knew how good you look to me, you would know how funny that is," Hawke replied.

Flaire smiled at him. "All right, come in and have a seat. Let me get ready. I think a picnic would be delightful. I'll be glad to go with you."

It took Flaire about forty-five minutes to make herself presentable, but when she emerged again, Hawke decided it was worth the wait. He escorted her outside, then helped her into the buckboard.

As they drove past the church, the number of horses and conveyances parked outside indicated that a service was in progress. As usual, Hawke felt a twinge of guilt. In his youth, his family had attended church regularly, but it had been a long time since he had been in one.

Just before they left town, three men stepped out into the

road in front of the buckboard. They held up their hands as a signal for Hawke to stop.

"You know them?" Hawke asked as they approached the men.

"Yes, they are members of the Regulators," Flaire said. "That's Nat Moody in front. The other two are Elmer Hooper and Jim Jarvis."

"I wonder what they want."

"I don't know, but you'd better stop. They can be very dangerous people."

Hawke stopped. "Yes, deputies, what can I do for you?" he asked.

"Where are you going?" Moody asked.

"I beg your pardon?" Hawke replied.

"I asked, where are you going?" the deputy repeated.

"Yes, I heard what you asked," Hawke replied. "What I don't understand is why you asked. Why would where I am going be any of your business?"

"We're deputies of the Salcedo Regulators Brigade," Moody said. "Where you are going is my business because, by God, I just decided to make it my business."

"You'd better decide again," Hawke said. "Because nothing that I do is any of your business. Ever. Now get out of the way."

Moody started to reach for his gun. "Mister, when I ask a quest—" Whatever he was going to say was interrupted in mid-sentence.

Shocked, he realized that somehow Hawke was holding a pistol, and it was pointed at him. Hawke was smiling, though there was no mirth in the smile. On the contrary, it was rather intimidating.

Moody blinked a couple of times, as if trying to figure out what had just happened.

"What the hell? Where did you get that gun?" he asked in surprise.

"It doesn't matter where I got it," Hawke said. "As you can see, I have it. Now, take off your gun belts, all three of you, and drop them into the buckboard."

"Now why the hell would we want to do a fool thing like that?"

"Because I'll kill you if you don't."

Moody smiled. "That's mighty big talk for a piano player. Do you know what it takes to kill a man?"

"Not much," Hawke answered. "And the less of a man you are, the easier it is." He cocked the pistol.

"Nat, I think the son of a bitch means it," one of the other deputies said in a clipped voice.

"You'd better listen to your friend," Hawke said. He made a little motion with his pistol. "Like I said, put your guns in the buckboard."

"Mister, you don't know who you are messing with," Moody said angrily, though he was now unbuckling his gun belt even as he was speaking.

The other two deputies did the same. All three of them put their guns and belts into the back of the buckboard.

"Now your boots," Hawke said.

"What? My boots? The hell you say!" Moody said loudly and angrily. "I'm not taking my boots off for you or for any man."

"You've got your choice," Hawke said. "You can hobble out of here without your boots or you can keep your boots and I'll shoot you in the foot. That way you can hobble in your boots."

Although Moody stood there for a moment longer, the other two deputies complied immediately. They sat down in the dirt of the road and began pulling off their boots.

"After I kill Moody, you two can drag him out of the

street," Hawke said easily. "I wouldn't want him to still be lying out here when the people are let out from church."

Immediately, Moody sat down with the others and began removing his boots. The entire front half of both of Moody's socks were missing, and his toes stuck out.

Standing up again, the three men dropped their boots in the buckboard, where they'd already dropped their guns.

"You want our pants too?" Moody asked with a snarl.

"You know, now that you mention it, that might not be a bad idea."

"Moody! You dumb son of a bitch!" one of the others shouted.

Hawke laughed. "I guess you can keep your pants," he said. Putting his pistol back in the holster, he snapped the reins against the team, and the buckboard started forward.

"You son of a bitch!" Moody shouted at him. "I'll have your ass for this!"

Hawke kept the team at a trot for several minutes so that, by the time he slowed them, the town was some distance behind them.

"I'm new to this area," he said. "You know any places that would be good for a picnic?"

"I . . . I can't believe what you did back there," Flaire said. Those were the first words she had spoken since the encounter with the deputies.

"Ah, don't worry about them. They're bullies," Hawke said. "I don't understand why Titus has them working for him."

"Is it possible that you don't know?"

"Don't know what?"

"What kind of man your friend Culpepper really is."

"He is a man who once saved my life," Hawke said. Seeing a grassy glade next to a stream, he pointed. "How about right there? It looks like a very nice place for a picnic."

"Yes, it does," Flaire said.

Hawke turned for the basket, but Flaire put her hand out. "You just go over there and relax," she said. "I'll take care of everything."

"All right," Hawke said. He climbed down from the seat, then helped Flaire down. Flaire took the basket over to the flat, grassy area, took out the cloth and spread it, then began putting out the food.

"Oh, my, it looks like Mrs. O'Neil outdid herself," Flaire said as she examined the spread. "Fried chicken, potato salad, biscuits, and a cake."

"And a bottle of wine," Hawke added. He walked over to look out at the stream. "I wonder if there are fish here?"

"Of course there are. My brother used to fish here all the time," Flaire said. "The meal is ready."

Hawke came back and sat down by the spread. Flaire was already seated, and Hawke was pleased to see that when he sat close to her, she made no effort to reposition herself. He opened the bottle of wine and poured them each a glass.

"You aren't from here originally, are you?" he asked.

"No. I'm from Missouri."

"What brought you here?"

Flaire sipped her wine, silent for a moment. "I may as well tell you," she said, and took a deep breath. "My brother killed two men back in Missouri. After that, he felt that it wasn't safe to stay."

"That seems prudent to me," Hawke said. "I take it the killing was justified. Otherwise, I doubt you would have come with him."

"If there was ever a case of justifiable homicide, that was it," Flaire said. She sipped her wine and for a long moment said nothing more. Hawke, sensing that she needed the period of silence, didn't press her.

"The men my brother killed were bushwhackers," Flaire

said, finally breaking the silence. "Do you know what bush-whackers are?"

"Yes," Hawke said. "They were irregulars who called themselves soldiers but more often than not were outlaws using the war as an excuse to steal."

"Yes, that's it exactly," Flaire said.

"But he didn't kill them just because they were bush-whackers, did he?"

Flaire shook her head. "No."

Hawke knew there was more to it, but he could see that it was still too painful for Flaire to talk about. He didn't press her.

"Whatever it was, it must've been very hard for you."

"Yes, it was very hard," Flaire said. She smiled. "But that is enough about me. What about you? I know that your father was a congressman. You must've come from a family of means. And yet, here you are, playing a piano in a saloon. How did you get here?"

Hawke sipped his wine before replying. "When the war was over, I just started moving," he said. "Oh, I stop from time to time, but I don't generally stay in any one place for too long."

Flaire laughed. "Is that a warning?" she asked.

"A warning?"

"Don't get the wrong ideas about anything. 'I don't stay in any one place for too long,' " Flaire said, repeating his comment.

"Oh. Oh, yes, I see," Hawke said. He smiled. "Well, I didn't intend it that way, but . . ."

"That's all right. I feel the same way," she said. "I don't know how much longer I'll stay here now that Eddie is dead. Let's just enjoy each other's company while we can."

"Good idea," Hawke said, pouring them another glass of wine.

"How did he save your life?"

"What?"

"A little while ago you said that Culpepper saved your life. How?"

"It was at Gettysburg," Hawke said. "My father had been killed at Fredericksburg, so the regiment now belonged to my brother. We were moved to the East and were ordered to flush some Union sharpshooters out of the woods at the foot of the slope of a hill called Round Top. We did it, though our casualty rate was very high. After that, we were ordered to take Little Round Top, the hill next to it, which we were told was undefended.

"Well, it wasn't undefended, and even as we were climbing the hill, more Yankees were pouring in from the other side. They had artillery, including canister, firing down on us. We were cut to pieces, and I was wounded. My brother, who was the commander at the time, ordered that we withdraw.

"What my brother didn't know was that I was too badly wounded to withdraw. I lay there with musket and canister fire falling all around me, certain that the next volley would finish me. Then, all of a sudden, someone grabbed me by the shoulders and started dragging me downhill until I was far enough out of range to be safely placed on a litter."

"Culpepper?"

"Yes," Hawke said.

"Well, I can see how you would be beholden to him, then," Flaire admitted. "But believe me, Mr. Hawke, Titus Culpepper is not the same man you once knew. He has changed."

"Most folks just call me Hawke, not 'Mister,'" Hawke said with a smile.

"You go by Hawke? Not your first name?"

"Mason is my first name. But I prefer Hawke."

"All right, Hawke it is," Flaire said, returning the smile.

Chapter 7

BY THE TIME MOODY, HOOPER, AND JARVIS RE-
turned to the office, they were limping on sore feet. Culpepper, Vox, and Bates looked up in surprise.

"What the hell happened to you?" Vox asked.

"What happened to us? That damn piano player took our
boots, that's what happened to us," Moody said.

"And you just let him do it?" Bates asked.

"We didn't have no choice. He took our guns too,"
Hooper added.

"But we aim to get 'em back," Jarvis said. Taking a rifle
from the rack, he jacked a shell into the chamber. Then he
took two more down and tossed them to the other two
deputies.

"What do you think you're doing?" Culpepper asked.

"There ain't no thinkin' to it, Colonel. I aim to kill that
son of a bitch," Moody said angrily.

"No."

"What do you mean, no?"

"No means no. I didn't stutter," Culpepper said. "You
aren't going to do anything to Hawke."

"Damn it! You think we're just goin' to stand around and
do nothing? I mean, this piano player is beginning to be a

real problem," Moody said. "First he cuts down Delaney and brings him back into town without so much as a fare thee well. And that was right in front of everyone, when everyone in town knew we had put up a sign tellin' people to leave the body hangin' there. Then, this morning, he took our guns and boots."

"What I want to know is, how the hell did he get your guns and boots?" Vox asked.

"Yes, I'd be interested in hearing that myself. There are three of you and one of him. Just how did that happen?" Culpepper asked.

"We wasn't expectin' nothin' like that to happen," Moody said. "All we done was stop him and that Delaney woman."

"Stop them from what?" Culpepper wanted to know.

"Just stop them. They were leaving town in a buckboard, and the whole thing looked a little suspicious to me. Especially her being Delaney's sister and all. We was just—"

"You were just meddling in something that is none of your business," Culpepper said. "Put the rifles back in the rack."

"What about our guns and boots?" Jarvis asked.

"My guess is he'll return them today. If he doesn't, you can go to him, hat in hand, and ask him to give them back to you."

Culpepper's guess that the guns and boots would be returned proved to be correct. Just before dark that evening, Ken Wright came into the office.

"Yes, Mr. Wright, what can we do for you?" Culpepper asked.

Ken made a motion with his thumb, jerking it toward the street.

"Mason Hawke rented a buckboard from me today," he said. "When he came back there were a few items in the back that he said might belong to you."

"Our guns!" Moody shouted, and darted through the front door, followed by the other two. Grabbing the guns and boots, they came back inside, then sat down and started pulling on the shoes.

"Damn, my feet is so sore I can barely get into 'em," Jarvis said.

"Thank you, Mr. Wright," Culpepper said.

"Colonel, if you don't mind tellin' me, how'd they wind up in the back of my wagon?"

"You mean Hawke didn't tell you?"

"No, sir. He didn' say nothin', 'cept he thought these might belong to some of your deputies."

"Ain't none of your business how he wound up with 'em," Moody said.

By now all three men had their boots on, and after strapping on their pistols, they walked around the room a few times, gingerly testing the boots against feet swollen from going a day without shoes.

"Let's just say my deputies got careless," Culpepper said. "I thank you again, blacksmith."

"Yes, sir, I'm glad to be of service to you," the blacksmith said, touching his eyebrow in a casual salute.

Moody waited until the blacksmith left before he spoke again.

"I'm beggin' you, Colonel, let me go settle scores with this man."

"Try it, and you'll be dead," Culpepper said.

"I can't believe you would go that far to defend him against one of your own men."

"Oh, I don't mean you'll be dead by my hand," Culpepper said. "Hawke would kill you."

"What if all three of us went up against him?" Hooper asked.

"Don't you understand? I'm talking about all three of

you," Culpepper said. "If all three of you go against him, all three of you will be dead."

"Wait a minute," Jarvis said. "He can't possibly be that good."

"Oh, he can, and he is," Culpepper said. "If you know what is good for you, you'll stay the hell out of his way."

It was four o'clock in the morning, and the saloon was dark except for the small golden bubble of light that came from the single candle on the open key lid of the piano.

Hawke sat at the piano playing "Les Jeux d'eau a la ville d'Este," a composition of his old piano instructor, Franz Liszt. The music filled the darkened room and spilled out into the street.

Abner Poindexter, a hostler for the West Texas Stage Company, was on his way to work when he heard the music. He stopped in front of the saloon and sat on the front porch to listen.

Maurice Baldwin, the baker, also heard the music, and after he got his dough rolled out and in the oven, he came over to join Abner.

Ken Wright had risen early to get the fire going in his forge. Hearing the music, he walked down the street to join the other two.

When the concert was over, the three men sat for a moment longer on the porch, then Poindexter stood up and brushed off the back of his pants.

"I reckon I'd better get that team put together or the folks plannin' on takin' the stage out this mornin' won't be able to make the trip," he said.

"You think he'll do this again tomorrow mornin'?" Baldwin asked.

"Oh, he be here tomorrow," Ken answered.

"What makes you think so?"

"Because he got the gift," Ken explained. "When the Lord give a man the gift, He also give him the need to use it. The music Mr. Hawke play in the daytime don't satisfy that need."

"Then I'm going to bring my wife tomorrow morning," Baldwin said.

"Yeah," Poindexter replied. "I think I'll tell my neighbor about it. He was in the saloon the day this fella arrived when he played that real pretty song. I bet he'd like to hear it."

With the music finished, the three men returned to their respective occupations.

Ken checked on his fire, then went back to his room to look at his latest work in progress. When Ken told the others that an artist had to practice his art, he knew what he was talking about.

Ken was a painter. He had never sold any of his paintings, had never even thought about selling them, because he was an artist for art's sake. Picking up the palate, he dipped a brush into a dab of ochre, then applied it to the canvas.

Flaire's thirteen-year-old brother Paul sounded the alarm, and when Flaire opened her eyes, she saw that her bedroom was as bright as day, illuminated by the burning barn.

"Everyone turn out! We've got to save the animals!" Flaire's father shouted.

Within seconds the family dashed out through the front door. They were still in their sleeping gowns, not taking the time to get dressed because every second lost decreased their chance of saving any of the trapped animals.

When they reached the front porch, they came to a sudden stop, shocked to see three mounted men out front. Backlit by the burning barn, they were in silhouette, as if they were ghost riders from hell. Their faces could not be seen.

"Who are you? What are you doing here?" Flaire's father asked.

"Delaney, you have a boy ridin' with the Yankee army?" one of the men called.

"I do," Flaire's father answered.

Flaire shielded her eyes against the glare of the fire, trying to see who the men were, but try as she might, she couldn't see their faces.

By now the animals in the barn were screaming in terror. The horses were kicking at the sides of their stalls, underscoring the snapping and popping of the fire.

"Why is it you didn't try to stop your boy from joining up with the Yankees?" the man asked.

"What? What are you talking about? We don't have time for all this. Listen to those poor animals," Flaire's father said. "Help us get them out of there!"

"Help you? Why, you damn fool, we started the fire," the man said.

"Why would you do something like that?" Delaney asked angrily.

The animals continued to scream, though there weren't as many screams now, as some of them had already succumbed to the flames.

"Papa, listen to them! The poor animals are dying!" Flaire cried.

"We've got to get to them," Delaney said, stepping down from the porch.

They were interrupted by a gunshot, then the one who had been doing all the talking yelled at Delaney.

"Delaney, the people's court of Platte County has tried you, found you guilty of treason against the South, and sentenced you to die."

"No!" Flaire's mother said.

By now the animals were silent. The barn was a roaring inferno and Flaire could feel the intense heat, even from where she stood.

"You and the boy have thirty seconds to say your prayers. Then the sentence will be carried out."

"The boy? Wait a minute! He's only thirteen!" Delaney said. The defiance was gone now, replaced by concern for his son.

"Your thirty seconds are up."

"No!" Flaire's mother screamed again, and grabbing her son, she pulled him to her and stepped in front of her husband, trying to shield the two of them with her own body.

Her action did nothing to prevent what happened next. The riders began firing. Flaire heard the bullets whizzing by her, saw them tear into the flesh of her mother, father, and younger brother. She screamed, and was still screaming, even when the firing stopped and the reports of the gunshots were but distant echoes.

Chapter 8

HAWKE ACCEPTED AN INVITATION FROM TITUS Culpepper to join him for lunch in the private dining room of the Ranchers' Hotel. The two-story edifice was not only Salcedo's only hotel, it was also the town's only brick building. It had been built in anticipation of a railroad spur line that never developed.

The hotel clerk recognized Hawke as soon as he came in the lobby, and he smiled broadly at him.

"You would be Mr. Hawke?" he asked, affecting what he was certain was a cultured accent.

"Yes."

"Colonel Culpepper is waiting for you in the private dining room. If you'll come this way, sir, I'll take you there."

"Thanks."

The lobby of the hotel was covered with a deep wine carpet; the wainscoting was light blue with gold trim, and the wallpaper featured huge baskets of flowers. The oak stairway was broad and only partially covered with a narrow runner of the same color as the carpet in the lobby. The polished wood of the steps was exposed on either side of the runner.

The clerk led Hawke across the lobby to a hallway that went behind the stairs. At the end of the hallway he opened a door and made a grand gesture with his hand, inviting Hawke to enter.

Culpepper was standing near the window in the back of the room, smoking a cigar. He turned when Hawke entered.

"Hawke," he said warmly. He chuckled. "I would thank you for dressing for dinner, but you are always well-dressed." Culpepper picked up a silver box, opened it, and extended it to Hawke. "Would you like a cigar?"

"Yes, thank you," Hawke said, taking one from the box.

Culpepper lit the cigar for him.

"I want to thank you for returning my men's guns and boots the other day," Culpepper said. He laughed. "You should've seen them limping around all day long. I tell you, they were mad as wet hens."

Hawke took several puffs, waiting until the cigar was well-lit before he exhaled, then spoke through a cloud of blue smoke.

"Well, I'm glad you aren't taking it personally," he said.

Culpepper dismissed it with a wave of his hand. "No, no, not at all. In the first place, those boys had no business stopping you like that. Or asking you where you were going. And in the second place, you did me a big favor. I think they have all three been getting a little too big for their britches. Or, in this case, boots," he added, laughing again.

"Why did they stop me?"

"Oh, I suppose they thought that, in some way, they were just doing their job," Culpepper said dismissively. "But don't worry about them, this won't happen again."

"They don't particularly worry me," Hawke said.

"No, I wouldn't think they would," Culpepper agreed.

A swinging door from the back of the room opened and a tall, thin man with a very narrow moustache came into the room. He was wearing a white jacket and a white hat.

"Monsieur Culpepper, shall I serve now?" he asked.

"Yes, thank you, Monsieur Mouchette, please do," Culpepper answered. Then, as the chef withdrew, Culpepper said to Hawke, "I hope you enjoy the meal I've had the chef prepare for you. Mouchette is a real Frenchman, you know. He works for the governor, but I brought him out from Austin just for this occasion."

Mouchette came back in, carrying a wine bottle and a corkscrew.

"Monsieur Mouchette, I would like you to meet Mr. Hawke," Culpepper said.

"Bon matin, Monsieur Mouchette. Très agréable pour vous rencontrer," Hawke said, before Mouchette could say anything.

"It is good to meet you as well, Monsieur Hawke. *Merveilleux! Vous parlez français!*"

"Yes, I speak French."

"Mr. Hawke is a pianist, Monsieur Mouchette. He once toured the continent giving concerts."

"How wonderful," Mouchette said.

"Tell Mr. Hawke what you have prepared for us."

"Le sein de canard aux abricots frais."

"Now, tell it in English, so I know."

"Breast of duck, in apricot sauce," Hawke said, translating it for Culpepper. "It sounds delicious."

"And with it, a nice Cabernet Sauvignon," Mouchette said, presenting the bottle he had brought with him.

After the men seated themselves, Mouchette uncorked the bottle in front of Hawke and let him test it. When Hawke nodded his approval, Mouchette poured it slowly.

"A little better than the raw whiskey and green beer you get over at the Golden Calf, isn't it?" Culpepper asked.

"You'll spoil me," Hawke replied.

"To the friends we lost in the war," Culpepper said, holding his goblet up.

"To absent comrades," Hawke replied.

The meal was served, and for a while there was nothing but the sound of eating. Finally, satisfied with one of the best meals he had enjoyed in a long time, Hawke pushed his plate away and looked across the table at Culpepper.

"All right, Titus," he said. "What's all this about?"

"What is what about?" Culpepper asked, refilling his glass.

"I know you well enough to know that you have something on your mind."

Culpepper chuckled. "You're right, I do," he said. "Hawke, I want you to come work for me."

"Work for you. You have a piano you want me to play?"

This time Culpepper's chuckle turned into a full-bodied laugh. "A piano to play," he said. "That's good. No, what I really had in mind was a combination of things. First of all, I want you to be my chief deputy. You've seen the caliber of help that I have. I need someone I can depend on, someone who can think on his feet and, quite frankly, someone who could rein in the . . . let's just call it enthusiasm, of the men who work for me."

"Is that what you call it? Enthusiasm?"

Culpepper shook his head. "All right, I'll admit, I was just trying to make it sound better than it is. The term I should have used is arrogance. I'm talking about their arrogance and obnoxious, even improper, bullying behavior. I can't afford too many incidents like what happened to you. If that had happened to the wrong person, it would have resulted in only two possible outcomes. Either my deputies would have killed the civilian, or the civilian would have killed the deputies. Quite possibly, a combination of both."

"You said there were two things you wanted," Hawke said.

"Yes," Culpepper replied with a nod. "I also want you to manage my campaign for Congress. After all, you have some experience in that area."

Hawke shook his head. "My father was a congressman, not I," he said.

"Nevertheless, there is that connection, that cachet," Culpepper said. "I think it would play well among the voters of this district. And, of course, we have the accomplishments of the Regulators to help."

"And you want me to be your chief deputy?"

"Yes."

"Vox is your chief deputy now, isn't he? Wouldn't he be a little put out if I took his job?"

"He might be. But that would be his problem, not yours," Culpepper said. "We're doing good work here, Hawke. You could be a part of it. And with you to keep a rein on my deputies, we could do even better work."

Hawke shook his head. "I thank you for the invitation," he said. "But I'm not much for joining volunteer organizations."

Culpepper ran his hand around the lip of his wine glass, making it sing.

"Maybe you misunderstand. Don't get the idea that you would be working without compensation, my friend," Culpepper said. "Join me, and you will be paid. In fact, you will be paid very well."

"You are talking about the nickel tax on beer?" Hawke said. "It doesn't seem like a nickel tax on beer would generate that much money."

"We don't just tax the beer," Culpepper said. "We tax every business in town. It all adds up, and it adds up very quickly."

"And the town goes along with it?"

"Yes, and gladly. Like I said, we keep the town safe."

"I see."

"Look, don't give me your decision now. I have to go to Austin for a few days. For one thing, I must file my intention to run. For another, I have some things to discuss with the governor. I wish you would accept my offer now, so I could leave you in charge during my absence. But since you won't, I'll have to leave Vox. At least give my offer some thought while I'm gone."

"All right," Hawke said. "I'll do that."

"That's all I ask," Culpepper said, once again lifting his wine goblet toward Hawke. Hawke returned it and the men drank a second toast.

In the wee hours of the next morning there were nearly a dozen people gathered in front of the saloon as Hawke, unaware of his audience, bent over the keyboard. The strains of Beethoven's Sonata Number 32 in C Minor held the listeners enraptured for nearly twenty minutes.

"It's like music from heaven," the baker's wife said as they walked away from the saloon at the conclusion of the concert.

Word spread throughout the town about Hawke's nocturnal concerts, and every morning at four, people would gather on the saloon porch, in the alley alongside, or in front of the stage depot next door, and they would listen.

"Did you hear the music last night?" they would ask each other the next day.

"It's like an angel come down from heaven to entertain us," another would say.

And Hawke, unaware of his growing nocturnal audience, was pleasantly surprised to see that the bowl in which tips were placed seemed to be getting fuller every day.

Chapter 9

THE HERD WAS COMING NORTH, NOT IN ONE large mass, but in a long plodding column, generally no more than three or four abreast. On an average day they managed twelve to fifteen miles, and while on the move, one of the cowboys would ride as point man ahead of the herd, scouting for water and graze. Flankers rode on either side of the herd, to keep it moving, while one man rode drag, bringing up the rear. This was the least desirable position because the cowboy who rode drag had to swallow all the dust.

In many outfits the least experienced man would have been selected to ride drag every day. But Justin Parker, who was the trail boss, was fair about it, and he rotated the position among all the men, even taking drag himself when it was his turn.

The hardest part of the drive was to get the cows moving each morning. By design, the campsites were picked where there was plenty of grass and water. In addition, there would be an occasional tree or an overhanging bluff to provide some respite from the sun. As a result, the cows were reluctant to leave. Every morning they showed all intentions of staying right where they were.

Sometimes the drovers would have to shout, probe the animals with sticks, and swing their ropes to get the herd under way. Eventually their efforts would pay off and the herd would begin to move. Then, once the cattle were moving, they would change from three thousand individual creatures into a single entity with a single purpose. The inertia the drovers needed to overcome to get the herd moving in the first place now worked in their favor as the cows plodded along all day long at a steady clip, showing no inclination to stop.

There was a distinctive smell to a herd of such a size. It came from sun on the hides, dust in the air, and especially from the animals' droppings and urine. The odor was pungent and perhaps, to many, unpleasant. To the cowboys, however, it was an aroma as familiar and agreeable as the smell of flour and cinnamon on their mothers' aprons.

After supper on the seventh day of the drive, the trail boss, Justin Parker, walked over to the campfire for a second cup of coffee. The coffee was poured by Moses Gillespie, cook for the outfit.

"Moses, how are we on supplies?" Justin asked.

"We could use some more taters, onions, and flour," Moses said. "And maybe a little more coffee."

"We'll reach Salcedo tomorrow," he said. "You can go into town there."

"What about the boys?" Moses said. "You going to give them a break?"

Justin turned to look at the hands. One man had finished eating and was lying down with his head resting on his saddle. The others were visibly tired and listless from the long drive, their conversations quiet and unanimated as they ate.

"Men, let me have your attention a minute," Justin called.

Everyone looked in his direction.

"Tomorrow we'll reach Salcedo. There's water and grass there, and Moses needs some supplies, so I plan to stop there for a while to give you boys a rest and to let the herd recover some of their weight before we drive them on up to the railhead at Marva."

"Are you going to let us go into town, boss?" one of the cowboys asked.

"I'll let three of you go in each night, and we'll stay long enough to give all of you a chance to visit."

"Yahoo!" one of the cowboys shouted, and the others joined him.

"How we going to select who goes in first?"

"Anybody have a deck of cards?"

Several of the cowboys pointed to one of their number. "Pete has a deck," one of them said.

Pete Malone nodded in agreement.

"All right, we'll draw high card. The two highest cards drawn will go in first."

"I thought you said three could go in."

"We're using Pete's cards, so he'll go in the first night. Seems only fair."

"Yeah, especially since they're his cards and he'd probably draw the highest one anyway."

"You sayin' I cheat with my cards?" Pete asked.

"I'm just sayin' you *know* your cards," the cowboy said, and the others laughed.

Pete presented the deck, and one by one the cowboys filed by until all nine hands from the drive had drawn their card. When they were finished, Dusty Moore and Kendall Stallworth were the other two cowboys selected to make the trip into town with Pete.

Pete and Dusty had been on several drives before, but it was Kendall's first. At sixteen, Kendall was the youngest cowboy in the outfit, and everything about the drive was a new and exciting experience for him.

"You know what we need to do, don't you, Dusty?" Pete

asked as he, Dusty, and Kendall were discussing their upcoming trip into town.

"What's that?"

"Well, think about it. Young Kendall here is a virgin. We need to get him fixed up with a woman. It's about time he got broke in."

"Good idea," Dusty said.

"You two don't have to get me fixed up. I can do it myself," Kendall insisted.

Pete shook his head. "Uh-uh, no you can't," he said. "Not if you don't know what you're doing."

"Oh, I think I could figure out what to do, all right," Kendall said.

"Uh-huh. And what if you get hold of a snapping turtle?" Pete asked.

"A what?" Kendall asked, confused by the question.

"A snapping turtle," Pete repeated.

"What is a snapping turtle?"

"Well, it's never happened to me, mind, but it happened to a fella used to ride for the Lazy M. Fella by the name of Slim. Well, don't know that he was borned with that name, that's just what all the other cowboys called him. Terrible thing, what happened to Slim."

"What happened to him?" Kendall asked.

"He got caught by the snapping turtle."

"You still ain't told me what a snapping turtle is."

"See, the fact that you don't even know what I'm talkin' about is proof that you're too young to try and pick out your own whore. 'Cause, sometimes, what happens is, when a man is on top of a woman, why she's liable to just snap shut on him. And when that happens, ain't no way you can get loose. That is, not without having a couple of your friends come pull you out. Ain't that right, Dusty?"

Dusty was trying hard not to laugh. "That's right," he said.

"Of course, if that does happen to you, why, I don't reckon you'd really have to worry all that much. I mean you've got Dusty 'n' me, and we'll come right into that whore's room and pull you out if need be. Not like poor ol' Slim." Pete took his hat off, held it across his heart, and, with a warning glance, indicated that Dusty should do the same. Seeing the other two do that, Kendall took his own hat off and held it across his chest.

"Poor Slim," Dusty said, shaking his head as he went along with Pete's story.

"Yes, sir, what happened to him was just awful. Well, it was awful for the whore too, but seein' as how it was her fault and all, I just can't feel as sorry for her as I do for Slim."

"What happened to Slim?" Kendall asked.

"Why, he starved to death," Pete said.

"Starved to death?"

"Yes, sir. You see, when she snapped shut on him like she done, well, there weren't no friends around to come pull him out. So they just lay there, the two of 'em stuck together like two boards nailed together till someone found 'em both dead from starvation."

"I remember that," Dusty said, joining in now. "It was about the most awfulest thing ever to happen over to the Lazy M."

"Oh," Kendall said in alarm. "Oh, I wouldn't want anything like that to happen."

"Well, you don't have to worry that much about it," Pete said. "If it happens, all you got to do is let out a yell, 'n' me 'n' ol' Dusty will come pull you out. Right, Dusty?"

"Right," Dusty said. "We'd do that for our pard, all right."

Over at the chuck wagon, Justin Parker and Moses Gillespie were trying so hard to suppress their laughter that tears were flowing down their cheeks.

* * * *

In Salcedo, Flaire was hosting a dinner for Hawke. She had prepared the meal in her own kitchen and was serving it in the dining room of her apartment behind the dress shop.

"Chicken and dumplings," she said as she brought the meal to the table. "I know it isn't as fancy as the meal you had with Titus Culpepper, but—"

"But I will enjoy it more," Hawke said, interrupting her. "And how did you know about my meal with Culpepper?"

Flaire smiled. "You would be amazed at how rapidly gossip gets around in this town. How do you think everyone found out about your early morning concerts?"

"What?"

Flaire laughed. "You don't know, do you?"

"Know what?"

"You don't know that early in the morning, when you play such beautiful music, you have an audience hanging around outside the saloon."

"No," Hawke said. "I didn't have any idea. What about you? Do you ever come to hear me?"

"Every morning," Flaire answered.

"But I don't play every morning. What happens on the mornings I don't play?"

"We have that covered too," Flaire said. "Mr. Baldwin and Mr. Poindexter go to work at about that time, every morning. If they see candlelight in the saloon, they know you are getting ready to play, and they spread the word. You should see it; it's like our own version of Paul Revere."

"Well, I'm glad you told me. I'll unlock the doors the next time so everyone can come in."

Flaire shook her head. "I don't think anyone would want to come in."

"Why not?"

"It's hard to explain, but I think everyone would prefer to

stay outside. There's something ... almost magical ... about listening to beautiful music under a sky full of stars. Besides, I think they like the idea of listening to you without you knowing about it."

Hawke smiled. "If that's the case, why did you tell me?"

"Maybe I like the idea of sharing secrets with you, without anyone else knowing about it," Flaire said. She spooned the chicken and dumplings onto his plate, then put the bowl down. "Tell me, how is it that you play the piano so beautifully? I mean, you certainly aren't like the average saloon piano player."

"My parents had a piano in our house," Hawke said. "According to my mother, before I could even talk, I would sit at the piano and try to play. As soon as I was old enough, they hired a piano teacher for me. When my teacher thought I was ready, I went to Europe to study, and I even made a concert tour."

"Oh, how grand!" Flaire said, smiling broadly. Then her expression changed to one of curiosity. "But I don't understand. With such talent, why are you not playing concerts today? Why are you playing in saloons?"

"I'm not sure I can answer that question," Hawke replied.

"What a shame. I'm sure it is the world's loss," Flaire said.

"Would you like to hear a concert?" Hawke asked.

"You mean other than the one you give in the wee hours of the morning? Yes, I'd love to."

Hawke shook his head. "No, I'm not talking about a concert that I would give. I'm talking about a concert given by Gottschalk."

"Gotts ... ?"

"Gottschalk. Louis Moreau Gottschalk. He is one of the finest pianists in the world, and certainly the finest in America."

"Oh! Well, if you think he is the best, then he certainly must be," Flaire said. "Where would this concert be given?"

"In San Antonio," Hawke said. "I figured we could catch the stage to Marva, then take the train to San Antonio. Of course, that means you would have to close your shop for a few days. Can you do that?"

Flaire smiled. "That's the beauty of being my own boss," she said. "When is this concert?"

"Next week," Hawke said. "If you would like to go, I'll make all the arrangements."

"Do you know Gottschalk?"

"Yes, I know him."

"Is he famous?"

Hawke chuckled. "Yes, he is famous."

"I've never met a famous person."

"Then I will introduce you."

"Oh, this whole thing is so exciting," Flaire said. "Yes, I would love to go. Of course, it will cause a scandal, but I don't care."

"Oh? Why should it cause a scandal?"

"We will be gone overnight, won't we?"

"Yes. At least for two nights."

"In view of what people are already saying about us, this will just add fuel to the fire."

"What are they saying?" Hawke asked.

"Are you kidding? First there was the picnic, which, because of the way you handled Culpepper's three deputies, wasn't exactly a secret. And now everyone knows I'm hosting a dinner for you. By the time we go off together, I imagine that half the town will have us in the middle of a torrid affair while the other half will have us secretly married."

"I wouldn't like to be a part of anything that would damage your reputation."

"Put your mind at ease on that score. I have no reputation to damage."

"Why do you say that?"

"I am a woman, running a business," Flaire explained.

"What's wrong with that?"

"Women don't run a business. It simply isn't done," Flaire said.

"How do they expect you to eat if you don't have some way of making a living?"

Flaire laughed. "Heavens, the public can't be bothered with such petty details as survival."

"By the way, if you ever get tired of making dresses, you could always open a restaurant," Hawke said as he enjoyed his meal. "This is absolutely delicious. Much better than the dinner I had with Culpepper."

"You are being kind. Untruthful, I think, but kind."

"No, I am being truthful."

"Well then, kind sir, I thank you for the compliment. So now, tell me. Are you going to work for *Colonel* Culpepper?" She emphasized the title, showing her disdain for it.

"You know about that?"

"I know only that he offered you the job. Some say you turned him down, others say you are waiting to make up your mind."

"So now the truth is out. You invited me to dinner just so you could find out whether I'm going to work for Culpepper," Hawke teased.

"No," Flaire said quickly—too quickly. Then, with an embarrassed laugh, she amended her answer. "Well, all right, but not just that. I'm actually paying you back for the picnic. But I do confess that I am curious about what you are going to do."

"Then let me satisfy your curiosity," Hawke said. "I turned him down."

"Oh. I'm sorry you did," Flaire said.

Surprised by her response, he looked up. "You're sorry? Wait a minute. I thought you didn't like Culpepper. What is it you said about the Regulators? That they had replaced one outlaw gang with another?"

"Yes, that is what I said."

"And, believing that, you still think I should have joined them?"

"Yes. Maybe if you had taken the job, you could have changed things."

"I doubt it," Hawke said. "The truth is, Culpepper isn't going to let anyone have any say in running the Regulators."

"I can believe that. Culpepper does strike me as that kind of person."

As Flaire cleaned up her kitchen after her dinner with Hawke, she thought about the feelings she had for him. He had already made it clear, in no uncertain terms, that he wasn't the kind of man who could, or would, settle down.

That was all right, she decided. She could accept that. She was just thankful that, apparently, she was able to feel something for Hawke. After her ordeal with the men who burned out the ranch and killed her family in front of her, she wasn't sure she would ever have been able to feel anything for a man.

Flaire's mother, father, and younger brother lay on the ground, their sleeping gowns covered with blood. No longer screaming, Flaire continued to stare in shock at her dead family. She was only barely cognizant of the fact that two of the riders had dismounted and were coming toward her.

"How old are you, girl?" one of them asked.

"Sixteen," Flaire answered dully.

One of them bunched her sleeping gown up in his hands,

then pulled it off. She was aware of the heat of the flames from the burning barn against her naked skin, but was so numbed by what she had just seen that she was powerless to react.

"Damn, lookie here at the way she's tittied up. Them ain't the titties of no little girl. This here is a woman, full-grown."

The two men who dismounted had their way with her, but compared to the shock of having just watched her family murdered, the rape barely registered with her. She lay on the ground, feeling the rocks digging into her back, listening to the snapping and popping of the burning barn, and smelling the fetid breath of first one and then his partner as they grunted on top of her.

Chapter 10

AFTER HIS DINNER WITH FLAIRE, HAWKE RETURNED to the Golden Calf. The saloon was crowded, so he sat down at the piano and began playing, sticking to the standards that would provide background music but would not be so intrusive as to keep the patrons from drinking.

Doc Urban and Cyrus Green were engaged in their usual game of chess, Darci was working the tables, and at least one poker game was in progress. Doc Urban took out one of Cyrus's rooks with a knight.

"Damn, I should've seen that," Cyrus said. He made a move to protect his remaining rook. "Doc, let me ask you something. Do you pay taxes to the Regulators?"

"You're damn right I do," Urban replied as he studied the board. "The taxes are as much as I charge most people, which means I have to almost double my charges in order to have any money left over after taxes."

"One hundred percent taxes," Cyrus said. He moved his bishop to challenge one of Doc Urban's knights.

"What do you mean, one hundred percent taxes?" Doc Urban asked as he took his knight out of danger.

"I mean we are paying one hundred percent taxes," Cyrus said. "I've been doing a little research. From what I can determine, one out of every two dollars that change hands in this town wind up in Culpepper's pocket."

"Well, now," Doc Urban said, looking up at his chess partner with renewed interest. "And here I thought you and Culpepper were joined at the hip. I've never seen one negative word about him in your newspaper."

"That's because I haven't printed one negative word about him. I was convinced, for some time, that he was our savior."

"And you no longer believe that?"

"Let's just say that I am having second thoughts."

"My, my. Mohammed has gone to the mountain. How, may I ask, did all this come about?"

"I've been getting a lot of letters-to-the-editor," Cyrus said. "Almost every one of them contains complaints about our surrogate police force. The people feel that we are overtaxed by an overbearing and overzealous band of . . . well, one word that pops up a lot is thugs."

"So now you, who once beat the drums for them, are turning against them," Doc Urban said. "Who would have thought?"

"Let us just say that I no longer intend to wear blinders," Cyrus replied. Then, with a broad smile, he said, "Check."

"Hawke," Doc Urban called as Hawke finished one of his songs. "Come here, this upstart newspaperman thinks he has me in check. Let me show you how I handle upstarts."

Answering the summons, Hawke came over to join them at the table. Darci, who was already bringing him a beer at the end of his set, put the beer on the table.

"You may watch as well, my dear," Doc Urban said to her.

Doc Urban took out Cyrus's offending rook with a bishop.

"Damn!" Cyrus said. "I'm sure there is an object lesson somewhere in there, but I can't see what it is."

"Where did you learn to play chess so well, Doc?" Hawke asked.

"When you spend twenty years at sea, you have lots of time on your hands," Doc said. "I played a lot of chess."

"Did you like being a sailor?"

"Oh yes, I liked it."

"Why did you leave?"

"Wait a minute," Cyrus said, looking at Hawke. "Do you mean the good doctor has never told you why he left the sea?"

"No, he hasn't."

"Tell him, Doc."

"Ahh, it's too long a story and everyone has heard it," Doc said with a dismissive wave of his hand.

"No, not everyone has heard it. Mason Hawke hasn't heard it," Cyrus said. "And I, for one, wouldn't mind hearing it again." Cyrus turned back to Hawke. "It's a hell of a story. I'm trying to talk him into writing a book about it, but he doesn't seem interested."

"Now you do have me curious," Hawke said. "I'd like to hear it."

Doc Urban drummed his fingers on the table for a moment, then nodded. "I'll tell it." He looked at Cyrus. "But don't you even think about touching the board until I'm finished."

"Don't worry," Cyrus replied. "I'll be too caught up in the story."

Doc nodded. "All right," he said. "It all began with a storm. In twenty years at sea, I had never encountered such a storm.

"I was on board the *Lydia Holmes* as a ship's surgeon, and we were forty-three days out of Coramantine with a load of hemp when the typhoon hit.

"The wind began blowing with gale force, and the ship was crashing violently through the waves. The crew managed to furl the topsail, but suddenly the great mainsail on the foremast ripped open from top to bottom.

"The captain sent men aloft to work on the torn sail, but

no sooner had they finished than the mizzen topsail tore loose and began flapping in the breeze, threatening to pull away and take with it the top part of the mizzenmast, which was now vibrating like a wand.

"Waves were battering the hull of the ship with the impact of cannon balls. The *Lydia Holmes* would be lifted by one swell, hang quivering over the trough between the waves, then slam back down into the sea, only to be caught up by another, even larger wave.

"Then, one monstrous wave stove in the side, and the captain gave orders to abandon ship. Well, you can imagine that if a ship like the *Lydia Holmes* couldn't weather the storm, the idea of getting into small lifeboats wasn't very appealing.

"But we had no choice, so we took to them, and even though we were lashed together, somehow the boats got separated during the night. The next morning I and six others found ourselves on the same boat in which most of the water and food had been stored.

"We searched for the other two boats but couldn't find them."

Doc stopped talking for a moment, and Hawke noticed that the others—Paddy and Mary, who were now listening, and Darci—remained silent, hanging on every word, even though they had all heard the story before.

"The real horror of the ordeal was my growing suspicion that one of the survivors, a man named Angus Pugh, may have set the other boats adrift during the night in order not to have to share the food and water.

"As our nightmare continued, we lost more people, and always in the middle of the night when we were sleeping. Everyone assumed that they were just unable to take it anymore and so slipped over the side. But I began to have the overpowering feeling—which I did not share with anyone—that Pugh might be killing them, to further reduce the demand on our rations. I was convinced that he was sparing me only because he might have need of a surgeon. I am ashamed that I shared my suspicions with no one else, but I was fearful that Angus Pugh might decide that he wouldn't need a doctor after all.

"At any rate, our numbers steadily decreased over the three weeks we were adrift, until we were picked up by a packet ship that was California-bound from Shanghai. By then only three of what had been fifteen original survivors were still alive."

"That's quite a story, Doc," Hawke said when Urban was finished. "Was that before or after the war?"

"During."

"During?"

"Yes. I served throughout the entire Civil War as a ship's surgeon on a merchantman that plied the Pacific, so I didn't fight for either side."

"Which side would you have fought for?" Hawke asked.

"To tell the truth, I'm not sure," Doc Urban said. "I think both sides had their points. I read about the war in all the newspapers, of course. But I never was quite able to figure out what it was all about."

"I have news for you," Hawke said. "Many of those of us who did fight in the war were never able to figure out what it was all about."

"Amen to that, brother," Paddy said quietly.

"Hey, Hawke," Cyrus said. "I was telling Doc, here, about a song the soldiers used to sing. It was a real pretty song, sort of sad. Had some woman's name."

Hawke smiled. "Would you be talking about 'Lorena'?"

"'Lorena,' yeah, that's it," Cyrus said. "I'd be mighty obliged to you if you'd play it."

"All right."

Hawke returned to the piano and slid easily into the song. The music was mesmerizing, the familiar and haunting melody underscored with an equally haunting but totally unfamiliar countermelody. In addition to the melody and countermelody, trills and ruffles moved through the tapestry of the music like a golden thread.

Conversation in the saloon stopped during the playing of the song, and a couple of men surreptitiously wiped away a tear, memories and emotions from their own war experiences evoked by the melody.

"Damn," Doc said when the song was finished. "You're right, Cyrus. That's about the prettiest thing I've ever heard." Taking out a dollar, Cyrus walked over to the piano and dropped it in Hawke's tip bowl. Doc did the same thing.

"Why, thank you, boys," Hawke said.

Several other patrons added their own contributions, making the tip bowl fuller than it had ever been since Hawke started playing at the Golden Calf.

One block down the street from the Golden Calf, Flaire sat on a sofa in her apartment with the window up, listening to the sounds of the night. Next door, Mrs. Underhill was berating her husband about something. Flaire could hear her high-pitched, carping voice, though, mercifully, she couldn't make out what the woman was saying.

A little earlier a baby had been crying, but he stopped, either because he was at the breast or had fallen asleep. A dog's yap had sent a screeching cat running.

Just down the street she could hear the sounds of the saloon . . . a woman's squeal over the unintelligible rumble of conversation. But above all, she could hear the piano.

Flaire realized then that the saloon had grown strangely quiet.

Except for the music.

Without the background noise of laughter and conversation, the music could be clearly heard spilling out of the saloon and rolling down the single street of the little town. The music was exceptionally beautiful, and for a moment she wondered what the piece was. Then, with a start, she realized it was *Lorena*, the beautiful but sad song that had become the love ballad of the Civil War.

And yet, even as she recognized it, she realized that she had never heard it played in such a way before. In its own way, she believed the song to be as beautiful as the music Hawke played during his early morning concerts.

Sometime during the evening, Deputies Vox and Bates came into the saloon. Bates took a table while Vox stepped up to the bar.

"Give me a bottle and two glasses," he said.

Paddy reached for the bottle. "You know, don't you, that I'm going to have to charge you for this," he said. "My arrangement with Culpepper is one free beer every time you come in. Beer, not whiskey."

"Yeah? Well now your arrangement is with me," Vox said. "Culpepper won't be back for at least another week. Maybe longer. Now give me the goddamn bottle," he demanded.

Shrugging his shoulders and making a mental note to take it up with Culpepper when he got back, Paddy gave Vox the bottle and two glasses.

"That wasn't so hard, was it?" Vox said. Carrying the bottle and two glasses over to the table, he sat down. But before he could pour the whiskey, Darci stopped by his table and, smiling, took the bottle from him.

"What are you trying to do?" she asked. "Put me out of work? Pouring is my job."

She poured into both glasses, and as she was doing so, Bates reached up under her skirt, a garment that came only to her knees, and grabbed her behind.

Darci's smile turned into a frown. "Please don't do that," she said, pushing his hand away.

"What do you mean, don't do that? Are you telling me you don't like it?"

"I don't like it."

"You're a whore. Men put their hands on you all the time," Bates said.

"Men who arrange for my services do," Darci said. "But even then, they must behave as gentlemen."

"Ha! A whore wanting her customers to be gentlemen," Vox said. "It'll be a cold day in hell before I'm a gentleman to any whore I'm with."

"Then that works out well. Because it'll be a cold day in hell before you are with this whore," Darci replied with a deceptively sweet smile.

She walked away from Vox's table and, seeing a frequent customer, painted the smile back on her face as she went over to talk to him.

"I don't know why Culpepper didn't make a deal so we could have women too," Bates said.

"Yeah, well, once he goes to Congress and I take over, I intend to make that deal," Vox said. "Damn, would you look at that?" he added.

"Look at what?" Bates asked, twisting around in his seat to see what Vox was staring at.

"That bowl on top of the piano over there. It's full of money. What you think that's there for?"

"That's his tips," Bates said.

"Tips?"

"Yes, tips."

"What's tips?"

"You mean you don't know?"

"If I knowed, would I ask you?" Vox asked.

Bates laughed. "I guess this shows what a cheap shit you are," he said. "A tip is what you give somebody when they do a good job."

As if on cue, Vox got up from the table, moved to the piano, and dropped some coins into the bowl on top.

"You played some real pretty songs tonight, Hawke," he said.

Hawke nodded in response, but if he spoke, he was too quiet for Vox to hear.

"How much you think is in that bowl?" Vox asked his companion.

"I don't know. I'd say around fifteen dollars, at least," Bates said. "Anyway, what do you care how much money is there?"

"I care, because half of it belongs to us," Vox said.

"How do you figure that?"

"Has he paid us any taxes that you know of?"

Bates smiled. "Nary a cent," he said.

"It's about time we collected, don't you think?"

"Yeah," Bates agreed.

Vox moved closer to Hawke and stood alongside him. "Hey, piano player, where at did you get all that money?" he asked.

Ignoring Vox, Hawke continued to play.

"Didn't you hear what I said?" He pointed to the money bowl. "Where at did you get all that money?"

"Leave him alone, Vox," Baldwin said. Baldwin was the baker and one of the original discoverers of Hawke's early morning concerts. "The rest of us are enjoying his piano playing."

"You want to spend the night in jail?" Vox warned Baldwin.

"No."

"Then stay the hell out of this. I'm just doin' my duty."

"Rousting the piano player is doing your duty?"

"I said, stay the hell out of this," Vox repeated. Then he turned back to Hawke, who had not stopped playing, nor had he given any indication that he was even paying any attention.

"I tell you what, piano player. I had no idea you was

makin' that much money. Seems to me like it's about time you started paying taxes like everyone else."

"I don't intend to pay taxes," Hawke said.

This was Hawke's first response to Vox, and even then he didn't quit playing the piano.

"What do you mean you don't intend to pay taxes?" Vox sputtered. "By God, you'll pay taxes just like everyone else."

Vox reached down into the bowl to pull out a handful of coins and bills. He had barely put his hand in when he let out a yell. "Argh!" he called out in pain.

The cause of the pain was the barrel of his own pistol, which Hawke had jerked from Vox's holster, then shoved up the deputy's nostril.

"Put it back," Hawke said menacingly.

"What are you doing? Are you crazy! I'll throw you in jail for this!"

Hawke pushed the gun up so far that Vox's nose began to bleed, then he cocked the pistol.

"I said put it back," Hawke said again.

Hawke's sudden and unexpected action brought all conversation in the saloon to an instant halt. Everyone looked on in shock.

With trembling hands, Vox put the money back in the bowl.

Hawke stood up then and, with the gun still shoved up Vox's nose, walked him back over to the table where Bates was watching, as shocked as the rest of the saloon.

"I think you two had better leave now," Hawke said.

"You got no right to run us out of here," Vox said.

"I've got a gun stuck up your nose," Hawke said. "Looks to me like that sort of gives me the right. Now, get out of here."

"Get up, get up!" Vox said to Bates. "I believe this crazy son of a bitch really will try to kill me!"

Not until Bates got up as well did Hawke pull his pistol from Vox's nose. There was blood on the end of the pistol, and blood running down across Vox's chin.

"What about my pistol?" Vox asked.

"This is the second time you've given it to me. Why don't you just let me keep it?" Hawke asked.

"Are you crazy? That's a twenty-dollar gun!"

Hawke wiped the barrel of the gun off on Vox's shirt. "Yeah, I can see that it's a pretty good gun," he said. "It has very good balance."

Still glaring at Hawke, Vox turned and left the saloon, with Bates trailing behind.

Hawke moved quickly to the bat-wing doors, then stepped over to one side. As he knew he would, Vox stepped back into the saloon, this time with what must have been a pistol belonging to Bates in his hand.

"Piano player!" Vox shouted angrily, bitterly. It was clear that if he had seen Hawke at that moment, he would have killed him, even if it meant shooting Hawke in the back.

Stepping inside was as far as Vox got, however, because Hawke, standing just beside the entrance, smashed Vox in the face with the butt of his own pistol. Vox went down and out.

"Come get him!" Hawke yelled into the darkness just beyond the door. "Come get him, or I'll pull him out back and feed him to the hogs!"

Hesitantly, cautiously, Bates stuck his hands inside, showing that he wasn't holding a gun.

"I ain't armed," he called from the porch.

"I know you're not," Hawke said. "Unless I miss my guess, that's your gun there, on the floor."

Bates came in. Like the eyes of a trapped rat, he glanced around the saloon. The arrogance and belligerence he normally displayed had been replaced with the look of fear.

Hawke emptied Vox's gun, then picked up Bates's gun from the floor and emptied it as well. He stuck both of the empty weapons down into Vox's pants.

"Get him out of here," Hawke ordered.

Grabbing him by his feet, Bates pulled Vox outside. Once on the porch, Vox started regaining his senses, but he was so groggy that Hawke didn't expect any more trouble.

He didn't come back.

Not until then did all the patrons in the saloon let out a collective sigh of relief.

Flaire worked on a dress of her own design, getting it ready for the trip to San Antonio. It was a beautiful dress, and if she sold it, it would cost much more than any of her customers would be able to afford.

If she hadn't made it herself, she wouldn't be able to afford it either.

The dress, called a "visiting toilette," was made of pearl gray faille, trimmed with bands of dark crimson velvet.

"My dear, you do such beautiful work," Emma Rittenhouse had told her. "With your talent, you should go to New York.

After the men left, Flaire lay on the ground alongside her family for the rest of the night. Sometime before morning, as the barn burned itself out, she fell asleep from pure exhaustion; physical, mental, and psychological.

Neighbors found her the next morning, drawn to the farm by the smoke that was still curling into the sky from the burned barn.

"My God, Helga, what happened here?" Chris Speer asked his wife as he stopped the wagon and set the brake. What had been the barn was little more than a charred pile of smoking lumber. What were at first unidentifiable lumps,

Speer now recognized as the burned carcasses of horses and cows.

"Why didn't the Delaneys get their animals out?" Speer asked.

"Chris!" Helga said, her voice tight. She pulled on her husband's shirtsleeve. "Chris, look."

Helga pointed toward the house, where four bodies lay on the ground.

"Gott im Himmel!"

Chris jumped down from the wagon and ran over to the bodies. "They've been shot!" he called back to Helga, who, clutching her shawl about her shoulders, had remained on the wagon. "They're dead! All of them!"

Flaire moaned then, and Chris turned toward her.

"Helga," he called. "Come see to the girl. She is still alive. And she is naked!"

Helga climbed down from the wagon then, and hurried over to attend to Flaire. Not seeing any wounds on her body, she picked up Flaire's nightgown and handed it to her.

"You had better put this on, child," she said.

"Mama!" Flaire said. "Papa!" Memories of what had happened the night before came flooding back to her and she started toward her parents.

Helga held her back. "No, child," she said. "You can't help them now."

Flaire went home with the Speers and stayed with them until her family had been buried. But like the Delaneys, Chris and Helga Speer were Union sympathizers in a county that was predominantly pro-South. Frightened that their farm would be next, Chris sold his place and he and Helga planned to move back to St. Louis, where they felt safer.

"We want you to come with us, child," Helga said. "You've become almost like a daughter to us."

"Thank you," Flaire replied. "I feel the same way about

you and Mr. Speer. But I fear that if I leave town, my brother won't be able to find me when he returns."

"I understand," Helga said. "Still, I wouldn't feel good about leaving you alone, with no means of support. Let me look around and see what I can find for you."

It took a few days, but Helga found a spinster seamstress by the name of Emma Rittenhouse, who agreed to take Flaire on as an apprentice.

"I can't pay anything," Miss Rittenhouse said. "But I will feed her and give her a place to stay." She smiled. "And if she is a good student, she will be able to make her own clothes."

Flaire had been totally unprepared for her reaction to the art of sewing. She loved it . . . loved taking bolts of cloth and turning it into beautiful things. She discovered a talent for designing, and quickly became such a valuable asset that Emma Rittenhouse's business increased and Miss Rittenhouse started paying her.

"You've gone far beyond me," Miss Rittenhouse said. "You have a God-given talent and you should study under someone who could do more for you. Perhaps someone in New York, or even Paris."

Although the suggestion that she was good enough to study in such places as New York or Paris was very flattering, Flaire knew she would never be able to do anything like that. But when the war ended and she moved to Texas, she felt very confident when she started her own business.

Chapter 11

IT HAD NOT BEEN MERE IDLE CONVERSATION with Doc Urban when Cyrus Green started talking about the exorbitant taxes the Regulators were extracting from the town. Cyrus was having an epiphany. He had been one of the first supporters of the Regulators Brigade, and a staunch defender of the brigade ever since its inception. And he had remained steadfast despite the complaints he was hearing about them from so many of the townspeople.

"You're like a ship underway," Doc Urban told him. "Once you have your course set, it is very difficult to come about."

Cyrus chuckled at the analogy. "You have a point there, Doc. But I have to tell you, as I told you before, I am now having second thoughts."

At first Cyrus had thought the complaints were because of the strictness with which the Regulators enforced the law. Spitting on the sidewalk could bring a cowboy a crack on the head and seven days in jail. Laws against public drunkenness were so rigidly enforced that the jails were filled every night with people who did no more than take a stutter step as they left the Golden Calf.

Each of these offenses brought fines that did not go to the

operating costs of the town, but directly into the coffers of the Regulators Brigade. What Cyrus was beginning to question more than anything else, though, was the taxation the Regulators had levied on the businesses of Salcedo. When the town council hired Culpepper, they also authorized him to recruit volunteers to serve in the Salcedo Regulators. At the same time, they vested Culpepper and the Regulators with law enforcement authority.

It wasn't until later that Culpepper returned to the council to ask that a tax be enacted that would enable him to hire and pay deputies.

"To run this operation right, it's going to take money," he said. "More money than my contract calls for. I am going to have to hire and equip deputies, and pay them well enough that they will risk their lives in our service. And the only way I can do that is if I am given the authority by the town council to levy taxes."

Although taxing authority had not been a part of the original contract, Cyrus Green, as mayor, had been an early supporter of the idea. But lately he had started paying attention to the people who were complaining. He also began adding up all the taxes the Regulators were collecting, and he was shocked by the figures.

Just from the people who willingly gave information, Cyrus figured that Culpepper and the Regulators were bringing in over two thousand dollars every month.

In addition, Cyrus know there were many who wouldn't share the information with him, either because they were frightened, ashamed, or genuinely felt that it was none of his business. He believed that if all those numbers were factored into the equation, the actual amount of money might be twice as much.

Cyrus had already asked Culpepper when he planned to

have the town council hire a new city marshal so he could
disband his Regulators.

"Soon," Culpepper answered whenever he was asked.
"Soon."

Cyrus used to wonder why Culpepper kept putting off the
hiring of a new marshal. Now he knew why. He hated to admit it to himself, but he was convinced that Culpepper had
no intention of ever giving up the position he held. Why
should he? What he had grabbed hold of was a money cow.

That gave Cyrus an idea for an editorial. Moving to his
layout table, he began setting type, starting with the larger
font for the headline.

WOC YENOM EHT

He looked at the head he had just set, able to read it as
easily backward as nearly everyone else could the right way.

THE MONEY COW

Cyrus's hands flew from type box to type box, selecting
the lead letters, headers, and spacers as he assembled them,
composing the editorial as he went along.

I have been accused of being a stubborn man,
someone who makes up his mind and will not
change it, even when confronted with ir-
refutable facts. Indeed, it is as difficult to pull
me away from a position once arrived at as it is
to stop a fast-moving train.

But that time has come. I am about to confess
that I have been wrong in my undying support
of that group of men known as the Salcedo Regulators Brigade. Perhaps others were as fooled

as I was, mistaking the vigilantes' routing of the Dawson gang as a service performed for the benefit of the public.

Subsequent investigation suggests that not to be the case at all. By eliminating the Dawson gang, and by getting the sanction of the mayor and town council, the encouragement of our citizens, and, I am sorry to say, the support of this newspaper, the self-appointed "colonel" Titus Culpepper has turned Salcedo into his private money cow.

We are living under a burden of taxes more loathsome than any taxes that have ever been imposed upon a society, and, as the Regulators are not an elected body, we have no means of political redress. Our only weapon would be to refuse to pay any further taxes to this oppressive group.

A further means of showing our disapproval would be to make certain that Titus Culpepper does not achieve any elected office. As of this writing, he is in Austin, filing for election to the United States Congress. I will go on record, here and now, as saying that this paper will not only not support him, but will do everything within its power to prevent his election.

Your letters on this subject are welcome.

On the afternoon of the day Cyrus Green's editorial appeared, several of the deputies gathered in the headquarters building to discuss what they should do about it.

"He has some nerve, printing something like this with the colonel gone," Deputy Hooper said, slamming the newspaper on the desk.

"Yeah," Deputy Moody said. "He wouldn't dare have done that with the colonel here."

"I think we ought to go over there and knock him around a bit," Vox said.

"Yeah, and tear up his damn shop," Hooper added.

"Hold on," Deputy Bates said. "We ain't goin' to do nothin' like that lessen the colonel tells us to."

"We don't need Culpepper's permission," Vox said. "He left me in charge while he's gone, so anything I say we can do, we can do." Both of Vox's eyes were black and his nose was swollen and discolored from the blow he had taken in the face the night before.

"Right!" Moody said.

"And I say we go over there right now," Vox said. "But don't just tear it up, let's burn the whole building down."

"You don't want to do that, Vox," Bates said.

"And why the hell wouldn't I want to do it?"

"Well, for one thing, it was the Dawsons doin' that to 'em that got the town all riled up in the first place, remember? Now you want to do the same thing and get them riled at us?"

"You think I care about whether or not the town is riled at us?" Vox asked. "What are they going to do about it? Nothing, 'cause there's nothing they can do. It's the town should worry about us, not us them."

"Maybe so, but if we do somethin' like that, the colonel can just kiss his chances of getting elected good-bye."

"Yeah, well, that's Culpepper's problem, not mine," Vox said.

"Maybe," Bates agreed. "But don't forget, when the colonel goes to Congress, you'll be taking over here."

Vox stroked his chin for a moment, considering that. Then he nodded.

"Yeah," he said. "Yeah, you're right. All right, we'll hold off for now. But you mark my words, when Culpepper gets back, he'll have a few choice words for our mayor."

Vox made it a point always to speak of Culpepper as

"Culpepper" and not the colonel. In that way, he set himself apart from the rest of the deputies, showing them that his position was elevated enough to allow that type of intimacy.

Gillis, who had not been told of Vox's adventure in the saloon the night before, was staring at him.

"What the hell are you staring at?" Vox asked irritably.

"I was just starin' at your face," Gillis replied. "Damn if you don't look like you was hit by a train. What the hell happened to you?"

"The piano player done it," Spellman said, barely able to suppress his laughter.

"The piano player done that to you?" Gillis said. "Damn, he don't look that tough to me."

"He was hiding behind a wall and he hit Vox when he wasn't expecting it," Bates said, covering for the chief deputy.

"And you're just going to let him get away with it?"

"No, I ain't going to let him get away with it," Vox said. "I figured on settling the score with him today, only the son of a bitch is gone."

"Where'd he go?"

"How the hell do I know where he went?" Vox replied. "He just tucked his tail between his legs and skedaddled. He's running from me, the cowardly son of a bitch."

"Nah, he ain't runnin' from you," Gillis said. "Him an' the Delaney woman took the stage out this mornin'. Hell, ever'-body in town is talkin' about it. Them runnin' off together like that."

"Runnin' off to do what?" Spellman asked.

"What do you think?" Gillis replied. "She's a good-lookin' woman. I figure he's just takin' her somewhere so's he can bed her without folks talkin' about it."

"That don't make no sense," Bates said. "Didn't you just say ever'body was talkin' about it?"

"I tell you what," Gillis said, grabbing himself unconsciously. "I sure wish I had knowed that about her before now. I wouldn't mind takin' her off somewhere my ownself."

"Yeah, and I'm sure she would go with you," Bates said sarcastically.

"I figure she would," Gillis said. "After all, women like that will go with just about any man.

The rims of the stage wheels were covered with steel bands, and they rolled over the hard dirt road with a quiet, crunching sound. As the wheels whirled around, dirt adhered to the rims for about half a revolution, then was thrown back in little rooster tails to be carried off by the whispering breeze. The sun was still early morning low in the east, and a morning mist wrapped itself around the cottonwood trees, clinging to the branches in flowing tendrils of lace.

There were five passengers on the stage: Hawke, Flaire, a young mother and her baby, and a whiskey drummer. The driver explained that the trip to Marva would take just over four hours, counting the time required for a change of teams at the halfway station.

As Flaire looked through the window at the wildflowers growing in colorful profusion alongside the road, she thought of her luggage back in the boot of the stage. In her suitcase was the new dress she had just finished making, and it excited her to think about wearing it.

The thought of going to a grand concert and then meeting the famous performer afterward was also exciting. But then, though she dared not admit it even to herself, so was the thought of making a trip with Mason Hawke.

Hawke was looking out the window on the opposite side of the stage from Flaire, but his attention was directed inside. The drummer was staring at him, and had been staring at him for some time now.

"Puxico," the drummer finally said, holding up his finger. "I knew it would come to me. That was you, wasn't it?"

"I beg your pardon?" Flaire asked, turning her attention back into the coach. "Did you address me?"

"Not you, ma'am. I was addressing this gentleman here. That was you at Puxico, wasn't it?"

"Yes, I've been to Puxico," Hawke said. He knew what was coming next. He'd been in this same situation many times before. He wished there was some way he could head it off, but knew that there wasn't.

"You've been to Puxico?" the drummer said. He laughed. "Is that all you have to say about it? Just that you have been there?"

"It's all I care to say about it," Hawke said.

"I'll tell you this: That was the damnedest thing I ever saw in my life. They was three of 'em drawed their guns on you, and you kilt all three of 'em, slick as a whistle."

"Oh!" the young mother said in alarm. Almost involuntarily, she scooted farther over in the seat, holding her baby closer to her.

Hawke could feel the woman's fear.

"I'm afraid you have mistaken me for someone else," Hawke said.

"Look, this isn't an accusation. Ever'one that saw it said there was nothin' you could do about it. They drawed down on you first."

"I said, you have mistaken me for someone else," Hawke said, more resolutely, almost menacingly, this time.

Finally the drummer caught on. "Uh, yes," he said. "Yes, now that I look at you more closely, I think I have made a mistake. I'm sorry."

"That's all right, it happens a lot," Hawke said. "I have one of those faces that everyone thinks they recognize."

Convinced that the drummer was mistaken, the young

mother visibly relaxed, and the fear left her face. The rest of the coach trip was uneventful.

They boarded the train at six o'clock that evening for the fourteen hour trip to San Antonio. Not until they were having their supper in the dining car did Flaire bring up what the drummer had said.

"That whiskey salesman didn't mistake you, did he?" she asked. "You are the one he saw."

"What makes you think that?" Hawke asked as he took a sip of his wine.

"He said there were three men who accosted you in Pux-ico."

"There were three men who accosted the person he was talking about," Hawke corrected. "I did not concede that I was that man."

"Maybe it is just a coincidence, but there were three men who accosted us on the day of our picnic," Flaire said. "I wondered how you could have handled the situation as easily as you did. This would explain it."

"Would it?"

Flaire reached across the dinner table to put her hand on his. "It's all right if you don't want to talk about it," she said. "I won't bring it up again."

"Thank you," Hawke said.

Flaire lay in her bed that night, rocked gently by the motion of the train, and listening to the sound of steel wheels rolling on steel track.

Despite Hawke's reluctance to concede that the drummer had not made a mistake, she was convinced that Hawke was the man he was talking about. She had seen him in action and knew that he was quite capable of performing the feat described by the salesman.

But it was more than his ability to do it; it was his willingness to do it. He had told the three men who accosted them on the day of the picnic that he would kill them. He had spoken the words as calmly as if he had just said that he would open the door for them, and it was that quiet, deadly calm that sent chills running down her spine. It was as if she had just heard the quiet, fluttering wings of the angel of death.

As she drifted off to sleep she thought about her brother, and remembered his reaction when she told him who killed her parents, then raped her.

It wasn't until both men were through with her and were readjusting their clothes that she actually looked at them. When she did, she recognized them, though something told her to give no sign that she knew who they were.

They were the Sumlin brothers. She knew them because they lived on a farm on the other side of the county. In fact, she knew that her brother Eddie, now away fighting with the Union Army, had gone fishing and hunting with them a few times before the war started. How could men who were once friends of her brother do such a thing as was done to her that night?

The third man did not dismount, so Flair never got a good look at him.

When Eddie came back home after the war, he learned of the murder of his parents and the rape and defilement of his sister. He also learned that it was the Sumlin brothers.

The war was over, and general amnesty had been granted for all, including the Sumlin brothers. The officials of the state of Missouri, and of Platte County, pleaded with neighbors, many of whom had been separated by the war, to put the war behind them.

Eddie rode over to the Sumlin farm and invited the brothers to go hunting with him, just as they did before the war.

The Sumlins, who had no idea Flaire had recognized them, accepted the invitation.

"Hell yes," Dewey Sumlin said. "I mean, you fought for the Yankees, we fought for the South, but that's all behind us now."

"Yes," Eddie said. "That's all behind us now."

They were three miles away, on the banks of the Missouri River, when Eddie called out to them. Turning, they saw him holding a shotgun, which was leveled at them.

"What you doin', Eddie? Don't be foolin' around like that," Loomis Sumlin said.

Eddie shook his head. "I ain't foolin'," he said.

"What do you mean, you ain't foolin'?" Dewey asked.

"I know that it was you boys who killed my ma, pa, and little brother. And I know it was you that shamed my sister."

The Sumlins grew white with fear, and Loomis held his hands out.

"Look here, Eddie, that was war," he said. "We wouldn't never done nothin' like that iffen you'da fought on our side like you shoulda."

"That wasn't war, that was murder," Eddie insisted.

"What do you call it if you kill us now? I mean, there ain't even no war goin' on now. It'll be murder."

Eddie smiled at them. "That's right," he said.

A ringing bell awakened Flaire, and she lay there in the dark of the little bedroom compartment, wondering if she had been dreaming or was merely recalling the story Eddie had told her.

The train whistle blew, and she sat up in bed, then pulled the curtain to one side to look out onto the depot platform. She had no idea what stop this was, a small town, in the middle of the night, but the depot was relatively well lit by several lanterns, and she saw a woman and two children welcoming a passenger who had just gotten off the train.

"Board!" the conductor called.

The train blew its whistle again, then started forward in a series of jerks until it finally smoothed out.

Flaire lay her head back on the pillow and stared into the darkness above. She knew she shouldn't feel joy over the fact that the Sumlin brothers were dead, but God help her, she did.

Then, feeling guilty for her thoughts, she silently made the Confessional Prayer.

Almighty God, Father of our Lord Jesus Christ, Maker of all things, Judge of all men; I acknowledge and bewail my manifold sins and wickedness, which I from time to time most grievously have committed by thought, word, and deed, against thy Divine Majesty, provoking most justly thy wrath and indignation against me.

I do earnestly repent, and am heartily sorry for these my misdoings. The remembrance of them is grievous unto me, the burden of them is intolerable. I have sinned in feeling joy over the death of Loomis and Dewey Sumlin, and I ask that you forgive me for such thoughts and that you forgive them for their deeds.

I ask too that you forgive my brother Eddie for committing murder against them.

Have mercy upon me most merciful Father. For thy Son our Lord Jesus Christ's sake, forgive me all that is past, and grant that I may hereafter serve and please thee in newness of life. To the honor and glory of thy name, through Jesus Christ, my Lord. Amen.

Shortly after she completed the prayer, Flaire fell asleep again. This time the sleep was dreamless, the demons gone.

Chapter 12

~~~

OUT AT THE BAR-Z-BAR HERD, WHICH WAS IN CAMP about four miles outside of Salcedo, Pete, Dusty, and Kendall, the three cowboys who were coming into town, were having a discussion. They were trying to decide whether they should wait until after supper before they came in or come in before supper and eat at a restaurant in town.

"It would be good to put somethin' in our belly other than Moses' grub," Pete suggested. "I say we go in and find us a café somewhere."

"If we wait until we get into town to eat, we'll have to pay for it," Dusty said.

"Well, of course we'll have to pay for it. I wasn't plannin' on gettin' it free."

"Yes, but what I'm sayin' is, if we stay here and eat Moses' grub, we won't have to pay for it. And that'll leave us more money to spend on drinkin'," Dusty said. "Besides, Moses is a good cook, and I wouldn't be surprised if his food ain't better'n what we'd get in town anyway."

"Yeah, his food's good all right, but how many women do you see eatin' with us out here on the trail?"

Dusty laughed. "You say that as if when we go into town

we're all goin' to go into a fancy café with a woman hangin' onto our arms."

"Well," Pete said, "maybe not. But we for sure ain't goin' to have no women eatin' with us if we stay here."

"I'm with Dusty," Kendall said. "I say we eat here, then go into town."

Pete was finally won over by the logic of the argument, and so it was that, even as the sun was a big red ball poised on the western horizon, the three young cowboys were just passing the WELCOME TO SALCEDO sign.

"'Obey our laws,'" Dusty read. He laughed.

"What you think is so funny?" Pete asked.

"The sign says obey our laws," Dusty said. "If a fella is going to obey 'em, he don't need no sign tellin' him to. And if he ain't goin' to obey 'em, a sign ain't goin' to make him do it."

"Dusty, has anyone ever told you that you are a strange man?" Pete asked.

"You think, maybe, we shoulda left our guns back with the herd?" Dusty asked.

"What?" Pete replied. "Hell no! Ain't nobody takin' my gun away from me. Why, I'd feel plumb naked without my gun."

"Moses never carries a gun," Dusty said.

"Well, come on, who's going to try anything with Moses? He's a—" Pete started, then stopped.

"He's a what?"

"You know."

"Colored man?"

"Well, yes, that, and he's also a cook. I mean people just don't pay no attention to a colored man or a cook. So, when you figure that Moses is both a cook and a colored man, why, what would he need a gun for in the first place?"

"Yeah, a gun would probably scare him to death," Kendall said.

"Oh, I hardly think that," Dusty said. "Don't forget, ol' Moses was a Buffalo Soldier."

The three cowboys approached a little house at the end of the street where two young children were playing in the yard. A ball rolled into the street in front of them, and they jerked back on the reins, bringing their horses to an abrupt halt when a little boy darted out for it. The boy picked up the ball, looked up and smiled at the three riders, then ran back into the front yard.

"Damn fool kids. They're going to get hurt one of these days if they don't watch out," Pete said.

"Ah, they're just kids," Kendall said. "Haven't you ever been a kid?"

Pete thought of the strict regimen of the orphanage, back in New York City. He had no memory of family, could not remember when he didn't live in the orphanage. He was released at sixteen, joined the army, and wound up out West where he took his discharge.

"No," Pete said. "No, I never was a kid."

"You know what, Pete? You are as full of shit as a Christmas goose," Dusty said.

Kendall laughed.

"Hey, what do you say we find us a whorehouse?" Dusty suggested. "A big one, where they got maybe eight or ten gals, and we could line them up against the wall and take our pick."

"What are you talkin' about, eight or ten whores?" Pete said. "Why, no bigger than this place is, I'll bet there ain't eight whores in the whole town."

"Maybe there ain't no whores at all in this town," Kendall suggested.

"Ever' town has a whore," Pete insisted. "I mean, it wouldn't be civilized if it didn't. A man's got to have his ashes hauled ever' now and again or he'll go plumb loco."

"Hey, Pete, have you ever been to a real whorehouse?" Dusty asked.

"Well, yeah," Pete answered. "I've been to Suzie's."

"Suzie's ain't no real whorehouse," Dusty said. "I mean, she's a whore, but a real whorehouse is a fancy place, with red curtains and gold-framed mirrors and the like. And they got a parlor with plush furniture where you can sit and palaver for a while before you choose up whatever whore is the one you want. Then you go upstairs with her."

"You ever been to a place like that?" Pete asked.

"No," Dusty admitted. "But I've heard tell of 'em."

As they rode through town, they could hear the guttural guffaw of a man laughing. They pulled rein in front of the saloon and tied their mounts at the hitching rail.

"This where we goin'?" Kendall asked.

"You see anyplace else?" Pete asked.

Kendall looked up and down the single-street town. "No," he said. "Don't reckon I do."

"Then this is where we're a'goin'," Pete said. "Let's go in."

The three cowboys pushed their way through the bat-wing doors and strode up to the bar.

Dusty put a quarter down. "Three beers," he ordered.

Paddy looked at the quarter. "Sorry, mister, but you ain't got enough money lyin' there for three beers," he said.

Dusty laughed. "Where at did you learn your cipherin', barkeep?" he asked. "Your sign outside says you're getting a nickel for a beer. That means three beers is fifteen cents."

"The beers are a nickel," Paddy said. "But you have to add another nickel each for the Regulator tax."

"Regulator tax? What the hell is a regulator tax?"

"The Regulators keep the peace in this town," Paddy said. "If you want three beers, you need to put another nickel down."

"Damn! I ain't never heard of such a thing," Dusty said,

putting a nickel alongside the quarter. "If I didn't have me a week's worth of trail-drivin' thirst, and if this here wasn't the only place for fifty miles around that a fella could get hisself somethin' to drink, I'd tell you to keep your damn beer."

"Ain't goin' be all that easy to get drunk iffen ever' beer cost a dime," Pete complained.

"Believe me, cowboy, sure an' in this town you are better off not getting drunk," Paddy said as he drew the beers for them.

The Homestead Hotel proudly advertised that it was the best hotel in San Antonio, with bathing rooms at the end of the hall on each of its three floors.

"Hot water is available at the turn of a handle," the advertisement boasted.

The bathing room was the first convenience Flaire availed herself of, and having taken her bath, she was now returning to her own room. She noticed, with some surprise, that her door wasn't locked.

That was strange. She was certain she had locked it before she left. Curious as to how the door could have gotten unlocked, she pushed it open and stepped inside.

She was startled by a large man who at first didn't see her come in. Her suitcase was open and her clothing, lingerie, and other items were scattered about on the bed.

"Who are you?" Flaire demanded. "What are you doing in my room?"

The intruder pulled a knife and brandished it menacingly toward her.

"You just keep your mouth shut, girly, and you won't get hurt," he said in a raspy voice. "Where do you keep your cash money?"

"Get out of here!" Flaire said. "Get out of here at once or I'll scream!"

"You open your mouth to scream and it'll be the last sound you ever make," the intruder hissed.

At that moment, Hawke happened to be walking by Flaire's room. A towel tossed over his shoulder, he was heading for the bathing room for his own bath. He heard the raspy sounding words, ". . . it'll be the last sound you ever make."

Slowly, Hawke turned the doorknob and eased the door ajar just far enough to determine that it wasn't locked. Then, suddenly, he pushed it the rest of the way open and moved in quickly behind it.

"What the hell?" the intruder said. "Who are you?"

"I'll be asking the questions now. What are you doing in Miss Delaney's room?" Hawke asked.

For just a moment the intruder's eyes reflected fear and surprise, then he saw that Hawke was unarmed and the fear was replaced with a smug smile.

"You'll be asking the questions, will you?" He chuckled evilly. "Well now, that's pretty bold talk for a man armed with nothing but a towel. You made a mistake, my friend. You made a big mistake."

The intruder crouched a little, then came up on the balls of his feet. He held the knife low in his right hand, palm up, the blade sideways. Lunging forward, he made a swipe with it, moving quickly and catching Hawke by surprise. The point of the knife opened up a cut across Hawke's belly, not penetrating, but deep enough to bring blood.

"Mister, I'm going to carve your heart out and feed it to the pigs," the intruder said.

It was obvious that the intruder, whoever he was, was skilled with a knife. He maintained a perfect knife fighter's position, balanced on the balls of his feet, ready to move either way as need be. The point of the knife, waving back and forth, reminded Flaire of the head of a coiled snake.

Realizing that she might well be witnessing a life and death struggle, she backed into the far corner of the room. Had Hawke and the intruder not been between her and the doorway, she would have fled.

"Girly, I'm goin' to let you watch me carve up this gent, then I'm going to start on you," the intruder said.

Hawke was now holding the towel in both hands, with one hand at either end. He held it out in front of him, as if he were measuring a fish, and he used the towel a couple of times to parry the intruder's knife thrusts.

Before then, Flaire had never noticed how fluid Hawke was on his feet. That his movements were so graceful, almost as if choreographed, became all the more beautiful, and frightening, because of the deadly implications.

The knife fighter continued to lunge at Hawke, growing more frustrated with each unsuccessful attempt. Hawke skipped back from him, warding off each thrust with his towel then scooting away as gracefully as if he were on a dance floor.

Flaire had never seen a bullfight before, but she had read about them and heard about them, and she knew that no matador could be more graceful or poised in the face of danger than Mason Hawke.

Then Hawke did a strange thing. He began twirling the towel up by making circular motions with his hands. When he had the towel rolled up tight, he flipped one end out, snapping the towel.

What might have been an act of play between two young boys took on a much more important role as Hawke aimed for and hit the intruder in the face. He got exactly the reaction he was looking for. The man let out a yelp of pain and put both hands up to cover his eyes. When he did that, Hawke kicked him in the groin, and when the man doubled over, Hawke spun him around, put one hand on the man's collar, the other on his belt, and started him toward the window.

The intruder opened his eyes just in time to see what was about to happen to him.

"No!" he shouted in fear. "Please, no!"

It was too late. Hawke, already committed, forced the intruder through the window, smashing out the glass with the man's head. A lift and a shove was all it took to send him screaming through the window and down to the alley below. He hit the ground with a sickening thud that could be heard all the way up in Flaire's room.

"We'll have to get you another room," Hawke said matter-of-factly. "You can't stay in a room that has no window."

There was blood on the broken shards of glass and on the windowsill.

The expression on Flaire's face was one of fear and shock. She was no longer frightened for her own safety, because that danger was eliminated. But she was stunned by the side of Hawke she had never seen before.

It wasn't that Hawke had gotten angry and reacted in rage. She could have understood that. What she could not understand was how he could do something so drastic and violent without showing any reaction at all. He had tossed the intruder out of the room with no more concern than if it had been a roach.

"Is he . . . is he dead?" Flaire asked in a weak voice.

"I don't know," Hawke replied. It was clear by the tone of his voice that not only did he not know, he didn't care, one way or the other.

As Hawke and Flaire left for the concert, they were met in the hotel lobby by a man who was wearing a badge.

"Miss Delaney," the sheriff's deputy said, touching the brim of his hat. "My name is Deputy Cumbie. I'm sorry to disturb you, ma'am, but I understand that you asked for a change of rooms."

"Yes."

"May I ask why?"

"What interest would the law have in Miss Delaney changing rooms?" Hawke asked.

"And you are?" Cumbie asked.

"Mason Hawke. I'm Miss Delaney's escort."

"And protector?"

"If need be," Hawke acknowledged.

"I see. Earlier today a man named Eduardo Vargas was found lying in the alley behind the hotel, suffering from two broken legs and a broken arm. He was thrown through the window of what was Miss Delaney's room. Miss Delaney obviously did not do it, and since you are her self-confessed protector, can you tell me anything about it?"

"I threw him out the window," Hawke said.

"And would you mind telling me why?"

"When I came back from my bath, he was in my room," Flaire said.

"Vargas admits to that, ma'am," Deputy Cumbie said. "But he claims to have been in your room by mistake. And he says that when he tried to explain it, Mr. Hawke, here, threw him out."

"He's lying," Hawke said. "He wasn't in there by mistake and he didn't try to explain anything. He had a knife and he attempted to use it on me."

"And how were you armed?"

"I had no weapon," Hawke said. "I was going to the bath when I heard him in Miss Delaney's room."

"And, unarmed, you went up against a man who was wielding a knife?"

"Yes."

"Sheriff—" Flaire started, but Cumbie held up his hand.

"I'm a deputy, ma'am."

"Deputy, Mr. Hawke is telling the truth," Flaire said. "When I returned to my room, Mister . . . Vargas, is it? Mr. Vargas was in my room, going through my things. When I accosted him, he pulled a knife and threatened to kill me. It wasn't until then that Mr. Hawke came in. They struggled and, somehow, Mr. Vargas went through the window."

Deputy Cumbie stroked his jaw for a moment as he studied both Hawke and Flaire. In their formal evening attire, a discussion involving a struggle with a knife-wielding assailant seemed incongruous, but Hawke did not back away from his story.

"Well," the deputy finally said. "The thing is, Eduardo Vargas is one of the lowest-life polecats in all of San Antonio. If he had a dozen priests backing him up, I wouldn't believe him. I'll accept your side of the story, ma'am. You came back to your room and found him rifling through your things.

"And you," he continued, looking squarely at Hawke. "I suppose, under the circumstances, you reacted as most anyone would." He chuckled. "Though many would not have had the success that you did. But—and here is what makes me leery of you—when you threw him out that window, you were on the second floor. Were you aware of that at the time?"

"Yes."

"Do you realize that if he had hit on his head, the fall could have killed him?"

"Yes."

"Did you bother to check on his condition?

"No."

"He broke both legs and an arm."

Hawke made no reply at all.

"Didn't you even think to inform the sheriff's office?"

"No."

"Why didn't you?"

"There was no need for any assistance from the sheriff's office," Hawke replied. "Miss Delaney was no longer in danger."

"That poor man lay out there in excruciating pain for well over an hour before someone found him."

Again Hawke didn't reply.

"I'll say this for you, Mr. Hawke. You are certainly one cold-blooded son of a bitch," Deputy Cumbie said. Again he tipped his hat to Flaire. "Ma'am, I hope you two have a good evening."

"The nerve of that man," Flaire said under her breath once the deputy was gone. "He practically accuses us of lying and assault, then he asks us to have a good evening."

Hawke laughed out loud. "It's his job," he said.

"I must say, you sure seemed to take his accusations easily."

"No sense in getting hostile about it."

"I agree," Flaire said. "But I will never be able to take such accusations lightly."

It wasn't that Hawke took the accusations lightly. That wasn't what bothered Flaire. Once again, what disturbed her was how cold he was about the whole thing.

The concert hall was filled to overflowing as men in formal attire and women in butterfly-bright dresses stood in little conversational clusters out in the lobby, waiting for the show to begin.

"Curtain call! Curtain call!" a young man was shouting as he passed through the lobby, alerting everyone of the imminent beginning of the show. "Curtain call!"

"We'd better take our seats," Hawke said.

Flaire started toward the door that led down into the auditorium, but Hawke called out to her. "No, we go this way," he said.

Flaire was confused as to why he seemed to be walking away from the auditorium, but she followed him without question. When they reached a flight of stairs, their passage was barred by a velvet rope that stretched across the entrance, as well as a uniformed usher.

"I'm sorry sir," the usher said, holding out his hand. "This is reserved."

"I have a letter authorizing me entry," Hawke said, showing it to the usher.

The usher read the letter, then shook his head and clucked his tongue.

"Very impressive," he said. "But I have instructions that no one is to be allowed upstairs."

"Read the letter again," Hawke said.

"I assure you sir that—"

"Read the letter again," Hawke ordered, this time with a hint of danger in his voice.

Flaire thought of what had happened back in the hotel, and she looked around quickly, hoping something similar wouldn't happen here. She wanted to tell the usher that if he valued his health, he would let them through. Evidently, the usher reached the same conclusion, for the challenge left his voice and an acquiescent smile crossed his face.

"Yes, sir, Mr. Hawke. You'll find your box at the top, and the far end of the hallway."

"Thank you," Hawke said.

Flaire had never been in any part of a theater but the mezzanine and she wondered why Hawke had pushed the usher so hard to let them come up the stairs.

"Here we are," Hawke said as he opened a door.

And then her curiosity increased even more, for this was a

completely private box, furnished by a single, overstuffed sofa. The view of the stage could not have been better.

"Oh, my, what this must have cost you," she said as they took their seat.

Hawke chuckled. "I hope you don't think I can afford this on what I make playing piano in a saloon," he said. "This was free."

"Free?"

Reaching into his inside jacket pocket, Hawke pulled out the same letter he had shown the usher and handed it to Flaire.

Please allow my friend, Mason Hawke, the use of the best private box in the house.

Louis Moreau Gottschalk.

"When did you get that?" Flaire asked.

"He is staying in the same hotel we are," Hawke said. "I met with him this afternoon."

"I hope you didn't threaten to throw him through a window to get it," Flaire said, then quickly put her hand to her lips. "Oh! I don't know why I said that!"

To Flaire's surprise and relief, Hawke laughed. "I didn't have to," he said. "But now that you remind me, it was an option."

The lights in the house were dimmed then, and the stage lights grew brighter.

The audience began applauding as a man came out onto the stage, then stepped to the front. He bowed once to acknowledge the applause then looked up toward the box occupied by Hawke and Flaire. Flaire saw that he had a receding hairline, dark, brooding eyes, and a sweeping moustache. He dipped his head slightly toward Hawke, and Hawke dipped his toward Gottschalk.

Gottschalk then walked over to the piano, flipped the tails of his coat back, and sat down to play.

"Oh," Flaire said quietly. "I know that song! You played it one morning."

"It's 'Gestern Abend War Vetter Michael da,'" Hawke said. "By Beethoven."

Flaire laughed. "What does that mean?"

"Yesterday evening my nephew Michael was there," Hawke said.

By the end of the concert, Flaire was pleased to notice that she recognized several of his pieces, not by name, but by familiarity as the result of Hawke's early morning concerts. Afterward, as the crowd was leaving, an usher appeared at the door of their private box.

"Mr. Hawke. Mr. Gottschalk has invited you to his dressing room."

"Thank you," Hawke said.

The usher led them through the upstairs hallway, then down a flight of stairs that brought them out behind the stage. He pointed to a closed door.

"There is his dressing room."

"Thank you."

Gottschalk opened the door on the first light tap.

"Hawke!" he said, reaching out to grab Hawke's hand. "It is so good to see you again. And who is this lovely creature?" he asked, smiling at Flaire.

"This is my friend, Flaire Delaney," Hawke said.

"Mr. Gottschalk, I very much enjoyed the concert tonight."

"Thank you, my dear. Come in, come in, I've ordered wine."

For the next several minutes Flaire sat spellbound as Gottschalk and Hawke exchanged stories. How easily

Hawke spoke of such people as Franz Liszt, Victor Hugo, and even Queen Victoria.

"You know, my dear," Gottschalk said to Flaire, "Mason Hawke is much too modest to say anything about it, but there was a time when he was one of the two or three best pianists in the world. Myself included in that top three, of course," he added quickly.

"Oh, I think that's a slight exaggeration," Hawke said. "Not about you, you certainly do belong there. But I never have."

"*Au contraire,* my dear fellow," Gottschalk said, wagging his finger. "Why, the maestro himself, Franz Liszt, is the one who put you there. He told me himself that of all the students he had over the many years, you were his most talented."

Finally, after the exchange of several more entertaining stories, Hawke bade his old friend good-bye, and he and Flaire left the theater for a nearby restaurant, for a late dinner.

They sat at a table in the back corner, a single candle lighting the distance between them.

For the first part of the meal, they discussed the concert, then Hawke expanded on some of the stories he and Gottschalk had told.

Flaire confessed that this was the most elegant thing she had ever done.

"I made this dress just for an occasion like this," she said. "Though, to be honest with you, I never really expected to be able to use it."

"The dress is beautiful," Hawke said. "And you are beautiful in it." He smiled. "Gottschalk may have thought all eyes were on him tonight . . ." Hawke chuckled. "In fact, I'm sure he thought all eyes were on him. But in fact, all eyes were on you."

Flaire smiled and ducked her head. "You mustn't tease like that, Hawke. You will turn my head with your flattery."

"Indeed, that is my intention," Hawke said.

They continued their conversation throughout the meal, and not until dessert and coffee were served did Flaire ask the question that had been on her mind all night.

"Hawke, why?" she asked.

Hawke had just cut a piece of his pie, and he held it poised on his fork for a moment while he considered Flaire's question. The fact that he didn't ask "Why what?" indicated to Flaire that this was, undoubtedly, a question he had asked himself many, many times.

"I don't belong in that world anymore," he finally said.

"But you do. Mr. Gottschalk spoke so glowingly of you. And he said that Franz Liszt said you were the most gifted pianist he had ever taught. God gave you that talent, and I know that you still have the desire . . . no, the *need*, to play. Tonight, an adoring crowd applauded Mr. Gottschalk's music."

"He earned the applause."

"And he was, no doubt, paid very well to perform."

"I'm sure he was."

"Here is what I can't understand, Hawke. You do the same thing, without the award of applause or money. You will sit at that piano at four o'clock in the morning for no other reason than your love of music."

"I play for myself now."

"You will excuse me for saying this, but that is a very selfish attitude. You should be playing for the world. You could have everything Gottschalk has, including the money and the recognition. Instead, you wander through the country like tumbleweed."

"It's not there for me anymore," Hawke said.

"What do you mean it's not there anymore? I know it is. Don't forget, I've heard you play."

"You've heard me play on a cigar-burned, beer-stained, upright piano. And most of what you have heard is music I played for the first time, when I was ten years old." He paused for a moment. "And if I were being honest with you, I probably played it better then than I play it now."

"That just means you are out of practice. You could get it back."

Hawke shook his head. "No," he said. "You don't understand. Music—real music, like we heard tonight—has to come from the soul." He took a sip of his wine before he continued in a pensive voice. "I no longer have a soul."

Flaire was about to challenge his statement, but on second thought, withheld her comment. When he said he had no soul, she could understand, more than anyone, just what that meant. She had left her own soul lying in the dirt of her father's farm, illuminated by the fires of hell.

Chapter 13

BACK IN SALCEDO, AT THE GOLDEN CALF SA-
loon, Pete, Kendall, and Dusty were still celebrating their
rare hours away from the herd. All three were drinking
steadily, though Pete had switched to whiskey.

"You better go easy on that stuff," Dusty cautioned. "You
ought to stick with beer, like me 'n' Kendall.

"Ah, the whiskey here is green, so it don't cost no more'n
a beer. Sure tastes awful, though."

"Then why are you drinking it?"

"Because you can get drunk faster on cheap whiskey than
you can on good beer," Pete explained.

"Well, I don't want to get too drunk," Dusty said.

"Sure you do. How the hell are you going to have any fun
unless you get drunk?" Pete asked.

"Yeah, but what if you get so drunk that, come tomorrow,
you won't remember the fun you had tonight?" Dusty asked.

Kendall laughed. "Dusty's got a point there," he said.

"I tell you what," Pete said. "You boys drink beer, I'll
drink whiskey. Then, tomorrow you two can tell me what a
good time I had tonight."

"Yeah," Dusty said. "Only, I thought part of having a

good time tonight was, we was going to all get us a whore. Where at's all them whores you been talkin' about?"

"Don't look like they got a lot of whores in here," Pete said, looking around the saloon. "'Ceptin' maybe that one over there."

He nodded toward Darci, who had been going from table to table, serving drinks. She had been to their table a few times already, and had smiled prettily at them each time.

"I'll go find out if we can afford her."

"Not her," Kendall said.

"What do you mean, not her? What's wrong with her?" Pete asked.

"Ain't nothin' wrong with her," Kendall said. "But I don't think she's a whore."

"Of course she's a whore. What makes you think she ain't?"

"Well, just look at her," Kendall said. "She's about the most beautiful woman I've ever seen."

"Have you seen how she is dressed?" Pete asked. "I mean, you ain't goin' to see clothes like that at a church social or a town picnic. No, sir. She's a whore all right."

Kendall shook his head slowly, as if trying to make sense of what Pete was telling him. "Why would a woman that beautiful be a whore?"

"Well, what else can she be?" Pete asked. "She's got a touch of the brush."

"She's got what?"

"She's part colored," Pete explained. "Can't you tell that by lookin' at her?"

Through the smoke-filled room, Kendall studied Darci as she worked the tables. At one of the tables, Darci paused, then laughed at something and reached out to touch the side of the man's face. Kendall could see by the expression in the customer's eyes that, for one brief moment, there was nobody else in the saloon but the two of them. It was a small, insignificant, yet intimate gesture, and Kendall put his hand to his own cheek, wishing she had touched him there in the same way.

"Well?" Pete asked when Kendall didn't respond.

"Well what?" Kendall continued to stare at Darci.

"Can't you tell that she is colored?"

"Oh, well, I don't know if she is colored or not. And I don't care. She is about the most beautiful thing I've ever seen in my life."

"I agree with Kendall," Dusty said. "I think this here bar girl is about the prettiest woman I've ever seen."

Pete smiled, then tossed down the rest of his whiskey, set the glass down, and wiped the back of his hand across his mouth. "Wait here," he said.

"Where you goin'?"

"I got some business to attend to."

Pete got up then and sauntered over to the end of the bar where Darci was now talking to another customer. Pete stood by, politely, patiently, until the customer left. Darci turned to him with a smile.

"Is there something I can do for you, cowboy?" she asked.

"That depends on what you do," Pete replied. "I mean, uh, besides carrying drinks to the tables."

"Are you asking if I can be bedded?" Darci asked. Despite the frankness of her question, the sweet, innocent smile never left her face.

Pete nodded. "Yes, ma'am, I reckon that is what I'm asking."

Darci looked up at the clock. "I can," she said. "But not until after nine o'clock. I have to serve drinks until nine."

"Are you the only whore?"

"Yes."

"Uh, well, there's three of us," he said.

"Don't worry, cowboy, you won't wear me out," she said with a lilting laugh.

"There's one I want you to be particular good to. He's a young'un, you see, and he ain't never been with no woman before."

"I'll do my best," Darci promised.

Pete led Darci back over to the table to meet Kendall and Dusty. Dusty was very gregarious, but Kendall stared at the table in embarrassment.

"This here is the young'un I was tellin' you about," Pete said, pointing to Kendall. "He ain't never had him no woman before."

"Oh, what a sweet boy you are," Darci said. She reached out and touched him, just as Kendall had seen her touch a customer earlier. "You and I are going to have a really good time."

Kendall felt a rush of sexual excitation, but because he had never experienced a feeling exactly like it before, he wasn't sure what it was. And, because his unexpected reaction embarrassed him, he blushed even more.

Vox, Hooper, and Bates came into the saloon then and found a table near the three cowboys.

"Paddy, a bottle and three glasses," Vox called.

Nodding at them, Paddy started toward the table with a bottle.

"Hell no, don't you be a'bringin' it," Vox said. He pointed to Darci. "That's her job, ain't it?"

Paddy nodded. "Yes, it is. But as you can see, she's busy right now."

Darci was still talking to the three young cowboys.

"I want the girl to bring us the bottle," Vox said.

Paddy sighed, shrugged his shoulders, then held the bottle out toward Darci. "Would you come get this and take it over to the deputies?" he asked.

"Hey, hold on there!" Pete shouted. "Wait your turn, mister. She's a'talkin' to us!"

"Sit down and cool off, cowboy," Vox suggested.

"Cool off, my ass. Who are you to tell me to cool off?" Pete replied. Noticing Vox's black eyes and nose, he laughed. "What happened to your face, mister? Looks to me like you done stood up when you should've sat down."

"It ain't none of your business what happened to my face," Vox replied.

"The piano player gave him that face," Darci said as she walked over to the bar.

"The piano player?" Pete replied. He laughed. "Are you sayin' a piano player beat you up like that?"

Dusty and Kendall laughed as well.

"Where at is this piano player?" Pete asked. "I'd like to buy him a drink."

"I'd like to know where he is too," Vox said. "I've got a score to settle with him."

"Ha! The only reason you came in here tonight is because you knew he wasn't here," Darci said as she started back toward the table with the bottle.

"Why you black bitch! I'm going to slap that grin right off your face!" Vox growled, and he started toward her.

"No, you ain't!" Paddy shouted, and when Vox looked at the bartender, he saw that Paddy was holding a double-barreled, twelve-gauge shotgun leveled at him. "You come one more step this way and I'm going to open you up like gutting a fish."

"By damn, you can't talk to me like that," Vox said. "I'm an officer of the law!"

"Right now you're not," Paddy said. "Right now you are nothing but an unruly customer who is threatening one of my employees."

"Vox, come on, let's go," Bates said. "We don't need to be stirring up any more trouble in here."

Vox stared at Darci, who was standing halfway between his table and the bar.

"Give me the bottle," he said, less threatening this time.

Cautiously, Darci extended the bottle, and he took it. She started to hand him the glasses, but he waved them away.

"We won't be needin' no glasses," he said. Pulling the cork from the bottle with his teeth, he spit it out on the floor. "Come on," he said to the others. "Let's go."

Paddy, remembering that Vox had suddenly burst back into the saloon the other night after Hawke ran him off, was ready for him this time. Not more than fifteen seconds after the three deputies left, Vox stuck his head back into the saloon.

Paddy was still holding the shotgun.

Vox saw it, glared at Paddy for a moment, then left again.

For the second time in less than a week, Vox had made an ignominious exit from the saloon. And for the second time in a week, the patrons in the saloon enjoyed a big laugh at his expense.

Neither Vox nor any of the other deputies came back. Within half an hour after the incident, it was almost as if nothing had happened. Cordial drinking and friendly conversations resumed, and the ongoing chess game between Cyrus Green and Doc Urban continued.

Sometime later Darci walked over to the table where the three cowboys were and reached out her hand. "It's after nine," she said. "Who wants to be first?"

"Let the boy go first," Pete suggested.

"No!" Kendall said quickly. "I . . . uh, would rather not be first."

"All right by me," Pete said. "I was just bein' nice to you." He stood up. "I'll be first."

Smiling, Darci took him by the hand and led him through the saloon and out the back door.

"Where they goin'?" Kendall asked.

"I imagine she's got herself a crib back there," Dusty said.

"A crib?"

"It's like a little one-room house," Dusty explained. "It's where whores live. And it's where they take their customers."

"Oh."

Half an hour later Darci and Pete returned. Pete had a satisfied smile on his face.

"That didn't take very long," Dusty said.

"It don't take long when you know what you're doin'," Pete said, grabbing himself suggestively. "Ain't that right?" he asked Darci.

"That's right, honey," Darci replied with a barely suppressed chuckle.

Dusty looked across the table at Kendall. "You want to go now?" he asked.

"No, no!" Kendall said. "You can go now. I'm not in a big hurry."

"Okay, but don't say I didn't give you the chance to go next." He stood up and smiled at Darci. "Darlin', if you think ol' Pete here was fast, you wait until you see how I operate."

Darci chuckled. "I can hardly wait," she said.

True to his word, Dusty and Darci were back within less than twenty minutes. Hitching up his trousers, Dusty looked at his two friends. Pete looked back at him, but his eyes were having trouble focusing.

"Damn, boy, you're damn near drunk already," Dusty said.

"Yep," Pete said. He giggled. "Good thing I went first, else I wouldn't have been able to do it at all."

So far, Kendall had made no effort to move, and Dusty looked over at him.

"Well, it's nut-cuttin' time, boy," he said. "You goin' to do it or not?"

"I'm goin' to do it, I'm goin' to do it," Kendall said. "Just don't rush me, is all."

Hesitantly, Kendall stood up, and looking around the room, saw that several of the customers were looking at him. He sat back down.

"What's wrong?" Dusty asked.

"Everyone is looking at me," Kendall said. "They'll all know what I'm doing."

"Well, hell yes they all know what you're doing," Pete said. "And ever' damn one of them will be wishin' it was them instead of you. Now, go on out there. Lookie there, she's over there at the bar, waitin' on you."

Darci came over to the table to get him. "Come on," she said, taking his hand in hers. "I don't bite. It will be all right, I promise you."

The touch of Darci's hand sent jolts of pleasure through Kendall and emboldened him to the point that he didn't care what the others might be thinking. He stood up.

"Just don't forget about the snapping turtle," Pete called out to him as he walked away from the table with her.

Kendall followed Darci through the back door of the saloon, across the alley, and into the small, one-room house.

"Is this here what they call a crib?" Kendall asked.

"Some folks might call it that, I reckon," Darci said. "But I call it my home."

Although the house was small, Darci had gone to great lengths to make it comfortable and homey. Frilly curtains hung on the windows, a crocheted doily was on the armoire, and her bed, turned down now because of previous use, proudly displayed a quilt with a wedding-ring pattern. Bright red pillows completed the decoration scheme of the bed.

Darci turned her back to Kendall and started undressing.

Kendall had never seen a nude woman before, and he watched, entranced. Darci knew exactly what she was doing, and she knew the effect she was having on him. Her measured, sensual disrobing slowly exposed her smooth, almost golden skin, until not one subtle curve or fold of her young, nubile body remained hidden. Kendall felt a fluttering in his stomach and he found it difficult to breathe.

Not until Darci was completely nude did she turn to face him. She was surprised to see that he had not taken off his clothes.

"Aren't you going to get undressed?" she asked.

The expression on Kendall's face was one of complete awe.

"Cowboy?" Darci asked again.

"You are the prettiest thing I've ever seen," Kendall said in awe.

Darci smiled at him. "Thank you," she said. "But aren't you going to get undressed?"

"Oh. Uh, yes ma'am," Kendall said. "Yes, ma'am, I'm going to get undressed." But he made no move to do so.

"Well?" Darci asked.

"Well?" Kendall repeated.

"When are you going to get undressed?"

"Oh. Uh, right now. But you have to turn around and not look."

Darci laughed. "Why not? You looked at me."

"Yes, ma'am, well, like I said, you're real pretty to look at. And I ain't never seen me a naked woman before. But I'd rather you turn around and not look at me."

"All right," Darci said.

Suppressing her laughter, Darci stared at the curtains until she heard him get in the bed behind him.

"All right, you can turn around now," Kendall said.

Darci turned toward the bed and saw that he was under the quilt.

"Are you going to let me get under there with you?" Darci asked. "Because if you don't, we aren't going to be able to do anything."

"Yes, ma'am," Kendall said. "You can get under here with me."

Darci climbed into bed, then pressed herself against him.

"Can I ask you a question?" Kendall asked.

"Ask whatever you want."

"Does it really snap shut?"

"What?" Darci asked, surprised by the question. She pulled away from him far enough to allow her to look into his face. "What are you talking about?"

"Down here," Kendall asked, pointing. "Does it . . . well, that is, Pete and Dusty told me that sometimes it will, uh, snap shut and trap me inside."

Darci laughed out loud.

"Well, cowboy, it never has before," she said. "And if it does, why, I can't think of anyone I'd rather have trapped inside than you."

Kendall smiled broadly, then felt his need for her growing. He reached for her.

"I'm ready now," he said.

"Oh yes," Darci replied. "I'd say that you are definitely ready."

It was almost an hour before Kendall returned to the saloon, and when he did return, Pete was so drunk that he was barely able to hold up his head.

"Boy," Dusty said. "It sure took you a long time."

"I reckon it did," Kendall said. "I don't reckon I'm as good as you two at it, but I liked it nevertheless."

"Well, we've had our ashes hauled," Dusty said. "Only thing left to do now is get drunk."

"Looks like Pete is already drunk," Kendall said.

"Yes," Dusty said, lifting his glass. "Better drink up. We've got a lot of catching up to do."

Chapter 14

～～

On board the Texas Southern train

THEY HAD LEFT SAN ANTONIO AT FIVE THAT EVEning, and would arrive in Marva at seven the next morning. After dinner in the dining car, Hawke and Flaire lingered at the table, engrossed in conversation. The window beside them, backed by the blackness of night, glistened with their reflected images.

The only other people still in the dining car were a couple of white-jacketed porters who were busy bussing the empty tables and cleaning the floor.

"Folks, we'll be closin' the diner in about fifteen more minutes," one of the porters said. "If you want another cup of coffee, this'll be the last call."

"Thanks, I'm good," Hawke said, putting his hand over his cup.

"Miss?"

"I'm fine, thank you."

All during dinner the two had talked. Flaire told of growing up, the only girl with two brothers. She shared some humorous stories with him, laughing sometimes, on the verge of tears at other times, realizing that she was the only one left in her family.

Hawke told Flaire about Tamara, a woman from his past, and the plans they had made.

"We were going to be married, then go back to Europe for a grand tour of the continent," he said. "But she died during the war."

Flaire put her hand across the table and rested it on Hawke's hand.

"Oh, Hawke, I'm so sorry," she said.

"Yes, well, I'm sorry that Tamara died. But I don't think we would have ever gotten married. The Mason Hawke she fell in love with is not the Mason Hawke who returned from the war."

The train passed over a trestle and the noise of the bridge reverberated throughout the car. When it was over, the porter returned to their table.

"Sorry to have to run you off, folks, but we're closin' down now."

"Thank you for allowing us to stay awhile," Hawke said, handing the porter a dollar.

"Thank *you*, sir!" the porter said, brightening at the large tip. The porter hurried around to hold the chair for Flaire as she stood.

They had adjacent rooms in the Wagner parlor car, and Hawke walked her to her room, then waited until she opened the door.

"Good night," Flaire said, stepping into her room quickly, as if denying any opportunity for him to kiss her.

"Good night," Hawke said.

It was well over an hour later when he heard a light knock on his door. Hawke had gone to bed, but the lantern was still burning because he was reading the San Antonio newspaper.

"Who is it?" he called.

"It's me," Flaire replied.

Getting up quickly, Hawke opened the door, causing a wedge of light from the aisle lantern to spill into the room. Flaire was standing in the doorway.

"Please let me in," she said. "I don't think anyone saw me and I don't particularly want to be seen standing outside your room."

Hawke moved to one side and she came in, then closed the door behind her.

"Is something wrong?" Hawke asked.

"No, nothing is wrong," Flaire said. She slipped off the long cotton duster she was wearing, and underneath, Hawke saw that she had on nothing but a silk-muslin chemise. The soft light of the lantern highlighted the thin garment, making it shimmer as if by its own golden light. Her nightgown draped her form like a filmy curtain, and the nipples of her breasts stood out in bold relief.

"Please tell me I'm not making a mistake," she said.

Hawke shook his head. "I can't tell you that," he said. "That's for you to decide."

"This isn't the first time I've come down here tonight."

"Oh?"

Flaire shook her head. "This is the third time. Each time, I stood here, right outside of your door, but I couldn't find the courage to knock. This time, I resolved to go through with it."

Hawke smiled, then put his hand on her shoulder. "I'm glad you did, but you shouldn't have had to take the chance of coming to me. I should've gone to you. Only, I didn't know if you would welcome me." He leaned down and kissed her.

"Hawke," Flaire whimpered, and her quivering lips opened on his in a kiss that was both tender and urgent.

"Yes?"

"I've come this far. The rest is up to you. I'm afraid I have neither the courage to take this any further nor the strength to resist."

"You've put me in an awkward position," Hawke said. "I don't want to take advantage of you."

"I came this far of my own free will. You would not be taking advantage of me."

Hawke needed no further urging to take the lead. He kissed her again, more urgently than before, and she responded by pushing her body against his.

Hawke reached down and scooped her up into his arms, then carried her over to the bed. He laid her on the bed and kissed her again, once more pulling her body against his, feeling her softness against the hardness of his muscles. His kisses became more demanding and Flaire became more responsive, positioning herself here and moving herself there to accommodate him. The tip of her tongue darted across his lips, then dipped into his mouth. The warmth Hawke felt erupted now to a raging inferno, and he began to pull at the hem of Flaire's chemise while removing his own clothes, until they were naked against each other.

Hawke moved his hard, demanding body over her soft, yielding thighs and, poised above her, paused for a moment, as if giving her one last chance to resist. When she made no move to stop him, he went ahead.

Moses Gillespie's wagon was loaded with the supplies the Bar-Z-Bar outfit would need to continue the drive. He had looked forward to coming into Salcedo because he had a particular friend who lived here and this would be the first time he had seen him in a long time.

Moses stopped in front of Sarge's blacksmith shop. The

shop was closed now but a square of light splashed through a curtained window at the back.

"Sergeant Wright!" he called from the wagon. "Are you in there, you worthless bag of piss and vinegar? Come out here and I'll whip your sorry black ass!"

There was a sound from inside the little cabin, then the door was pushed open, sending a bar of light splashing out to fall dimly on the forge, anvil, and tools of his trade.

Ken Wright's large frame filled the door.

"Who the hell is that?" he called. "Who's out here?"

"What do you mean who's out here? I'm out here," Gillespie said. "Private Moses Gillespie, company cook, reporting." He saluted.

"Moses!" Ken said, smiling broadly. "Why you ugly old dried-up fart. What are you doing here?"

"I'm cooking for the Bar-Z-Bar outfit," Moses said. "We're moving a herd up to the railhead and we're planning to camp for a few days just outside of town."

"Well, climb down from that wagon and stay awhile," Ken invited.

"Wait, wait," Moses said. Turning, he began digging through a pile of canvas just behind the seat. After a moment of searching, he found what he was looking for and, triumphantly, held up a bottle.

"Never let it be said that Moses Gillespie visited a friend empty-handed. You do have a couple of glasses, don't you? Or do we have to pass the bottle back and forth?"

"It wouldn't be the first time you and me drank right from the bottle," Ken said. "But I've got some glasses. Come on in."

Hawke stuck his head through the door and looked up and down the aisle. Not seeing anyone, he signaled for Flaire to come outside. Then he walked her back to her own bedroom compartment.

Flaire shivered.

"Are you cold?"

"No," she said.

"Frightened?"

"A little."

"Nobody has seen us."

"That's not what I'm frightened of."

"Ah," Hawke said, nodding. "You're having second thoughts about what we did?"

"Yes. Well, not second thoughts about what we did, exactly. But I am having second thoughts about what you must think of me. Especially since I threw myself at you tonight."

"Flaire, what happened tonight changes nothing about what I think of you. Before, and after, I thought of you as a beautiful, intelligent, and charming young woman."

"I hope I didn't give you the wrong idea. I'm not like this, I . . . I don't know what got into me. I'm not a tramp, Hawke. Please don't think that I am."

Very gently, Hawke put his finger across her lips to shush her. Then he lifted her face to his.

He began to speak in a soft, rhythmic, almost melodious voice:

> *"Then since we mortal lovers are,*
> *. . . Ask not how long our love will last;*
> *But while it does, let us take care*
> *. . . Each minute be with pleasure past."*

"Oh," Flaire said. "Oh, that is lovely! Did you write that?"

"I wish I could claim credit," Hawke said. "But it was written many years ago, by a man named George Etherege."

Bending down toward her, he kissed her. "Good night," he said.

"Good night," she replied with a satisfied smile. He waited until she was safely inside with the door closed before he started back toward his own compartment

At the blacksmith shop, Moses looked around at Ken's quarters and shook his head.

"My oh my, you got yourself a real nice place here, Sarge," he said.

"Thanks," Ken said, getting a couple of glasses down from the cupboard.

As Ken poured the drinks, Moses continued to look around. He saw a bow and a quiver of arrows, and he pointed to it.

"Where'd you get that?"

"You remember our Indian scout, Keytano?"

"Yeah, sure I remember him."

"He made it for me, gave it to me when I left the army."

"Do you know how to use it?"

Smiling, Ken picked up the bow and fitted an arrow into it. It wasn't until then that Moses saw a target on the wall on the far side of the room. There were a lot of holes in the target, indicating that bow shooting had become one of Ken's pastimes. He noticed also that there were very few holes outside the center disk of the target.

Ken loosed the arrow and it flew straight and true across the room, burying itself in the exact dead center of the bull's-eye.

"Damn, Sarge!" Moses said, impressed. "You are good with that thing."

"You want to try?" Ken offered, extending the bow toward him.

"No thanks," Moses said. "I'd probably wind up shooting you in the foot or something. Or worse, shooting myself in the foot."

Ken laughed, and Moses walked over to stand in front of a painting. It showed a mounted trooper at a gallop. He was twisted around in his saddle and firing his rifle back at pursuing Indians. One of the Indians was falling from his horse, having been hit by the trooper.

The trooper was black.

"This is a great painting," Moses said.

"Thanks," Ken responded. The glasses now full, he handed one to Moses.

"Where'd you find a painting like that? I didn't think anyone had ever painted a picture of colored soldiers."

"I painted it," Ken said.

Moses looked around in surprise. "You painted it? I didn't know you were a painter."

Ken chuckled. "I didn't either until I got out of the army. I came here and started this business." He took in the place with a wave of his hand. "And I'm doing real good too. But it's kind of lonesome here with no other colored folk around.

"Don't get me wrong, some of the folks here is real nice. But for someone like me, there's just not that much to do. So, I got me some paints and brushes and canvas, and next thing you know, I was paintin' pictures."

"Damn. You good, Sarge. You really good." Moses studied the painting for a moment longer before turning back to Ken. "You loved the army, didn't you?"

"Yes."

"So tell me, then, why you got out. I mean, you was a sergeant and everything. You had it made."

"Sit down," Ken invited. "I'm going to tell you a story."

Moses settled back in the proffered chair and took a swallow of his whiskey as Ken began talking.

"As I recollect, this happened about six months after you got out. A bunch of Injuns went bad and started spreadin' their mischief aroun', burnin' a ranch here, killin' a few miners and prospectors there . . . the kind of thing they're good at doin'. But there wasn't enough of 'em off the reservation to send out more'n a single company, so Colonel Hatch sent out just one troop of cavalry, D Troop."

"That was your troop as I recollect," Moses said.

"Yes, and Cap'n Bailey was the CO. You remember him?"

"Yeah, sure I remember him. I thought he was the best officer in the regiment. But after I got out, I heard tell that he got hisself into some kind of trouble and got court-martialed. What was all that about?"

"You goin' to let me tell the story or not?"

"Yeah, sure, Sarge. Go ahead," Moses said.

Ken was a good storyteller. And, like Ken, Moses was a veteran of dozens of field campaigns against the Indians, so it was very easy for Moses to project himself into the story Ken began telling.

"After Boots 'n' Saddles, we set out after the Injuns. The plains was stretched out before us, sort of like motionless waves, one after another. As we come over each wave, why, we would see us another one ahead, and beyond that another one still.

"You've been on the march, Moses, you know what it's like; the jangling equipment, squeaking leather, and that sort of dull thudding sound the horses' hooves make."

"Sure I know," Moses said.

"They was a lot of grasshoppers out then too. Don't know as I ever seen so many before or since, and the horses stirred 'em up so's they whirred ahead of us. And, underneath, well, the dusty grass give off that smell. I can't quite describe it."

"You don't need to describe it to me, Sarge. Once you smell that smell, you don't never forget. And I done smell that smell a million times," Moses said, taking another swallow of his whiskey.

"Well, sir, we find us a burned-out wagon, and a man and woman. The man was already dead but the woman was still alive. She died pretty soon after we found 'er, but before she died, she told us that the injuns carried off their colored girl they had workin' for 'em.

"About that time a courier come from the fort with the message that we been ordered to come back. But Cap'n Bailey said we ain't comin' back till we find the girl the Injuns took."

"Did you find her?"

Ken was quiet for a moment. "We found her," he said. "The Injuns had her staked out, and when we got to her, it was already too late. She was dead. But the Injuns knew we would come for her, so they was just waitin' there, usin' her for bait. They hit us pretty hard and we got three good men killed right off, and four more was wounded. We had to pull back to the rocks, but we couldn't take our wounded with us, so the Injuns got 'em."

Ken paused for a moment and took a drink before he continued.

"One of the men they took was Travis Jackson. Jackson 'n' me was particular good friends. Back when I was boxin', Jackson would train with me. And when I quit boxin', why, Jackson, he come too, and he join the army with me."

"Yes, I remember Jackson," Moses said.

"Well, sir, them heathens stake Jackson out in front of us, and they skin him alive. Jackson screamed somethin' terrible before he died, and we had to listen to 'im.

"Damn, Sarge, him bein' your particular friend an' all, that musta bother you somethin' awful," Moses suggested.

"Well, it bother all of us, but it didn't bother nobody any more'n it bother Cap'n Bailey. Him bein' the commander 'n' all, he figure he was to blame. So he tied himself a white flag to the end of his saber 'n' he walk down to see could he make a deal with the Injuns."

"Whoa, now, how you goin' to deal with Injuns?" Moses asked. "I ain't never known them to make no deals with anyone."

"Oh, they deal all right," Ken said. "If you make 'em the right offer, they deal. And Cap'n Bailey, he done just that. He tell 'em as how he was our chief, and how killin' him would be bigger medicine than killin' the three soldiers they be holdin'. Do you understand what I'm sayin', Moses? What Cap'n Bailey done is, he trade hisself for the three troopers the Injuns ain't started killin' yet. A white officer, doin' that for three colored privates."

"So, what happened?" Moses asked. "The Injuns didn't take his offer?"

"Oh, yes, they accept his offer, all right."

Moses shook his head. "No, they couldn'ta done that. Otherwise he wouldn't have still been alive for the army to court-martial him.

"Yes, sir. Well, the only reason Bailey didn't get killed is 'cause the Injuns wanted to kill him slow. So they tortured him for the rest of that day and into the night, cuttin' on 'im here, burnin' 'im there. And they wasn't nothin' we could do about it, 'cept listen to him scream.

"Come night, though, we was able to sneak down and get 'im. We cut Bailey free and brought him back."

"I guess I can see why you have sort of a special feelin' for 'im, then," Moses said.

"Then, when we get back to the fort, the army has Cap'n Bailey arrested for disobeying orders and putting his command at risk. They say they ordered him back, and when he went after the girl, he disobeyed those orders. And durin' the court-martial, they told how the girl was already dead when we found her so, what Bailey done was, he got four men killed for no good reason."

"What about him tradin' himself for the men the Injuns had captured?" Moses asked.

Ken shook his head. "The court didn't let his lawyer say nothin' about that. They said that had nothin' to do with the charge of him disobeyin' orders. He was found guilty and they give him a dishonorable discharge."

"That don't sound fair," Moses said.

"There wasn't nothin' fair about it," Ken said. "Bailey got his discharge, but he didn't know nothin' but the army. And, with that kind of discharge, there didn't nobody want to have anything to do with him. So, about six months after he got out of the army, he shot hisself."

"Damn," Moses said.

"When I heard about that, I decided I didn't want no part of an army that would do that to one of their own. So, when my time come to reenlist, I just take my discharge and get out."

"But you loved the army, Sarge. You always said that."

"Yes, I loved the army. But this was something I figured needed to be done. I owed that to Cap'n Bailey."

"So, after you leave the army, you come here?"

"Yes. Bein' as I'd been a farrier sergeant while I was in the army, well, it just seem natural to me I should open up a blacksmith shop. So that's just what I done. I took my army pay I'd saved up, come to a place where they didn't have no blacksmith, and started one up."

"Do you ever miss the army?" Moses asked.

Ken nodded. "There don't hardly a day go by that I don't think about it. What about you? Do you miss it?"

"I miss the men we was with. But I got me a good job cookin' for the Bar-Z-Bar." Moses smiled. "And I got me a wife and two chilrun."

Ken smiled broadly. "The hell you say! I knew you married that laundress. Sally was her name?"

"Yes, Sally Harrington."

"So, you got yourself a wife off soapsuds row, huh? Well, good for you. I didn't know you had any kids, though. That the reason you got out?"

"Yeah. Well, when Sally lose her job on the post, I didn't make enough money as a private to support a family. Then she got a job with the Zigenhorn family. Mr. Zigenhorn, he own the Bar-Z-Bar, and he offer me a job to cook for the outfit, so whenever my time come up, I got out."

"I remember that," Ken said. "I said then that the army was losin' a good man, and I tried to get them to promote you to corporal."

"Like I say, I miss the army some, but me 'n' Sally, we got us a good life, Sarge. A real good life." He ran his hand through his hair. "And here be the best thing. There ain't no chance now of me gettin' my scalp lifted. Yes, sir, Sally is real happy to know that ever'time I go out, I'm goin' to come back."

"I'm glad for you, Moses," Ken said. "I'm really glad."

"Maybe, someday, you can come out to the ranch and meet Sally an' my kids," Moses said. "Let me fix you a dinner like I used to when we was soldierin' together."

"I'd like that," Ken said. "I'd like that very much."

Chapter 15

DOWN THE STREET FROM THE BLACKSMITH SHOP, in front of the Golden Calf, Pete, Dusty, and Kendall were leaving. But Pete, who was by far the most inebriated of the three, barely made it out to the street. Stumbling at the top step, he grabbed hold of one of the porch supports to keep from falling.

"Better be careful there, Pete," Dusty said. He pointed to a horse apple very near the step. "You could wind up face-down in a pile of horse shit."

Kendall laughed.

"You two boys jus' don' be worryin' none 'bout ol' Pete Malone," Pete said. "I'm doin' jus' fine, thank you very much."

Pete tried again to step down from the porch but missed the steps. Only the fact that Kendall was standing close enough to grab him kept him from winding up exactly where Dusty said he would.

Kendall helped him down, then led him over to his horse.

"I sure wouldn't want to be inside your head in the morning," Dusty said. He chuckled. "I don't want to be inside my head in the morning."

"That's 'cause you're durnk," Pete said.

"I'm durnk?"

"Yep. You're durnk," Pete repeated. Then, catching himself, he said the word slowly. "Drunk. You're drunk."

"We're all drunk," Dusty said. "Except for Kendall. Kendall isn't drunk."

"Maybe not, but ol' Kendall got his ashes hauled tonight," Pete said. "You a man now, ain't you, Kendall?"

"Yes," Kendall said proudly. "And you know what else? You was lyin' about that snappin' turtle thing. Darci told me that don't never happen."

"Well, maybe it don't happen to Darci, but that don't mean it don't happen," Pete said.

"Come on, Pete, get mounted," Dusty said. "We have to get back out to the herd. Parker is going to roust us out of the blankets before daylight tomorrow. You know damn well he is."

"Yeah, I know it," Pete agreed. He tried to mount his horse, but fell and wound up on his back in the street.

"Damn, Pete, you plannin' on sleepin' there? Or you goin' to come on out to the herd?" Dusty asked.

"I'm goin' out to the herd. Just hold your horses," Pete insisted, and he stood up and tried, again, to mount his horse. The horse, sensing something was wrong, didn't stand still, but began twisting around in circles.

Kendall laughed. "Hold your horses? You the one needs your horse held."

"Damn, hold still, will you?" Pete said to his horse. He draped his arms across the saddle for a moment, as if preparing himself for another try. Then he looked around.

"Hey, where at's Darci?" he asked. "I didn't get to tell her good-bye."

"Darci is with someone else," Dusty said. "Which you woulda seen if you hadn't been so drunk."

"She went with someone else?"

"Yes."

"Damn. What'd she go and leave with somebody else for? I thought after tonight she'd be in love with us."

"She's in love with ever'one," Dusty said.

Smiling, Pete wagged his finger at Kendall. "Yeah," he said. "But I think she loves our boy Kendall most of all."

"Come on, Pete, get mounted. I don't want to spend the rest of the night out here in front of the saloon," Dusty said.

Once again Pete was pushing his horse around in circles as he tried to put his foot into the stirrup, making another ineffective attempt to mount.

"Kendall, he ain't never goin' to get up on that horse unless me 'n' you throw him belly down across it," Dusty said.

"I guess you're right," Kendall said. He and Dusty dismounted and started toward Pete when they saw Moses coming slowly up the street in his wagon.

"Moses," Dusty said. "What are you doin' here?"

"I came in for supplies, remember?"

"How long it take you to get supplies?"

"Not long," Moses said. "But I've been visiting with the blacksmith, another gentleman of color."

Pete made another unsuccessful try to mount his horse, again chasing him in circles. But when he fell this time, he didn't get up.

"Damn, he's passed out," Kendall said.

"Put him in the back of the wagon," Moses said. "Then tie his horse on. I'll take him back."

"Yeah, that's a good idea," Dusty said. "He'd prob'ly like that better'n goin' all the way back belly down across his horse."

Dusty and Pete picked up the unconscious cowboy and lay him unceremoniously in the back of Moses' wagon. Then, after tying Pete's horse to the back of the wagon, they mounted their own horses and started out together.

They were halfway down the street when Vox, Bates, Moody, and Hooper suddenly stepped out into the road in front of them.

"Where do you people think you're goin'?" Vox asked.

"We're going back to the herd," Dusty said. "What's it to you, anyhow?"

Vox shook his head. "No, you ain't," he said. "You boys is going to spend the night in jail. All of you."

"What for?" Kendall asked.

"For bein' drunk."

"We aren't causin' anybody any trouble," Moses said.

"Don't make no difference whether you're causin' trouble or not. You are drunk in the street, and that is public drunkenness. That is also against the town ordinance. Come on, you're going to jail. All of you."

"Mister, we ain't goin' to no jail," Dusty said. "So, the best thing you can do is to just get the hell out of our way and let us get on back to the herd."

"Get down off them horses and drop your guns," Vox ordered. "Or else."

"Or else what?" Dusty said. "You think just 'cause you say shit, we goin' to squat and ask how much? Now, get out of the way and let us through."

"Mister, I'm tellin' you and your friends, for the last time. Get down off them horses and unbuckle your gun belts."

"And I'm tellin' you to get out of the way, or I'll run you down," Dusty said, urging his horse forward.

Moody suddenly reached for his gun.

"Oh, shit! Dusty, they're drawin' on us!" Kendall shouted.

Dusty and Kendall pulled their own guns and six desperate men brought their guns into play.

For the next ten seconds bright flashes of light bounced off the facades of the buildings fronting the street as the flame patterns flared from the barrels of the guns. Crashes of gunfire, like thunder, echoed through the town as the guns flamed and roared.

The citizens of the town of Salcedo had heard gunfire many times before. Most of the time it was no more than the exuberance of an inebriated cowboy shooting his gun into the air.

But the gunfire that night was different. It was more urgent, and in some cases the shots overlapped, so it was obvious that more than one gun was being fired. These gunshots had an evil, death-dealing sound, and all who heard them felt the hackles rise on the backs of their necks. They knew, without being told, that one or more men had died.

All over town people got up, walked to their windows and stared out into the black of the night. Most of them couldn't see anything because the street was dark and unlit by street lamps.

Many of them shrugged and went back to bed. But some people got dressed and went out to the street to make a more thorough exploration. There, they saw others on the same quest, shadows within shadows moving through the darkness toward the center of town.

They spoke quietly among themselves, and their numbers grew as others came out from their own homes to join them.

"What was all that shooting?"

"Prob'ly just some drunken cowboys."

"No, didn't sound like just drunken cowboys havin' a good time."

"It sounded more serious to me."

"Yeah, sounded like that to me too, shots on top of shots."

"Look, down there. There's several people gatherin'."

By the time they reached the center of town, they could see by the ambient light of nearby buildings that there were, indeed, several people gathered. They also saw that the shots had been much more than drunken celebration.

* * * *

Moses Gillespie, who was unarmed, had been caught in the melee. Hit twice, he tumbled forward from the wagon seat and was draped across the footboard of the wagon, head and both arms hanging down, his blood pooling in the dirt beneath him.

Dusty was sitting in the street, holding his hands over a wound in his stomach, desperately trying to staunch the flow of the blood pouring through his spread fingers.

Kendall had been hit also, but it was no more than a nick in the arm. Of the four cowboys, only Dusty and Moses had been hit. Kendall and Pete had come through the battle totally unscathed. Passed out in the back of the wagon, Pete was blissfully unaware of the drama that had just played out around him.

"Who's hit?" Vox shouted.

"Looks like Moody is down," Hooper replied.

"Anyone else?"

"None of us except for Moody," Bates said. He laughed. "Woo wee! We sure as hell shot them cowboys up good, though."

"Oh, Jesus! Oh, Jesus it hurts!" Dusty was saying. Kendall was on his knees beside his friend, tending to him as best he could.

That's Moody," a townsperson said, pointing to one of the deputies who was lying in the street.

"Is he dead?"

"I don't know. He ain't movin'."

"There's two more over there," another said, pointing to Kendall and Dusty.

"I know who them boys is. I seen 'em in the saloon earlier tonight. They're cowboys from a herd that's passing through."

"Was they causin' any trouble?"

"No, they was just drinkin' and keepin' pretty much to themselves, as far as I could tell. Didn't look like they was botherin' nobody."

"There's another'n, over there, hangin' down from the wagon. He ain't movin' none. Looks like he's dead."

"Get a doctor!" Kendall pleaded from his position next to Dusty. "Somebody, please! Ain't there a doctor in this town?"

"Get up," Vox said, grabbing Kendall by his shirt and jerking him to his feet. Vox turned toward his two deputies, both of whom were tending to the deputy that was wounded. "How's Moody?" he asked.

"I think he's dead," Bates replied.

"You think he's dead? Or you know he is dead?" Vox asked.

"He is dead."

"Then what the hell are you wastin' your time over there with him for?"

Turning to the two cowboys, Vox smiled triumphantly. "Well, Moody's dead and that's murder. That means you boys is goin' to hang, right here, right now."

"You can't do that, Vox," one of the townspeople said. "That would be lynchin'."

"Who said anything about lynching?" Vox replied. "Hooper, you go wake up Judge Watermeyer. I want to be legal, but I intend to get these sons of bitches hung before mornin'."

"Can we please get a doctor for my pard?" Kendall asked, looking over at Dusty. Vox's deputies had dragged Dusty over to the wagon, and he was sitting, leaning back against the wheel.

"Somebody go get Doc Urban," one of the townspeople said. This was Poindexter, the hostler for the stage line.

"No," Vox said. "Leave the doc be."

"But this man is hurt bad," Poindexter insisted. "Wouldn't be right not to get a doctor to look after him."

"No need in wastin' a doctor's time on him," Vox said. "He's prob'ly goin' to be dead in a few minutes anyway. And even if he don't die from the gunshots, we goin' to hang him."

"Well can I at least try to stop him from bleedin' to death?" Kendall asked.

Vox nodded at the deputy who was holding Kendall, and the deputy let him go. Kendall took off his shirt then started tearing it into strips to make a bandage.

Judge Watermeyer came out into the street then, obviously hauled from his bed because he was still tucking his shirt down into his pants. In keeping with the dignity of his office, his shirt had a collar, and he was wearing a jacket. "I heard gunshots. What's going on here?" he asked.

"We're goin' to have us a trial," Vox said. "And you can't have a trial without a judge."

"What do you mean you are going to have a trial? You mean now, in the middle of the street, in the middle of the night?"

"Yes, right here, in the street, where it happened," Vox said. "And we're going to have it right now. Somebody get some torches lit," he added, looking around in the dark. "We got to see what's going on here."

"Where's Culpepper?" the judge asked. "Is he back in town yet?"

"Don't you be worryin' none about Culpepper. Culpepper ain't got nothin' to do with this," Vox said angrily. "I'm in charge." He pulled his pistol and pointed it at Judge Watermeyer. "Now, by damn you are going to hold this trial, or I'm goin' to shoot you where you stand!"

"This isn't a court of law! You are asking me to condone a lynching, and I can't do that."

Vox pulled the hammer back on his pistol. "Then I'll just kill you and do the judgin' myself," he said.

"No, wait!" Judge Watermeyer said in sudden fear. "All . . . all right," he stuttered.

By then a few torches were burning and the scene was eerily lit in a pale, wavering light that cast deep shadows, painted skin orange, and made the eyes look as if they were reflecting the fires of hell itself.

"What's going on here?" Paddy O'Neil shouted, coming out into the street then. Looking around at the carnage, he gasped.

"My God!" he said. "Vox, you insane bastard, what have you done? These men were just in my saloon. They weren't bothering anyone!"

"You know the ordinance against public drunkenness," Vox said. "You should've kept 'em in your saloon until they sobered up."

Looking around, Paddy saw Kendall, shirtless, and with his arms tied behind his back. He also saw Judge Watermeyer standing near one of the torches. There was a pained expression on Watermeyer's face.

"Judge, you aren't going along with this, are you?"

"I . . . I have no choice, Paddy," the judge replied.

"Well I don't intend to let it happen," Paddy said. He pointed to Kendall. "Let him go."

"Get out of here, O'Neil, before you get hurt," Vox growled.

"I will not get out of here," Paddy said. He started toward Kendall but got only a few steps before Vox nodded at Bates. Stepping out behind Paddy, Bates brought his gun down, sharply, on the saloon keeper's head. Paddy went down.

The gathered townspeople gasped in surprise and quick anger.

"Anybody else want to protest what's going on here?" Vox called.

His offer brought no responses, so he turned to Judge Watermeyer and nodded. "All right, Judge, let's get this thing started," Vox ordered.

Judge Watermeyer cleared his throat, then nodded in acquiescence. "This court is now in session," he said. "What are the charges?"

"The charge is murder," Vox said. "These here four murderin' sons of bitches killed Moody."

"What are you talkin' about? We didn't murder him!" Kendall said angrily. "You started shooting first. All we done was shoot back."

"If you'da come down off your horses, give your guns up, and come to jail like I told you to, none of this woulda ever happened," Vox said. "You woulda just slept off your drunk in our jail, then gone on home tomorrow. Now, a good man has been kilt, and the four of you is goin' to hang. Killin' a lawman in the performance of his duty is murder. And it don't matter none whether the lawman is shootin' at you or not. Ain't that right, Judge?"

"I'm afraid so," the judge replied hesitantly.

"Which one of you killed Deputy Moody?" Vox asked.

"What? How the hell do I know?" Kendall replied. "We was both firin' at him."

"Judge, I'm goin' to call Bates and Hooper as witnesses," Vox said. "They was the other two deputies with Moody and me when we tried to arrest these men. Bates, you and Hooper, get over here and take a look at the defendants."

The two deputies stepped up to the front of the wagon.

"You," Vox said to one of the men holding a flaming torch. "Put that light over here so the witnesses can see."

The torch was held very close to Kendall's face, and he squinted his eyes and held up his hand, as much to shield himself from the heat as to block the light.

"Are these the men that was shootin' at us?" Vox asked.

"Well, hell, Vox. You know damn well they was," Hooper said.

"Just answer the damn question," Vox demanded. "You are a witness in a trial. Now, are these here four men the ones that was shootin' at us?"

"Well, two of 'em was shootin'," Hooper said. "Him and him." He pointed to Kendall and Dusty. He pointed to Pete. "That one was passed out drunk in the back of the wagon, and the one that was drivin' the wagon, well, he never got off a shot before we killed him."

"You started shootin' at us first," Kendall insisted.

"You'll get your turn to talk," Vox said. "Right now I'm doin' the talkin'." Vox turned to Bates. "Now let's hear from you. You go along with what Hooper has to say?"

Bates nodded. "That's the way it was," he added. "These two here, this one standin' in front of the wagon and the other'n, the one sittin' on the ground by the wheel, was shootin' at us. But I think the colored man was shootin' at us too."

"He couldn't have been shooting at you. He didn't even have a gun," Kendall said. "Moses never carries a gun."

"Now, Judge, I'm callin' myself as a witness," Vox said. "And the way I seen it, all we done was tell these men they was drunk and they was goin' to have to spend the night in our jail. Just one night, that's all we was goin' to ask of 'em. But the next thing you know, they started in to shootin' at us. And the way I remember it, they was all four shootin' at us."

"You are a lying sack of shit," Kendall said. "Moses didn't even have a gun, and Pete was passed out drunk. Only me 'n' Dusty was shootin' at you."

"Aha!" Vox shouted triumphantly. He pointed at Kendall. "So, you admit that you was shootin' at us?"

"Yes, but you drew your guns first," Kendall said.

"And you admit that you did shoot back?" Vox asked.

"Hell yes, we shot back," Kendall replied angrily.

"Do we really need this trial to go on any longer, Judge?" Vox asked. "We did draw our guns, but that was to enforce the arrest. We had no intention of shooting until they began shooting. And you just heard this cowboy admit that they were shooting at us. The way I see it, that is a confession."

Judge Watermeyer sighed and shook his head. "I don't like it," he said. He looked at Vox. "I don't like any of this. Why can't we wait until tomorrow morning, when they can get a lawyer to defend them?"

"'Cause there ain't goin' to be no tomorrow mornin' for them," Vox replied.

"What do you mean? What are you talking about?" Judge Watermeyer asked.

"Simple. I aim to hang these sons of bitches right here, to-night, just as soon as you declare them guilty."

"In that case, I have no intention of declaring them guilty."

"You got no choice in it, Judge," Vox said, again pointing his pistol at Judge Watermeyer. "You either declare these sons of bitches guilty or I'll shoot you where you stand."

Judge Watermeyer began shaking in fear. "All right, all right," he said. "I want it noted by all here that I am rendering this decision under duress. But because I have no choice, I find the defendants guilty as charged."

"Get some rope," Vox ordered. "We'll hang these bastards right here, right now."

"Where?" Bates asked.

Looking around, Vox saw a large brace protruding over the boardwalk. The sign on the brace read:

CASTLEBERRY'S
BOOTS
AND
LEATHER GOODS

"Get that sign tore down," Vox said. "Let's get this hangin' done."

Within moments the sign was taken down and ropes were tossed over the support arm.

"Vox, this here one is dead," one of the townspeople said of Dusty.

Vox walked over to Dusty and kicked him, hard. Dusty gave no reaction. "Well, it don't matter none whether he's dead or not. The judge has just found him guilty, so we are going to hang him."

"What about the colored man in the wagon?" another asked.

"Him too. We're goin' to hang all four of them."

Judge Watermeyer shook his head. "No, sir," he said. He pointed to Pete. "That one was passed out drunk when the shooting started. He didn't have anything to do with what went on here, and you aren't going to hang him."

"He's as guilty as the others. It don't matter that he was passed out drunk, he was with 'em."

"No, sir," the judge said again, more resolutely this time than before. He shook his head and pointed his finger at Vox. "You aren't going to hang him!" he said.

"By damn, Watermeyer, you better be careful there, or you'll wind up hangin' right alongside them," Vox said.

"The only way you're going to hang that other man is if you hang me too," Judge Watermeyer said, suddenly finding some backbone.

"Well, don't think we won't hang you."

"Vox," Poindexter said. The stage depot hostler was standing in the front row. "You don't think we are just going to stand by and let you hang the judge, now, do you?"

"You think you can stop me?" Vox asked.

"I don't know," Poindexter said. "But I aim to try. You think you can take on the whole town?"

"So far I don't see nobody but you mouthin' off about it," Vox said.

"And me," Baldwin added. "You ain't goin' to hang the

judge. And you ain't goin' to hang the drunk," the town baker said.

"All right, all right!" Vox said angrily. "We won't hang the drunk, and we won't hang the judge. But we sure as hell are goin' to hang the other three, whether they be already dead or not."

Kendall was standing on the back of the wagon with his hands tied behind his back. Dusty and Moses were beside him, their already dead bodies hanging from the ropes around their necks.

"No!" a voice cried from the crowd. "No, don't hang him!"

Looking toward the sound, Kendall saw Darci coming from the direction of the saloon, running toward the wagon.

"Get that whore out of here," Vox growled, and one of the townsmen took her away, gently.

"Are you goin' to at least put a hood over his face, Vox?" someone from the crowd asked. "For God's sake, man, at least do that."

"All right, if somebody's got somethin' for me to use, I'll do it," Vox said. "This here is a legal hangin', it ain't murder."

"No, I don't want a hood," Kendall said quietly, shaking his head. "When I meet my Maker, I want Him to see my face, so that He may judge me innocent of any wrongdoing."

"Have it your way," Vox replied. He dropped the noose over Kendall's head, then stepped down from the wagon and walked up to the head of the team.

Oddly, even though Kendall was standing on the brink of eternity, he felt no stomach-wrenching fear. Instead, a sense of calm came over him. He was not a regular churchgoing man, but he had been to church a few times, and now a phrase he once heard the preacher use came to him.

Kendall was experiencing a "peace that passeth all understanding."

Gone was the anxiousness he had felt earlier. He was going to die now, and he knew it. He stood on the wagon and accepted it as calmly as if he were waiting for the visit of a friend.

After all, he told himself, isn't death a friend? Death will come to everyone, and once it has arrived, what difference does it make how long one had been able to hold it off? A person who has been dead but an hour differs not from one who has been dead for a thousand years.

"Have you got any last words, mister?" someone from the crowd called up to him.

Kendall looked out over the crowd of people who had gathered to witness the execution. He had no idea how many were there, and he was amazed that so many had showed up in the middle of the night.

He looked over the heads of the crowd. Down toward the end of the street he saw a small house with a dim light on inside. He thought of the little boy and the little girl he, Pete, and Dusty had seen playing in the front yard of the house when they had ridden into town earlier. He hoped the children were peacefully asleep, unaware of the atrocity taking place in their town.

He looked back toward the townspeople again. From his newly arrived rapprochement with death, he was able to observe them casually, objectively. Many had looks of sympathy or sorrow. Some looked horrified, others merely curious. What did surprise him, though, was the fact that there were a few who had expressions of almost eager anticipation on their faces, as if they were actually enjoying the gruesome spectacle they were about to witness.

Kendall wanted to laugh at them, to tell them that they weren't actually going to see anything; that his body might feel the hangman's noose, but he wouldn't be in his body. His soul would be free.

"Cowboy," the judge said, calling up to him. "If you'll let your neck be relaxed, it'll snap like a twig and be over in a second. Tighten it up 'n' it's likely to take a little longer."

"Yeah? How do you know that?"

"It isn't breaking your neck that kills you. You die by strangulation, but if your neck is broken, you'll pass out, and you won't be able to feel anything. I've seen folks tighten up, then kick for nearly half an hour."

"Oh, well, then thank you," Kendall said calmly. "I shall heed your advice."

Vox stood back from the horses, holding a whip in his hand. He drew it back, held it for one long moment, and looked up at Kendall.

"You got'ny last words, cowboy?"

"Yeah. It'll be a cold day in hell before I visit your town again."

A few who were close enough to hear him chuckled. Others shuddered, as if there was some hidden meaning to the comment.

That moment when Vox was holding the whip aloft was all the time that remained between Kendall and eternity. It was just a brief moment in the lives of those who stood on the ground watching, but it was a lifetime for Kendall.

The question was, how best to make use of the time remaining?

Looking toward the back of the crowd, Kendall saw Darci, barely illuminated by the flickering torchlight. She was standing with her back to him, unable to watch him hang, and he wished she would turn around so he could see her one last time.

He thought of how pretty Darci was. He was glad that he was dying a man, and a small, enigmatic smile passed across his face as he recalled everything they had done earlier that night.

"Look at that," Poindexter said in awe. "He's smiling. They are about to hang this poor soul and he is smiling. That has to be the bravest son of a bitch I ever saw."

Those were the last words Kendall would ever hear.

The whip snapped sharply over the head of the team, and the horses leaped forward. Kendall felt himself dropping off into space.

"No!" Pete shouted.

The jerking forward of the wagon had awakened him, and when he sat up, he saw three men hanging.

"Stop that wagon and get him!" Vox shouted.

Hooper and Bates jumped onto their horses and chased the wagon down, then, turning it, they brought it back. Pete was on his knees in the back of the wagon, staring at the bodies of his three friends, trying hard to comprehend the horror of the moment. By now Kendall had quit kicking.

"What is this?" Pete asked in a weak, horrified voice. "What happened?"

"Mister, you just better be glad you was passed out drunk," Vox said. "Otherwise, you would be hanging up there with them."

"My God! My God!" Pete said. It was more of a prayer than an oath.

"Throw his ass in jail," Vox ordered with a jerk of his head.

"Come on, you," Bates growled.

"The hell you say! I'm not goin' anywhere with you. I want to know what's going on here!"

Bates nodded at Hooper, and from behind Hooper hit Pete over the head with the butt of his pistol. Pete went down.

Chapter 16

⌒⌒

THOSE WHO HAD NOT BEEN ACTUAL WITNESSES to the events of the night before learned about it the next morning. Going out into the street, they were greeted with the grizzly sight of three men hanging from the support arm of what had been the advertising sign for Castleberry's leather goods store.

Cyrus Green was so incensed by the sight that he did something he had never done before. He put out an extra.

THREE MEN HURLED INTO ETERNITY

Last night, while decent men and women slept in their beds, the evil machinations of that group of outlaws who call themselves the Salcedo Regulators Brigade were in play.

Four cowboys were attempting to return to their herd when they were accosted by Deputy Rufus Vox. In the absence of Titus Culpepper, Vox is acting as chief of the Regulators Brigade.

One of the young cowboys was drunk, but because he was asleep in the back of the wagon, he neither represented a danger to the town nor was he disturbing the peace.

Two of the men had been drinking at the saloon, but those who saw them, both in the saloon and when they left, have testified to this reporter that they were comporting themselves in a gentlemanly manner.

The fourth was a man of color, the cook of the Bar-Z-Bar cattle outfit. He had come into town to replenish the outfit's supplies, and as such, was providing a source of income for our town's businesses. The cook was driving the wagon filled with purchases made in our town when he, and the three cowboys with him, were stopped by Deputies Vox, Bates, Moody, and Hooper.

After an exchange of words, gunfire erupted, resulting in Deputy Moody's death, as well as the death of the colored cook and one of the cowboys. The other cowboy, after a trial that was absent any guarantee of rights to the accused, was hanged. In a move that can only be described as gratuitous cruelty, the dead cowboy and the cook were taken from their death's repose and strung up alongside the hanged man.

Only the young cowboy who was passed out drunk in the back of the wagon was spared, only thanks to the courageous stand of Judge Watermeyer.

It is time that we, the citizens of Salcedo, took an equally courageous stand. Therefore I, as editor of the *Salcedo Advocate*, do hereby, and on this date, call our citizens to arms.

Gene Welch pulled his wagon up to the front of Castleberry's, then stopped. Ken Wright was with him, and when the undertaker stopped the wagon, Ken climbed up onto the wagon seat and took out a knife. He looked into the face of Moses Gillespie.

The expression on Moses' face could be described more as one of surprise rather than pain or horror. He had died by gunfire, not by hanging.

As Ken cut through the rope he thought of the conversation he and Moses had the night before, when Moses said that his wife no longer had to worry about his not coming back. It didn't seem right that he had survived Indian battles only to be murdered in the street.

"Moses, when you get up there to Fiddler's Cyrus, I know you'll be sayin' hi to all your old friends. But do me a favor and look up ol' Travis Jackson for me, will you? I want you and him to hold a place for me. I'll be up there bye and bye."

Welch overheard Moses' comment. "Fiddler's Cyrus?" he asked. "What's Fiddler's Cyrus?"

"It's a place where all cavalrymen go when they die," Ken explained as, the rope now cut, he lowered his friend's body, gently, into the back of the wagon.

"I've never heard of such a thing," Welch said.

"You wasn't never a cavalryman."

"Is that just a colored cavalry thing?"

"Mr. Welch, when it come to the army, they be only two races. Those who are cavalry, and those who ain't."

Ken cut the other two men down and put them in the wagon as well.

"Hey! Who said you could cut them men down?" Deputy Bates shouted, coming quickly up the street.

Those who had gathered on the boardwalk and out in the street in front of Castleberry's leather goods shop stepped aside. Bates pushed his way through them until he was standing no more than a couple of feet away from Ken.

"Did you hear the question I asked you?" Deputy Bates asked. "Who gave you permission to cut those men down?"

Welch hesitated for a moment.

"You go ahead, Mr. Welch," Ken said. "Get these men seen to. I'll talk to the deputy."

Welch snapped the reins over the back of the team and they moved forward.

"Hey, you! Come back here!" Bates shouted in anger. "Damn you! Don't you drive off when I'm talking to you!"

The deputy pulled his pistol and pointed it at Welch.

"Bates! Put that gun down!" Baldwin shouted. The baker was one of those who had gathered around to watch the bodies be removed.

"The hell I will," Bates replied. "If he don't bring them bodies back I'm going to shoot him."

Ken reached out and wrapped his hand around Deputy Bates's wrist and began squeezing.

"Ahh!" Bates called out in pain.

Ken squeezed harder, and the deputy dropped his pistol. Reaching down, Ken picked up the pistol, then swung open the cylinder and emptied it. Putting the bullets in his own pocket, he handed the gun back to Bates.

"You damn near broke my arm, you black bastard!" Bates said angrily, rubbing the joint in pain.

Ken looked over at the banister that protected the boardwalk from the street. The banister was a round piece of wood, at least one inch in diameter.

"No, sir, Mr. Bates," Ken said. "If I want to break your arm, your arm would done be broke now. Just like this."

Ken slammed the side of his hand down against the banister, and it snapped into two pieces. The crowd gasped in awe at the demonstration of strength.

"All I done was keep you from killin' somebody that was just doin' his job."

"That's right, Bates," Poindexter said. "If you had shot Welch in front of us it would've been murder. Not even Culpepper could have got you out of that."

"You don't understand," Bates said as he continued to gingerly rub his wrist. "I wasn't really goin' to shoot him. I was just tryin' to make him put them bodies back."

"Why?"

"Why? Well, because Vox didn't say we could take them down, that's why."

"Get on back to your business, Bates," Baldwin said. "Whatever that is. And leave this be."

Glowering at Ken and the others, Deputy Bates started back up the boardwalk toward the Regulators' headquarters.

Cyrus Green was just arriving, and the two men passed on the boardwalk. Cyrus handed Bates a copy of his newspaper.

"I ain't payin' you no penny for your newspaper," Bates growled.

"You don't need to," Cyrus said. "Today, this paper is free for every citizen of the community."

"Free?"

"Yes."

"All right," Bates said. He took the paper, but made no effort to read it. Instead, he just continued his purposeful stride toward the headquarters of the Regulators.

"Here you are, folks," Cyrus called as he reached the gathering. "This is an extra, a special edition of the paper, and it costs you nothing."

"Cyrus, why are you putting out a free paper?" Poindexter asked.

"Because I've got something to say and I want everyone in town to read it," Cyrus replied. "Gather around folks, it's hot off the press. Take one for yourself and one for your neighbor."

Hawke and Flaire had breakfast at the train depot in Marva, then walked over to the stage depot to catch the coach for Salcedo. For a while it looked as if they would be the only passengers, but just before the coach left, a man, his wife, and two children joined them.

"I'm glad we made it," the man said once he had his family on board. "If we had missed the coach, we would have had to take a hotel room tonight, and the cost of hotel rooms are so dear."

"I'm glad you made it too," Flaire said, smiling at the family.

"We've been to see Grandma," the little boy said.

"Well, I'm sure she was happy to see you," Flaire said.

"You're the fella that's playin' the piano down at the Golden Calf, aren't you?" the man asked Hawke.

"Yes."

"I thought so. I don't frequent taverns, so I've never heard you play, but folks who have say you are very good."

"He's one of the best pianists in the entire world," Flaire said proudly.

The man laughed. "Well, I can see he certainly has a supporter in you," he said.

Flaire shook her head. "Oh, I'm not the only one who thinks this. We are on our way back from San Antonio, where we attended a concert given by the great Gottschalk. Mr. Gottschalk himself said that about Mason Hawke."

Hawke stared through the window in embarrassment. He wished Flaire wouldn't take on about him so, but he was glad there were other people on the stage. After last night, the intimacy of the two of them alone in the coach might have been a bit awkward.

When Justin Parker discovered Pete, Dusty, and Kendall's empty bedrolls the next morning, he was a little aggravated, but not entirely surprised.

What did surprise him was the fact that Moses hadn't returned either. That was totally unlike the cook.

"Hey, boss," one of his drovers said. "What are we going to do for breakfast?"

"Make some coffee, eat some jerky," Justin said.

"Jerky?"

"If you want to try and make some biscuits, be my guest," Justin said.

"I can't make biscuits. Not like Moses, anyway."

"Nobody can make biscuits like Moses," one of the other drovers said. "Where is Moses, anyway? Wasn't he supposed to come back last night?"

"Yes," Justin said. "And so were the others."

"Didn't none of 'em come back? Damn, they musta had a high ol' time last night. Want me to ride into town and see where at they are?"

"No," Justin said. "I'll go myself."

The others watched as Justin saddled his horse then rode off toward Salcedo.

"If he finds them boys layin' up with whores this mornin', I sure wouldn't want to be in their boots," one of the cowboys said. Then, slapping the heel of his hand against his forehead, he said, "What am I saying? I'd love to be layin' with a whore right now."

The other cowboys laughed.

When Justin reached the town, he recognized the wagon Moses had been driving. It was loaded with supplies and parked in front of the blacksmith shop. Dismounting, Justin stepped under the overhang and looked around.

"Hello the shop!" he called. "Hello, is anyone here?"

Ken came around the corner then, carrying an armload of wood.

"Yes, sir," Ken said. "What can I do for you? Your horse throw a shoe?"

"No," Justin said. He nodded toward the wagon. "I want to ask you about that wagon."

Ken shook his head. "That belongs to a cattle drive outfit that's camped just out of town."

"Where's Moses?"

Ken ran his hand through his hair and sighed. "You must be Mr. Parker," he said.

"I am," Justin said. He nodded toward the wagon. "When Moses didn't come back last night, I figured to come in and see what happened to him. Also, three of my drovers." He chuckled. "They must've had themselves quite a time last night. Not that surprising, I guess, for my drovers. But it's not like Moses to do something like that."

"Any of those boys kin to you, Mr. Parker?" Ken asked.

Parker shook his head. "Kin to me? No. Why would you ask that?"

"'Cause if any of 'em was kin, I would try and be more gentle with the news I got for you."

Parker's eyes narrowed. "What news?"

"Moses is dead," Ken said. "So are two of your cowboys."

"My God! What happened?"

Ken told about the confrontation the night before, then the shootout, followed by the trial and hanging.

"Wait a minute! Are you telling me that they had a trial in the middle of the night? In the street?"

Ken nodded. "Yes, sir."

Parker shook his head in confusion. "I've never heard of such a thing. You said Moses and two of my drovers were dead. What about the third one? Where is he?"

"They got him down in the jail now," Ken said.

"Thanks," Parker said. He started back toward his horse.

"Mr. Parker?" Ken called.

Parker turned toward him.

"Moses Gillespie be a friend of mine for a long time. We had a nice long visit last night, before all this happened. He told me you was a good man. I thank you for treatin' him so good."

"You don't have to thank me, mister," Parker said. "Black or white, Moses Gillespie was one of the best men I ever had the privilege to know."

"I'd like to take Moses back home to his wife, if you don't mind."

"I'd pay you to take all three of them back," Justin said.

"No, sir," Ken replied. "I mean, I take all three of 'em back, but I don't want no pay for doin' it."

"Anything you need? A wagon? Supplies?" Justin asked.

"No sir, I got all I need."

"No wonder Moses was such a good man, with friends like you," Justin said.

"That's the other way around, Mr. Parker. Moses had friends like me because he was such a good man."

Justin nodded, then remounted and rode on down the street. Ken watched him for a moment, then went back to his pile of wood and started stoking the fire for his forge. He was alone in the shadows of the back of his shop, and he was glad. That way, nobody would be able to see his tears.

Chapter 17

THE TENSION IN THE AIR WAS PALPABLE FROM THE moment the stage rolled into Salcedo. At first Hawke wasn't sure what the difference was, then he figured it out. Instead of the normal flow of traffic, mounted and on foot, there were little conversational groups of people scattered about.

Six were standing in front of Beadle's general store, four in front of the bank, a few in front of Heissler's apothecary. But the largest number of people were clustered in front of Sikes's hardware store and as the stage rolled by, Hawke saw what they were looking at.

In the window of the hardware store, propped up for all to see, was a black lacquered casket with the top half of the lid open. Deputy Nelson Moody was in the coffin, wearing a suit and a white shirt.

Seeing Moody in a suit and white shirt was nearly as shocking as seeing him dead.

"Hawke, did you see that?" Flaire asked, putting her hand on his.

"Yes, I saw it," Hawke replied.

The stage stopped in front of the depot, and Poindexter came out immediately, to take care of the team.

Hawke helped Flaire disembark, then he walked up to the front of the stage.

"What happened, Mr. Poindexter?"

"You saw the body?"

"Moody? Yes, I saw him in the window of the hardware store."

"Mr. Welch has three more bodies in the back," Poindexter said.

"Who are they?"

"Well, they ain't town folk," Poindexter said.

"A shootout?"

"Yes, we had a shootout, all right. Then we had us a hangin'," Poindexter said. "You see, there's a herd passin' through, and last night some of the cowboys come into town. Next thing you know, Vox is tellin' 'em he's going to throw 'em in jail, one thing leads to another, and they start shooting."

"What had they done that Vox was going to throw them in jail?" Hawke asked.

"That's the question everyone in town is askin' now," Poindexter said as he led the stage team into the corral. "From all I've heard from folks that was in the saloon last night, them cowboys wasn't botherin' anyone. But then, just as they was makin' a quiet exit from town, Vox and his deputies jumped them."

Poindexter continued with the story, telling of the hanging in the middle of the night, describing the scene as it was illuminated by flickering torchlight.

"Is Culpepper back yet?" Hawke asked when Poindexter finished with his story.

"No," Poindexter said. "I think he's got three or four more days before he comes back. But if he don't come back soon, he ain't goin' have no town to come back to."

"Hawke, I have to get back to my shop," Flaire said. "I have a fitting to do this morning."

"All right, I'll walk you down there," Hawke offered, and picking up the luggage, he walked her back to the apartment behind her store.

There they exchanged an awkward kiss, then she went inside. Hawke, under the excuse that he had better get back to work as well, went down to the Golden Calf.

The Golden Calf saloon was practically empty when Hawke got there, though there were several people sitting around one of the tables in back. Seeing tears running unchecked down Darci Benoit's cheeks, Hawke walked quickly back to the table.

"I hear we had a busy night," Hawke said as he handed his handkerchief to Darci.

"Thank you," she said, and dabbed at the tears.

"How much have you heard?" Paddy asked, a large bandage wrapped around his head from the blow he'd taken.

Hawke nodded. "I heard a little about it," he said. "Poindexter said that Vox hung some cowboys last night."

"Yes."

"What did he do, lynch them?"

Doc Urban shook his head. "No. Crazy as it sounds, they were legally tried and convicted. Vox held court in the street."

"How can there be a legal trial in the middle of the night?"

"Judge Watermeyer is a circuit judge. That gives him the authority to convene a court anywhere and anytime he pleases," Doc Urban responded. "So what Vox did was to roust Judge Watermeyer out of bed and made him hold court."

"He seemed like such a sweet boy," Darci said, dabbing at her eyes.

"Who was a sweet boy?"

"Well, they all were nice men, but the youngest one was so sweet."

"Did you hear that two of the men were already dead when Vox hung them?" Paddy asked.

"Poindexter said something to that effect, but I wasn't sure I heard him right."

"You heard him proper, all right," Paddy said. "The colored driver and one of the cowboys was already dead but Vox hung 'em anyway."

"That man must be insane."

"You know, so far I've kept my mouth shut about what's been going on around here," Doc Urban said. "I've tried to stay out of things, figuring it wasn't my place to take a stand one way or another. But this is getting out of hand."

"I don't think any of this would have happened if the colonel had been here," Paddy said.

"I'm not so sure of that," Doc replied. "I think it might have happened whether Culpepper was here or not. He had to know what kind of men he hired. Hell, everyone in town knows that Vox ain't worth a bucket of warm piss, and they've known that from day one."

"Still, Culpepper has done some very good things for this town," Paddy insisted.

"I don't know," Hawke replied. "I'd like to think that it wouldn't have happened if Culpepper had been here, but if there is one thing I do know about Titus Culpepper, it is that he is a calculating and deliberate man. You can believe that he knew what kind of men Vox and the other deputies were when he hired them. And if he did know, then he hired them for a reason."

"What would that reason be?" Doc asked.

"Maybe intimidation," Hawke said. "It is easier to control people if you have them intimidated."

"By controlling people, you mean control the town, don't you?" Doc asked.

"Yes," Hawke agreed.

"I can't believe that," Paddy said.

"Why not?" Doc asked.

"Robberies, assaults, and just plain brutish behavior are all down now," Paddy said. "That's all due to Culpepper."

"Paddy, do you know what happens if you put a frog in warm water?" Doc Urban asked.

Paddy chuckled. "No, I can't say as I do, Doc. But I'm pretty sure you are about to tell me."

"Frogs are cold-blooded creatures, you see. So, if you put one in warm water, they appreciate it, and they will just stay there and enjoy it. But here's the thing. If you heat it up a little, the frog won't hop out. If you heat it more, he still won't hop out. You can keep on heating that water, and heating it until it reaches a boil. By that time it is too late. At almost any time up until then, the frog could jump out, but he won't. He will just stay in that water until he is dead."

"So, what are you saying, Doc? That we are frogs in a pan of water?" Paddy asked.

"Something like that, yes," Doc said.

Cyrus Green came into the saloon then, walked over to the bar, and lay down a stack of papers. Paddy looked over toward him.

"Hey, Mayor, what are you doing bringing in newspapers today? Your next issue isn't until Wednesday, is it? I'm not sure I can sell another issue this fast."

"I don't want you to sell these, Paddy. I want you to give them away."

"Give them away? To who?"

"To every man, woman, and child in this town who can read," Cyrus said resolutely.

"You sound like a man on a mission," Doc Urban said, getting up and walking over to the bar. He grabbed a few papers, one for himself and one each for the others at his table.

"You're damn right I'm on a mission," Cyrus said. "My

mission is to run Culpepper and every one of his deputies out of town. Preferably on a rail."

Cyrus looked at Darci then, and saw that her eyes were red from crying.

"Did something else happen?" he asked.

"Darci was in love with one of those cowboys that was killed last night," Paddy said.

"Oh!" Cyrus said. "Oh, Darci, I'm so sorry. Which one? You knew him from before?"

"I wasn't in love with him," Darci said. "At least, I don't think I was. I wouldn't know, because I've never been in love before, and I don't know how it feels. Also, I just met him last night."

"Last night?"

"The cowboys were her customers last night."

"Yes, I heard they had been in here."

"No," Paddy said. "I mean they were Darci's customers last night. Special customers," he added pointedly.

"Oh. And they made that big an impression on you, did they?"

"Not all of them," Darci replied. "But one of them . . . the young cowboy that they hung. He was . . . he was . . ." Her lip quivered and, unable to finish her sentence, she began crying again.

"They did seem like nice young men," Paddy said. "They just came in to let off a little steam from the drive. They drank a lot, as you would expect, and they got a little drunk, but they weren't mean drunks. I think every customer in the place would agree that they weren't mean drunks."

"Yes, well, drunk or not, those boys deserved better than they got," Cyrus said.

"I wonder how Culpepper will react when he learns what happened here," Paddy said.

"I don't know about the reaction," Cyrus said. "But I'll bet he already knows what happened here."

"He knows? How does he know?"

"Because this morning I sent a telegram to Governor Hubbard."

While the newspaper editor and Paddy were talking, Doc Urban had been reading Cyrus's editoral. Now, he flicked the paper with the back of his hand.

"You've got something here, Cyrus," he said. "I hope the town pays attention to you."

"What does he say?"

"He says we need to take the town back," Doc Urban said. "I think so too."

"Maybe we should wait," Paddy suggested.

"Wait for what?" Doc asked.

"Wait until Culpepper gets back in town," Paddy said. "He's the one that's in charge. He's the only one that can put a stop to this."

"What do you think, Hawke?" Cyrus asked.

Hawke held up his hands and shook his head. "Uh-uh," he said. "This isn't my town."

"What do you mean, it isn't your town?" Doc asked. "You're living here, aren't you?"

"You might say I'm just passing through," Hawke replied. "All I want to do is play a few tunes on the piano. Looks like you are getting ready to open a ball here, and I don't care to be invited."

"You don't care to get invited?" Paddy chuckled and shook his head. "Excuse me for laughing, Hawke, but seems to me like you invited yourself when you took Vox's gun away from him the other night."

Cyrus laughed as well. "Poor Vox. He has been having a hard time of it here lately. First Hawke takes his gun away from him, then last night Paddy ran him out of the saloon."

"Yes, but I was holding a loaded shotgun on him," Paddy said. "I didn't reach down and snatch Vox's own gun from his holster before he knew what was going on."

"You ran Vox out of the saloon?" Hawke asked.

"I'll say he did," Doc said, and both Doc and Cyrus launched into the story, telling in great and often contradictory detail exactly what happened. By the time they were finished, everyone was laughing so hard that they were wiping away the tears. In fact, the gaiety teemed totally incongruous with the mood of the rest of the town.

Hawke looked once more around the empty saloon.

"Paddy, it doesn't look like you'll be needing much in the way of a piano player for a while. If you don't mind, I think I'll take a walk around the town."

"You go right ahead," Paddy said. "With all that went on last night, it don't look like we're goin' to be doin' much business this mornin'."

Chapter 18

~~~

AFTER HAWKE LEFT THE SALOON HE WALKED
around town for a while, gauging the reaction of the people
to recent events. The entire town seemed incensed about it,
but nobody had any idea what should be done.

Finally, Hawke found himself in front of Flaire's shop and
realized, with a smile, that he had deceived no one, not even
himself. This had obviously been his destination all along.
The sign on the door announced that she was open for business, so Hawke pushed it open and stepped inside.

"Lily is back here, Mrs. Perkins," Flaire called. "Come on
in, I think you are going to like what you see."

Hawke stepped into what Flaire called her fitting room.
There, he saw a young girl of about sixteen, wearing a full-
skirted dress and standing perfectly still while Flaire was on
her knees on the floor, hemming the bottom of the skirt.

"I don't know about Mrs. Perkins, but I think she looks
beautiful," Hawke said, smiling at the young girl, who
ducked her head in embarrassment.

"Hawke," Flaire said. She stood up and brushed the wrin-
kles from her dress. "I thought you were Lily's mother."
Flaire's speech was slightly impeded because she had a
mouth full of straight pins.

"No, I'm sorry, it's just me. You must be Lily?" he said to the young girl.

"Yes, sir."

"Lily is leaving tomorrow for finishing school," Flaire explained. "It's too bad she didn't leave yesterday, before all the nasty business of last night. She and her family arrived in town early this morning, before they cut the bodies down."

"You saw them?" Hawke asked.

"Yes, sir," Lily said. Her cheeks had flushed red in embarrassment when Hawke first came into the room, but now they turned white as she recalled the gruesome sight she had encountered when her mother and father brought her into town that morning.

"I'm sorry you had to see something like that," Hawke said. "No young girl should have to see anything like that."

"No," Flaire said. "No, they absolutely should not."

Flaire said the words with such feeling and conviction that Hawke looked at her in quick surprise. Then he remembered that she told him her parents had been murdered in front of her.

"Have you read Mr. Cyrus's extra this morning?" Hawke asked.

"No," Flaire said. She got back onto her knees and resumed pinning up Lily's skirt. "He dropped a copy of the newspaper off a short while ago. It's in there on the counter, but I haven't had the opportunity to read it yet."

"Read it as soon as you can," Hawke said. "He really lets the Regulators have it."

"Are you still supporting Culpepper?" Flaire asked.

"Well, don't forget," Hawke replied, "Culpepper had nothing to do with what happened last night. It was Vox and his deputies."

"Do you think, for one minute, they would do that if they didn't have Culpepper's approval?" Flaire challenged.

Hawke shook his head. "I'd like to believe that," he said. "But Titus knew the kind of men he was hiring. And knowing that, he had to expect something like this, sooner or later."

"Now you can understand why I said you should have taken him up on his offer to make you his chief deputy," Flaire said as she continued to pin up Lily's dress hem. "If you had, none of this would have happened."

She made the comment casually, but Hawke saw the truth of it. She was right. If he had accepted Culpepper's offer to become chief deputy, the four men who had died last night might still be alive.

"Yes," he said quietly. "You are right."

Flaire realized then that her remark had hit home, and she looked up quickly.

"No, Hawke," she said. She shook her head. "I didn't mean that the way it sounded. You're not the blame for this."

"I know I'm not the blame for it," Hawke said. "But I could have prevented it."

"You couldn't have known this was going to happen. Nobody in town could have predicted it, and we've lived here a lot longer than you have," Flaire said.

"I suppose so," Hawke said.

Flaire finished with the pinning and stood up again to look at the young girl.

"Twirl around for me, would you please, dear?" she asked.

Lily twirled.

"Take a look in the mirror," Flaire said.

Lily walked over to look at herself in the full-length mirror. A wide smile spread across her face. "Oh, Miss Delaney!" she said. "It's beautiful. This is the first grown woman's dress I've ever had. You are so talented."

"It's easy to make a beautiful dress when you have a beautiful young woman to wear it," Flaire said modestly. "What do you think, Mr. Hawke?"

"Where are you going to go to finishing school?" Hawke asked.

"Waco."

"I think the young men of Waco will be struck blind by your beauty," he said.

Once again the young girl blushed.

When Parker dismounted in front of the jail, he was surprised to see that the sign out front said nothing about it being a sheriff's or city marshal's office. Instead, it advertised the building as HEADQUARTERS, SALCEDO REGULATORS BRIGADE.

He wasn't sure what such a group was, but something about it didn't quite ring right with him, and he was a little apprehensive as he pushed the door open. There were three men, all wearing badges, and all involved in a heated discussion.

"I say we go down there and get this settled once and for all," one of the men said. He clutched a newspaper in his hand and wadded it up and shook it. "This is the second time he's wrote somethin' like this."

"Gillis is right," one of the other two men said. "The time to stop this is now, before it goes any further."

"Excuse me," Parker said, interrupting the conversation.

"Yeah, what do you want?"

"Is the sheriff in?"

"We ain't got no sheriff."

"Well, then, the city marshal."

"We ain't got one of them either."

"But you men are all wearing badges. What are you?"

"Didn't you see the sign out front?" Gillis asked. "We're Regulators. I'm Deputy Gillis. What can I do for you?"

"My name is Justin Parker. I'm ramrod of the Bar-Z-Bar

herd, parked just outside of town. I understand there was a problem with some of my men last night."

"That's right."

"What happened?"

"We tried to arrest them for public drunkenness," Gillis said. "They started shootin' and we shot back. Now, three of your boys is dead, and we got us another one back there in the jail for accessory to murder."

"Accessory to murder?"

"They kilt one of our deputies," Gillis said. "That makes the fella we got back here an accessory to murder."

"I'd like to talk with him, if you don't mind."

Gillis looked over at one of the other deputies. "Why don't you take him back there, Spellman," he said. "Let 'im visit for a spell."

"Yeah, all right. Come along, mister," Deputy Spellman said. Spellman took a key ring down from a hook and opened a door that led into the back of the building. The place was dark, dank, and smelled of urine, vomit, body odor, and sour whiskey, even though the cells, three on either side, were empty. At the back of the hallway, forming the top part of a U, the cell was occupied.

"He's right back there, the cell in the middle," Spellman said, pointing. "Knock on this door when you are ready to come out."

"Thanks."

Spellman closed the door behind him, and Parker heard the lock being turned. For a moment he felt apprehensive about being locked in here, though he was sure his fear was without foundation.

Parker started toward the far end of the hallway. He still didn't know who, among the three cowboys, was still alive, and who was dead, and the shadows were too deep for him to see into the cell.

When he reached the end, he saw Pete lying on the bunk, staring straight up.

"Hello, Pete," Parker called gently.

When Pete looked toward him, Parker could see that the young cowboy's eyes were bloodshot and bleary. He didn't know, though, if that was from crying or from being drunk. He finally decided that it must be a little of both.

"Mr. Parker!" Pete said. "I'm sorry," he said. "I'm sorry to have gotten you into all this." Pete got up and moved quickly toward the bars that separated him from his boss. He wrapped his hands around the bars. "I'm sorry," he said again.

"Yes, well, things like this happen," Parker said.

"Can you get me out of this place?"

"I'll do what I can," Parker said. "Pete, what the hell happened last night?"

Pete shook his head. "As God is my witness, Mr. Parker, I don't know what happened."

"You must have some idea. What do you remember?"

"I remember being in the saloon, drinking with Dusty and Kendall. There was a girl there, I remember that. But I don't remember another thing until I woke up this morning."

"They say they are holding you as an accessory to murder."

"Accessory to murder? What are they talkin' about? I didn't murder nobody."

"You don't remember a shootout in the street? Or someone being hung?" Parker asked.

"Seems to me like I can recall seeing the three of 'em hangin' there, but it's not very clear to me. All I know is what they told me when I woke up this morning. They said Moses was dead too."

"That's right."

"Well now see, that's another thing I don't understand. How did poor old Moses get involved in this? I mean, me 'n' the others was drinkin' pretty heavy, but Moses wasn't even with us. What did they kill him for?"

"I don't know. I was hoping you could tell me." Parker started back toward the front.

"Mr. Parker, you are going to get me out of here, aren't you? I'm afraid these crazy sons of bitches might decide to hang me too."

"Yes, don't worry. I'll get you out of here." Parker called back over his shoulder. He made the promise, though for the moment he had absolutely no idea how he was going to do it.

Titus Culpepper was having his breakfast in the Capitol Café, an eating establishment right across the street from the Capitol building, whose customers were either members of the Texas legislature or people who had business with the Texas state government.

"Mr. Culpepper?"

Looking up from his pancakes, Culpepper recognized Murray Adams, the governor's personal secretary.

"Yes, Mr. Adams?"

"Governor Hubbard would like to see you, sir, at your earliest convenience."

"At my earliest convenience?"

"Yes, sir."

Culpepper took one more swallow of his coffee, then touched the napkin to his lips.

"How about now?" he asked.

"That would be very good, sir. I'll take you to him," Adams said.

Culpepper followed Adams out of the café. Austin was a busy and bustling community, not only with the offices of the state capital, but also because of the state university. Carriages, shays, wagons, buckboards, and horses crowded the street, and the two men picked their way across with some difficulty.

A street corner preacher was haranguing a small audience in front of the State Railroad Commission. He wore chin whiskers that pointed straight out, rather than down, and as he made his points, he stabbed at the air with a bony finger.

". . . an' here's another reason why God don' want the railroad. All that steam kills the grass so's the cows can't graze. And them heavy engines shakes the earth something fierce, an' that makes the women sturl. Why, they'll come the time to where won't be a single woman in the entire state of Texas able to have chilrun."

Culpepper chuckled at the preacher and, shaking his head, followed the governor's personal secretary up the foot-polished concrete steps into the Capitol building. He had no idea why Governor Hubbard had asked to see him personally, but he was sure it had something to do with his announced intention to file for Congress. Perhaps the governor was going to offer his support.

There were a few soldiers scattered around the Capitol building, wearing Yankee blue. There was a part of him that still recoiled at the sight of a blue uniform, but he had learned, long ago, to live with it.

Adams led Culpepper through the building and down a long hallway until they reached an ornate door. Cornices and a peaked roof over the door set the office apart from the many other office doors. Over the top of the door, in gold-leaf lettering, were the words: OFFICES OF THE GOVERNOR.

Adams opened the door and they went inside. This was the governor's outer office, and another clerk looked up as they came in.

"Mr. Adams, Governor Hubbard asked that you wait out here. Mr. Culpepper, you can go right on in, sir."

"Thank you," Culpepper said, smiling broadly. Getting the governor's endorsement would be quite a coup and would just about guarantee his election.

"Governor Hubbard, it's good to see you," Culpepper said, crossing the governor's office with his hand extended.

Richard B. Hubbard had been a lieutenant governor to Richard Coke, becoming governor when Coke quit to become a United States senator. Hubbard was tall, with a full head of dark brown hair and a large, bushy beard.

"Mr. Culpepper, just what in the world is going on in your town?"

"I beg your pardon?" Culpepper asked, surprised, not only by the governor's question, but by his demeanor.

"You do know Mayor Cyrus Green, I presume?"

"Yes, of course I do. He is not only the mayor, he is also the editor of our newspaper."

"Mayor Green sent me this telegram this morning," the governor said, showing it to Culpepper.

MEMBERS OF THE SALCEDO REGULATORS,
USING THE AUTHORITY OF THEIR BADGES,
MURDERED THREE MEN IN COLD BLOOD LAST NIGHT.
THE CITIZENS OF SALCEDO ARE BEING HELD
HOSTAGE BY THIS GROUP OF OUTLAWS, FOUNDED
AND COMMANDED BY TITUS CULPEPPER.

Culpepper's eyes narrowed and he drew his mouth into a tight line as he read the telegram.

"Governor, I assure you, I have no idea what this is about," he said, handing the telegram back.

"Well, there has to be something to it," the governor said. "Or do you think the mayor manufactured this from whole cloth?"

"I don't know."

"What is this group of Regulators anyway?"

"We have been unable to keep a town marshal, and the sheriff is too far away to offer any protection. So we formed the Regulators to keep the peace. You may recall, Governor, we got rid of the Dawson gang a while ago."

Governor Hubbard stroked his chin. "Yes, yes, I do remember that. And, as I recall, they were a bad bunch."

"I'll say they were. About as bad a bunch as you would ever run across," Culpepper insisted. "Believe me, Governor, there were no tears shed when those boys went to meet their maker."

"What about Edward Delaney?" Governor Hubbard asked.

"I beg your pardon?" Culpepper asked, surprised to hear Delaney's name mentioned.

"I'm told that he was recently hanged after a trial that was, at best, questionable."

Culpepper shook his head. "I don't know where you are getting your information, but it is wrong. Delaney had a fair trial, complete with a judge and jury. Besides which, he was also wanted for murder in the state of Missouri. If we hadn't hung him, we woulda had to ship him back to Missouri so they could hang him. Look, Governor, I'm not tellin' you anything new when I tell you we've got outlaws in this state. I know that you have had to deal with them ever since you took office. First there was that business with John Wesley Hardin, then there was the riot down at Sandy Point."

"That's the truth," Hubbard replied. "I sometimes think that Coke didn't go to the U.S. Senate, he ran from this office."

"Well, we've had to put up with the same kind of thing back in Salcedo. And the citizens were getting sick and tired of the criminal elements in their town. They needed something done, and we were the cure."

The governor sighed and combed his hands through his great, bushy beard. "That may be the case," he said. "But we can't have the cure as bad as the sickness."

"I agree, Governor. I don't know what this is all about, but I intend to find out."

"Do more than find out, Culpepper," the governor said. "If you want my endorsement for your candidacy, then I expect you to clear this matter up. I'll not have any of my constituents . . ." He looked at the telegram again. ". . . held hostage by your band of Regulators."

"I'll take care of it, Governor."

In Salcedo, Culpepper's surrogate, Rufus Vox, wandered around town on the day after the hanging, letting it be known by all who saw him that he was the one in charge.

Nobody knew for sure where Rufus Vox came from. Like many in the small town of Salcedo, he had shown up after the war. What nobody could understand was why, of all his deputies, Culpepper had chosen the man who seemed the least suited for the job. A few suggested that it might be because Vox and Culpepper had served together during the war. Others questioned that, though, saying that Culpepper had fought in some of the major battles, whereas Vox never got east of the Mississippi River.

For a while after he arrived in town, Vox hung out with a group of rowdies, displaced souls from the war who drank, gambled, and fought, all without any visible means of support.

Ed Delaney was a part of that group as well, though he was always on the periphery, having been a Union soldier during the war, while the others were Confederates. If Delaney had any friends in the group, it would be Vox.

When Culpepper began forming the Regulators Brigade, he recruited all of his deputies from that group. The town council quickly complained that the men he was hiring were hardly representative of the best Salcedo had to offer. Culpepper replied that the men he hired were exactly what he wanted.

"These men are going to be asked to put their lives on the line," he said. "I don't need choir boys to do a job like that."

"I aim to get myself hired on as a Regulator," Ed Delaney told Vox one night over a bottle of whiskey they were sharing in the alley behind the saloon.

"Hah," Vox said. "I never woulda figured you wanted to be a lawman." He took another swallow of the whiskey, then handed the bottle to Delaney.

"I don't want to be a lawman," Delaney replied. "I hate the law and I hate anyone who has anything to do with it."

"Then I don't understand. Why do you want to join up with the Regulators?"

"Because of Culpepper," Delaney said. He finished the bottle, then threw it at the privy, smashing it against the wall of the outdoor toilet.

"Hey! I'm in here!" someone called.

Both Vox and Delaney laughed.

"How'd you get to be such a good friend of Culpepper? He fought for the South, you fought for the North."

"In the beginnin' he fought for the South," Delaney said. "But toward the end, he was nothin' but an outlaw. I know what he done, and I aim to take care of him, soon's I get the chance."

"What do you mean, you know what he done?"

"There was three of 'em," Delaney said, without being any more specific. "I already took care of two of 'em. And I don't figure to get any rest until I've took care of Culpepper as well."

"You ain't makin' a hell of a lot of sense, Delaney," Vox said. "What is it you think Culpepper done?"

"It ain't what I think he done, it's what I know he done," Delaney said, tapping his temple with his finger. Then he went into great detail, telling Vox exactly what he knew about Culpepper and how he found out.

"He don't know that I know," Delaney said when he finished the story. "But I plan to tell him."

"When are you goin' to tell him?"

"Just before I kill the son of a bitch," Delaney said.

Although Vox and Delaney often got drunk together, when it came to personal advantage, Vox could and would discard any friendship if he stood to gain by it. Armed with the information he had gleaned from his drunken discussion with Ed Delaney, Vox went to Culpepper.

"I've got something you would like to know," he said.

"What?"

"Uh-uh, it don't work that way," Vox said, shaking his head. "You make me your chief deputy in this here group you're puttin' together, then I'll tell you what I know."

"You've got to give me a hint, just so I will know whether or not the information is worth anything," Culpepper said.

"What if I told you that Delaney plans to kill you?"

Culpepper was silent for a long moment, then he said, "I didn't think he knew."

"Then it's true? What he said about you and them other boys really happened?"

Culpepper nodded. "Yes. When Delaney and his sister first showed up in Salcedo, I was a little apprehensive. But when neither one of them said anything, well, I figured it was just a coincidence that they were here. I mean, if he really did know, why hasn't he done anything before now?"

"He told me he was waitin' for the right time," Vox said.

"Well, we'll just have to make sure the right time never comes, won't we?" Culpepper suggested.

"We?" Vox replied.

Culpepper smiled. "If you help me out with this, I think I can make it worth your while."

Culpepper was the one who came up with the idea how to get rid of Delaney. But he depended upon Vox to carry it out for him.

It was easy enough to do.

Delaney was a bad poker player, but that didn't keep him from playing. So when he got into a game with Billy Tyrone, a hide tanner who lived in a little house just on the edge of town, Vox saw to it that Delaney lost his horse.

"How could I be so dumb as to bet my horse?" Delaney complained after the game that night.

"Hell, you was cheated," Vox said.

"You think so?"

"Do I think so? I know so. Hell, I seen Tyrone take an ace from the bottom of the deck oncet, an' there ain't no tellin' how many times he done it when I didn't see him."

"You did? Why didn't you say something?"

"And get myself shot? No sir," Vox said. "But I tell you what I would do if I was you . . ."

"What?"

"I'd wait until the son of a bitch was asleep tonight, then I'd go out there and get my horse back."

"You're right," Delaney said. He nodded. "You're right. That's damn well what I'm goin' to do."

The next morning, Vox's very first act as Culpepper's newly appointed deputy was to arrest his erstwhile friend. He was waiting for him when he returned to town with the stolen horse.

In exchange for his "quick action in finding the horse thief and bringing him to justice," as Culpepper put it, Vox became chief deputy. At least, that was the published reason as to why Vox, who was no more qualified than any of the other deputies, was made chief.

The real reason was the secret Delaney had told him, the secret that was now shared only between Vox and Culpepper.

Chapter 19

IT WAS ABOUT TEN O'CLOCK IN THE MORNING
when Judge Watermeyer came into the saloon. Buying a bottle of whiskey and getting a glass, he went to a table in the
back, where he opened the bottle, filled the glass nearly to
the brim, and began drinking.

After the first glass, Darci came over to sit at the table
with him. He acknowledged her presence with a nod, but
said nothing. Quietly, she reached across the table and put
her hand on his.

The judge was a fourth of the way through the bottle when
Doc Urban walked over to him.

"Judge, could I give you a little medical advice?" he offered. "If you are going to be drinking that hard, you might
want to eat something. Especially this early in the day."

"Yeah, Judge," Paddy said. He still wore the bandage, the
result of his encounter with the deputies the night before.

"How do you feel?" the judge asked.

"I've got a headache," Paddy answered. "But other than
that I feel all right." He forced a smile. "I'm just glad they hit
me in the head. We Irish are hard-headed, you know."

Paddy had tried to crack a joke, hoping to chase away
some of the judge's melancholy, but it didn't work.

"Listen, why don't you let me have my Mary fix you something? Some ham and eggs, maybe? I won't charge you nothing."

"No," the judge replied.

"That much whiskey on an empty stomach, to a man your age, could kill you," Doc said. "Especially since you aren't used to drinking like that."

Judge Watermeyer looked at Doc Urban. "How long would that take?"

"At the rate you are going, not long," Doc Urban said.

"That wouldn't be soon enough," Judge Watermeyer said. Pointedly, he took another swallow.

"As long as I've known you, I don't think I've ever seen you drunk."

"I've never been drunk," Judge Watermeyer said. "Not once in sixty-two years."

"Then why start now?"

"Do you have to ask? Are you the only one in town who doesn't know what I did last night? I made a mockery of the judicial system, and I sent a man to the gallows."

"Yes, and from what I hear, you kept another man from hanging," Doc said.

Justin Parker stepped into the saloon then, and seeing everyone gathered around a table in the back, walked toward it. He was a big man, and the anger he exuded was palpable.

Unnoticed by anyone, Hawke, who was just returning from his visit with Flaire, also entered the saloon. Not wanting to intrude into what he figured was an intense discussion of the events of the night before, Hawke sat at a table in the shadows on the far side of the room.

"I'm told I might find the judge in here," Parker said.

"Who are you?" Paddy asked.

"The name is Justin Parker. I'm ramrod of the herd that's camped just outside town."

"Mr. Parker, I want you to know how sorry we are about what happened to your men," Paddy said.

"You're sorry? Three good men dead and all the hell you can say is you are sorry? Well, mister, sorry isn't good enough."

"Take it easy, Mr. Parker," Doc said. "If you notice the bandage on the bartender's head, that is the result of a skull fracture he got while trying to save your men. None of us are responsible for what happened last night. And believe me, we are as sick over it as you are."

"That's not quite true," Judge Watermeyer said. He took another drink of his whiskey. "I am responsible for what happened last night."

"Who are you?" Parker asked.

"I am Judge Watermeyer."

"Is it true, what the blacksmith said? Did you really hold a trial in the middle of the street in the middle of the night?"

"I'm afraid that is true."

"You are one sorry son of a bitch! If you weren't so old, I would tear you apart with my bare hands! By damn, I just might do it anyway," Parker said angrily.

"No, please!" Darci said, stepping in front of him. "It wasn't his fault!"

"What do you mean, it wasn't his fault? He's the judge, isn't he?"

"I was there last night," Darci said. "I saw everything that happened. The Regulators pointed a gun at Judge Watermeyer's head. If he hadn't conducted the trial, they would have killed him. Then they would have hung Kendall anyway. And not only Kendall, they would have hung Pete as well."

"At least they didn't hang Pete," Paddy put in. "Aren't you the least bit curious as to why they didn't hang him?"

"All right, why didn't they hang him?"

"Because Judge Watermeyer stood up to them," Doc Urban said.

"He told them that if they hung Pete, they were going to have to hang him as well," Darci said.

"And by then half the town stepped in to stop them."

"Yeah? Where was the town earlier?" Parker asked.

Doc shook his head. "I wish I could answer that for you, Mr. Parker. But the truth is, except for Paddy, who got clubbed over the head for his efforts, and the judge, who nearly got himself killed, nobody did anything in the beginning."

"Why didn't they? How could everyone just stand around and watch an innocent man be hung?" Parker asked.

"Maybe if I had called their bluff the first time," Judge Watermeyer said. "Maybe I could have stopped them then."

Doc Urban shook his head. "I don't think so," he said. "They had a blood lust on last night. If you had pushed it too far before they got it satisfied, they would have killed you."

"I'm sorry, Mister . . . Parker, is it?" Judge Watermeyer said. "I've no words to tell you how sorry I am."

"Yeah," Parker said. He nodded, then sighed. "Yeah," he said again. He stood there for a moment, trying to regain his composure.

"Can I get something for you?" Darci asked.

"I could use a drink."

"Whatever you want, Mr. Parker. It's on the house," Paddy said.

"Whiskey would be fine."

"Darci, would you? Get the bottle from under the bar."

Nodding, Darci hurried over to the bar, poured a generous glass, and brought it back.

Parker took a swallow of the whiskey, then looked at the judge. "I just came back from talking to Pete. He says they're holding him for accessory to murder. Is there something you can do to get him out?"

"I can issue a release order," the judge said. "But I don't know that it will do any good."

"Why not?"

"Because if they decide to ignore the order, I can't enforce it."

"Issue the order," Hawke said. "I'll enforce it."

Everyone turned toward the sound of the voice, surprised to see him sitting over in the shadows.

"Who are you?" Parker asked.

"I'm the pianist in this establishment."

"You're the what?"

Hawke pointed to the piano. "I play the piano in this saloon," he said.

Parker snorted. "You are a piano player, and you are going to enforce the judge's order?"

"Believe me, cowboy, when I tell you that if Mr. Hawke chooses to do so, he can enforce the judge's order," Paddy said.

"Really?"

"He is the man I would want on my side," Doc Urban added.

Hawke did not join in the conversation. He merely sat calmly and quietly at the table, awaiting Parker's response to his offer.

Parker studied Hawke for a moment, impressed with his confident demeanor. Finally he nodded.

"All right," he said. "I'd be glad for you to enforce the order."

"Paddy, get me a paper and pen," the judge said. "I'd better write out the order while I am still sober enough to write."

"You aren't carrying a gun, Mr. Parker?" Hawke asked as they walked toward the Regulators headquarters.

"No," Parker replied. "Oh, my cowboys like to carry them, but I rarely wear one. The damn thing just gets in my way. I guess I should've brought one with me."

"No," Hawke said. "You won't need one. And if your men hadn't been wearing guns last night, none of this would've happened."

"Moses wasn't wearing a gun," Parker said.

"Touché," Hawke said.

"I beg your pardon?"

"It means you have a point," Hawke explained.

When they reached the headquarters building, Hawke pushed the door open and Parker went in first.

"Vox, this here is the man I was tellin' you about. He's the ramrod of the—" Gillis stopped in mid-sentence when he saw Hawke come in through the door behind him.

"You!" Vox said angrily. "What the hell are you doing here?"

Hawke looked around the office. In addition to Vox, there were five more deputies present.

"We have a court order, signed by Judge Watermeyer, ordering you to release your prisoner. Show him the paper," Hawke said to Parker.

The cowboy held out the paper Judge Watermeyer had given him.

"I ain't interested in no piece of paper," Gillis said.

"I assure you, it is a binding order, demanding that you release Pete Malone to me," Parker said.

Vox showed the note to Spellman and Cole, the other two deputies with him.

"Is this the judge's writing?" Vox asked.

"How the hell would I know? I can't even read," Spellman said.

"It is the judge's writing," Parker said.

"Why should I believe you?"

"Because I watched him write it. So did Mr. Hawke."

"That a fact?" Vox asked.

Hawke nodded, but said nothing.

"So what if the judge did write this order? What makes you think I'm going to obey it?"

"Because I will kill you if you don't," Hawke said easily. The words were spoken as calmly as if he had just asked the time.

"Mr. Piano Player, maybe you haven't noticed it, but you are a little outnumbered here," Vox said.

"I've noticed."

He pointed to Parker. "And this fool isn't even wearing a gun. What are you going to do? Draw on all six of us?"

"No. Just you."

"You do realize, don't you, that if you do that, you'll be killed?" Vox asked.

"That is a very distinct possibility," Hawke agreed.

"And the cowboy, here, will be killed," Vox added.

"Yes, that is also a possibility," Hawke said.

"Just a possibility?"

"There is also a possibility that some of you will be killed."

"Well now, we are just full of possibilities this morning, aren't we?" Vox chided. "Can't you do any better than that?"

"Oh yes," Hawke said. "I can do better than that. There is one absolute."

"And just what would that one absolute be?" Vox asked with a smirk.

"You will absolutely die," Hawke said.

Gauging the intensity in Hawke's eyes, the smirk left Vox's face. Tiny beads of perspiration broke out on his upper lip.

"Uh, let me take a look at that judge's order again," Vox said. The paper was lying on the desk in front of him, and he picked it up and looked at it.

"Yeah," he said. He licked his lips and cleared his throat. "Yeah, this looks like the judge's handwriting, all right. Spellman, go back there and let that cowboy out of jail."

"Don't you think we ought to wait until the Colonel comes back and let him—"

"I'm in charge here," Vox said sharply. "And I said let him out of jail. Now! We've got no choice. This here is a judge's order."

"All right, whatever you say," Spellman said, reaching for the keys.

"You," Vox said, looking at Parker. "I'd advise you to get on back to your herd and don't be coming back to Salcedo."

"Mister, all the horses in Texas couldn't drag me back to this hellhole of a town," Parker said.

At that moment Pete appeared. Seeing Parker, he smiled.

"You did it," Pete said. "You got me out."

"Come on," Parker said to his cowboy. "Let's get the hell out of here."

Titus Culpepper looked out the window of the train. It was dark, but a full moon reflecting off the desert sand presented a landscape of silver and shadow. Close by the tracks, little squares of golden light moved rapidly over the track ballast, measuring the train's speed.

He had no idea what had happened in his absence, but he was willing to bet any amount of money that Vox was the cause. He had taken a calculated risk when he made Vox his chief deputy, but Vox had put him between the rock and the hard place. Vox had information about him that he didn't want out, especially now that he was running for the United States Congress.

He wished Mason Hawke would have accepted his offer. Vox would have protested, and maybe gotten himself killed in the protest. That would have taken care of a lot of his problems.

Maybe he should have been more specific as to the amount of money Hawke could have made. No, that wouldn't have made any difference. Money had nothing to do with it. Hawke had turned him down because he didn't want to work for him. Hawke always did think he was a little better than everyone else.

It was like that when they were children together, back in Georgia. In front of the church, once, Hawke found a little cloth bag. When he looked inside, he saw that it contained several dollars.

Culpepper offered to keep quiet about it, if Hawke shared the money with him. But Hawke took the money inside to the preacher. As it turned out, it was money from the church building committee, and at church the next Sunday, the preacher praised Hawke for finding it and turning it in. Hawke thanked the preacher but said that Culpepper deserved some of the praise because they had been together when he found it.

Culpepper's father talked to him that evening. "Boy, you are lucky Mason Hawke was with you," he said. "If you had been alone, I know damn well you would've kept it, and you would have wound up in a lot of trouble."

It was the same way during the war. Hawke saved his life once, and was promoted to sergeant because of it. That made Hawke his platoon sergeant.

Then came the battle of Gettysburg. When they were ordered to withdraw from Little Roundtop, Hawke was wounded. Culpepper pulled him off the battlefield. It was an act that had more the appearance of bravery than the fact. In truth, Culpepper was abandoning the field anyway, and it didn't require a great deal of effort on his part to pull Hawke to safety. And, in his mind, it finally put him one up on Hawke.

For three years Culpepper had fought for whatever pay the army gave him, and even though he eventually made sergeant, he hardly ever had enough real spending money to buy himself a drink. Then he heard about the war in the West, and how certain guerrilla organizations were supporting themselves by whatever contraband they could come by.

When Lee's army quit the field at Gettysburg, Culpepper didn't return to Virginia with him. Instead, he went west. He didn't completely abandon the Confederate cause; he just chose his battles more carefully, selecting to fight with those organizations that could provide him with a little more incentive.

When the war ended, hundreds of thousands of Confederate soldiers returned to the South to find their fortunes expended and their homes gone. Culpepper, by contrast, headed for Texas with a substantial poke he had acquired during his guerrilla activities.

One of the reasons he went to Texas was so that he would be with other southerners, men who would recognize his service but would not be aware of all of the details. He was quick to point out that he had participated in such battles as Shiloh, Chickamauga, and Gettysburg, but said nothing about the guerrilla operations of the last two years, including the source of his poke.

Just two weeks before the end of the war, Culpepper had stolen a Confederate money shipment of fifteen hundred dollars in U.S. currency.

It was not until Vox came to him with the information that Ed Delaney planned to kill him that Culpepper felt threatened. Forewarned is forearmed, he thought, so he arranged to set up the horse-stealing incident. That was all he needed to take care of that little problem.

"I know you was the one," Delaney told Culpepper seconds before the noose was put around his neck. "I know you was the one, and when you get to hell, I'll be waiting for you."

"Mr. Culpepper?" the conductor said, taking Culpepper from his thoughts and memories.

"Yes?"

"We'll be arriving in Marva in about ten minutes, sir. I just thought you might like to know."

"Thank you," Culpepper said.

He wondered what would be waiting for him when he returned.

The name of the ranch, Bar-Z-Bar, was in wrought-iron letters, worked into a gate that arched across the road that led up to the ranch house.

It had been a hard, three-day wagon trip, and Ken was glad to see that his goal was finally in sight. He was driving the same Bar-Z-Bar wagon and team that Moses had brought into town, while his own horse, tied on at the rear, followed along behind. At least it would only take him two days to return home.

Ken slapped the reins against the back of the team, urging them on up the road toward the big white house that sat like a wedding cake on top of a small rise.

A rabbit hopped up in front of him, bounded quickly down the road, then darted off to one side just as Ken reached the front of the house. Before he could get down from the wagon, a man stepped out onto the front porch.

"Something I can do for you, mister?" the man called.

"Would you be Mr. Zigenhorn?" Ken asked.

"I am."

"I have a letter for you from your foreman, Mr. Parker," Ken said. Climbing down from the wagon, Ken walked over to the front porch and held the letter up toward the short, red-faced man.

"What do you have under the canvas?" Zigenhorn asked as he took the letter.

"The letter will explain everything," Ken said.

Curious, Zigenhorn began reading. Then, when he realized what the letter was saying, he looked up sharply.

"You have them with you?"

"Yes, sir," Ken replied. "I have all three of them."

A black woman stepped out onto the front porch then. She was wearing an apron, and dried her hands with it as she looked at Ken. Recognizing him, a smile crossed her face.

"Sergeant Wright!" she said. She laughed. "I remember you. Starch in your shirt, none in your trousers. What are you doing here?"

"Sally . . ." Zigenhorn said. He cleared his throat. "I have some bad news for you."

"Bad news?" Sally asked. She looked at Ken. "Sergeant Wright, do you know about this?"

Ken looked toward the ground. "I'm sorry, ma'am," he said.

"No," Sally said quietly, now realizing what they hadn't yet told her. Seeing the wagon behind Ken, Sally jumped down from the porch and ran to it. "No," she said a little louder.

"Mrs. Gillespie . . . Sally, I'm sorry to be the one to—" Ken started, but that was as far as he got before Sally lifted the tarp and saw three pine boxes. It was obvious to her what the boxes were.

"No!" she screamed. "Oh, Lord in heaven, no!"

Sally collapsed in front of the wagon. Startled, Ken rushed to her.

"Is she all right?" Zigenhorn asked anxiously.

"She be completely passed out," Ken said.

"It's probably the best thing for her right now," Zigenhorn said. "Bring her in here."

Ken scooped her up in his arms, then followed Zigenhorn into the house.

"In here, on the sofa," Zigenhorn offered, pointing to his parlor.

Mrs. Zigenhorn came running in then. "Keith, what is it?" she asked. "What's wrong with Sally?"

"It's Moses," Zigenhorn answered. "He's dead."

"Dead?"

"And so are Kendall and Dusty."

"What . . . what happened?"

Zigenhorn handed his wife the letter.

"Oh, my," she said after she read it. "What a terrible thing to happen. Are those people barbarians?"

"Not all of them are," Ken said. "Just some."

"Who are you?"

"I'm the blacksmith in Salcedo."

"Sally recognized him," Zigenhorn said. "She called him Sarge."

Ken nodded. "Moses and I were in the Ninth Cavalry together."

"Well, I thank you for bringing them all back to us," Mrs. Zigenhorn said.

Kendall and Dusty were buried in the little cemetery in the nearby town of Risco. Because he was black, they wouldn't let Moses be buried there, so Zigenhorn told Sally she could pick a spot on the ranch, anywhere she wanted, and they would bury him there.

"I know just the spot," Sally said. "There's a shade tree on a hill that looks out over the whole ranch. It was a place where Moses used to go sometimes when he just wanted to think about things. I believe he would like to lie there."

"Yes, I know the place you are talking about," Zigenhorn said. "It is a beautiful spot. That's just where we'll bury him. And I'll get the grave marker made up."

Moses was buried the next day, and Ken stayed for the funeral, making only one request. He asked Zigenhorn if he knew of anyone who could play Taps for Moses. As it turned out, there was someone, a cowboy on the adjacent ranch, who had been a bugler in the army. Zigenhorn made the arrangements, and on the day of the funeral, the man showed up carrying his bugle under his arm and wearing an army uniform that was still recognizable but had clearly seen better days.

At the appropriate time, the bugler raised his instrument to his lips and began to play.

The notes rolled long and sweet from the bugle, reaching the nearby hills, then returning in a sorrowful echo.

> *Day is done*
> *Gone the sun*
> *From the lake*
> *From the hills*
> *From the sky*
> *Soldier rest*
> *Rest in peace*
> *God is nigh.*

Sally stood next to Ken, and at one point leaned on him, inviting him to put his arm around her to comfort her.

Moses' two children, a boy, four, and a girl, two, looked on, disturbed by the fact, and not quite understanding why their mother was crying.

Chapter 20

THERE HAD BEEN AN UNEASY PEACE IN TOWN FOR the few days between the hanging and Culpepper's return. One of the first things Vox did was show Culpepper the editorial Cyrus had written.

"I thought about goin' over there and smashin' up his printin' press," Vox said. "But I decided we should prob'ly wait for you before we done anything like that."

"Yes," Culpepper said. "It's just too bad you didn't start thinking a little earlier. If you had, we wouldn't be in this mess."

"So, what do we do now, Colonel?" Bates asked. "I mean, we can't just sit around here with our thumb up our ass while Cyrus writes stuff like this about us."

Culpepper drummed his fingers on the newspaper article for a moment, then sighed. "We'll do whatever we have to do," he said. "But for now, I'll go talk to Cyrus. Things would go a lot easier if we could get him back on our side."

Cyrus had his shirtsleeves rolled up to his elbows and he was cleaning his press when the little bell on the entry door tinkled. Looking up, he saw Culpepper, and for a moment he felt a little twinge of fear. But Culpepper was alone, and

Cyrus figured that if he had anything planned, he would have brought some of his deputies with him.

"When did you get back?" Cyrus asked. He poured some solvent onto his hands and used it to clean away the back ink.

"I rode down from Marva this morning," Culpepper said. "Sounds like we had a little excitement here while I was gone."

"Is that what you call it? Excitement?" Cyrus asked.

"No, I guess that's not a very good word for it," Culpepper agreed. "I read your editorial about the trial and the hanging," he continued. "I want you to know that I'm sorry it happened, and I assure you it wouldn't have happened if I had been here."

"It was the same as your being here," Cyrus replied. "Vox was your appointed man, and you left him in charge."

"Yes, but that's my point," Culpepper said. "Vox was in charge, not I."

"There is an old military adage . . . *Colonel*," Cyrus said, emphasizing the word colonel. "You can delegate authority, but you cannot delegate responsibility. Surely you, being a military man, know that. The final responsibility for what happened was yours, whether you were here or not."

Culpepper nodded. "Yes, I know," he said. "Look, I've talked to Vox. In fact, I have talked to all of them. I realize they have been getting a little out of hand lately. But it won't happen again. I would like to know what it would take to regain your support."

"Right now, Colonel, the only way you can regain my support would be to first, disband the Regulators, then resign from your position."

Culpepper shook his head. "No," he said. "I won't do that."

"Suppose I put that in the form of an executive order?"

Cyrus said. "As mayor, I am telling you to disband the Regulators and resign your position."

"You have no authority to issue such an executive order," Culpepper said. "I have a contract. Neither you nor the town council can demand my resignation. Nor can you disband the Regulators, since I, and not the town council, put them together."

"Did you have any further business with me, Mister Culpepper?" Cyrus said. This time he emphasized the word mister. "Because if you don't, I have to get ready for my next edition."

"Your next edition," Culpepper said. "Yes. It would be unfortunate if something happened that prevented you from getting out another edition."

"Are you threatening me?" Cyrus replied angrily.

"Let us say I was just making an observation."

"Make sure you get coal oil on the printing press," Vox said. "And on all the type. If his type is melted down into lead slugs and the press is burned up, the son of a bitch won't be puttin' out no more papers against us."

Vox, Bates, and Jarvis worked quickly in the dark, splashing coal oil all over the inside of the newspaper office. Hooper stood at the front window, keeping an eye out.

"Seen anybody on the street?" Vox called.

"No," Hooper replied. "It's all clear."

"All right, boys, let's back on out of here and I'll set a match to it," Vox said.

"I can't believe it," Cyrus said. "What are you doing, Doc, letting me win this game so I'll keep playing you? Check."

"Mate," Doc Urban conceded.

"Paddy, a round of beers, on me," Cyrus said happily. "I won!"

"At the risk of giving you a big head, Cyrus, you are a worthy adversary," Doc said. "You do win from time to time, you know."

"Yeah, about one out of every ten games," Cyrus said.

Darci brought beers over to Cyrus and Doc. "Congratulations," she said.

"Fire! Fire!" someone shouted, running into the saloon.

"Fire? Where?" Cyrus asked, standing up quickly.

The citizen looked directly at Cyrus. "It's your place, Mayor. The newspaper office is burnin' like hell."

"My press! My type!" Cyrus shouted, rushing outside with the others. They got no farther than the street before they realized that any attempt to save the building would be useless. It was totally invested, and the flames that licked high into the air were already painting the false fronts of all the other buildings on both sides of the street with a flickering orange glow.

The very next day after the fire, Cyrus Green called the town council into an unscheduled session to discuss what should or could be done about the Salcedo Regulators Brigade.

"Gentlemen, I thank you for coming," Cyrus said after the meeting was called to order.

"Cyrus, I'm real sorry about the fire," Maurice Baldwin said. Because this wasn't their regular monthly meeting, Baldwin was wearing his apron, having come straight from his bakery. Around him there was the not unpleasant aroma of freshly sifted flour.

The others expressed their regrets as well.

"You got'ny idea what caused it?" Garland Castleberry asked.

"Is there any question?" Cyrus replied.

"Are you saying that Culpepper did it?" Castleberry asked.

"I have no proof," Cyrus said. "But if I were a betting man, I would bet that he did it."

"Who would you get to take that bet?" Paddy asked. "After that editorial you wrote the other day, I don't think there is anyone in town who doubts that he did it."

"Yes, well losing my shop is my problem," Cyrus said. "The way I see it, we—that is the town—has an even bigger problem, and that is what to do about the Salcedo Regulators Brigade."

"I say we get rid of them," Baldwin said.

"I don't know that we can do that," Poindexter said. Though he worked as a hostler for the stage line, Poindexter was also the vice mayor. A political enemy of Cyrus Green's, he had been very vocal in his opposition to granting Culpepper any authority back when the town council made the arrangement.

"I told you," he went on, "back when we first started talking about giving this man as much power as we did, that it was all going to come back to haunt us some day."

"You did at that, Mr. Poindexter, you did at that," Cyrus agreed. "And I will gladly confess that you were right and I was wrong. In fact, I was the biggest drum beater for hiring him. But I ask that you put our political differences aside now, so we can concentrate on this problem."

"Just so that everyone knows I'm not the cause of the problem," Poindexter said.

"Abner, will you for chrissake quit politicking?" Baldwin said. "We all know you were against it. The problem now is, what do we do about it?"

"Well, it seems pretty obvious to me," Castleberry said. The whole incident of the hanging had been particularly galling to Castleberry, because it had happened right in front of his store. "I say we fire them. We fire them all."

"Ahh, gentlemen, there is the rub," Cyrus said. He sighed. "We can't fire them."

"What do you mean we can't fire them?" Castleberry replied. "You seen what they done the other night. Hell, not only did they string up those cowboys—right in front of my store, I might add—they slapped Paddy O'Neil around when he tried to stop 'em. If that isn't cause to fire them, then nothing is. And not only that, they threatened to kill the judge, here, if he didn't go along with them. Isn't that right, Judge?"

Although Judge Watermeyer was not on the council, he often sat in on their meetings to provide legal counsel whenever required. When Castleberry reminded everyone how the judge had been frightened and intimidated, the judge looked toward his feet in shame and embarrassment.

"I should not have let them have their way," Judge Watermeyer said.

"Hell, nobody is blamin' you, Judge. You didn't have no choice in the matter, we all seen that," Baldwin said, picking up Castleberry's argument. "But I agree with Mr. Castleberry. The way they treated the judge is just another reason why we need to get rid of them."

"Look, Maurice, Garland, you both know that I agree with everything you have to say," Poindexter said. "But this is exactly the situation I warned the council about when we did this. Cyrus is right when he says we can't fire Culpepper. We did not appoint a town marshal. We entered into a contract, appointing Titus Culpepper as a private law enforcement agent. He is not an official municipal agent subject to our control, he is a private law enforcement agent, empowered to enforce the ordinances of the council. That's why we can't fire him."

"Of course we can fire him. We hired him, didn't we?" George Heissler, the druggist and a member of the council, said. "All we have to do is tell him that we no longer require his services."

Cyrus shook his head. "I wish we could, but it's not as easy as that."

"What do you mean it's not as easy as that?" Baldwin asked. "We are the town council, for crying out loud. It's like George said, we hired Culpepper, so we can fire him."

"No. As Abner explained, we entered into a legal contract with Culpepper granting him the authority to act as a law enforcement official. A binding contract. I don't think we can just unilaterally dissolve that contract without facing a lawsuit. What do you think, Judge?"

Judge Watermeyer closed his eyes, pinched the bridge of his nose, and thought about the question for a moment. Then, with a sigh, he shook his head.

"I wish I could dispute you, but I'm afraid you are right," he said. "If you withdraw from the contract, Culpepper will have grounds for a lawsuit against the town. He would not only retain his position, he would break the town treasury."

"The son of a bitch has about broke us now," Baldwin grumbled.

"By damn, we ought to be able to do something," Heissler said.

"They are here until their contract expires, or until they commit an actionable violation of that contract, neither of which has occurred," Poindexter said.

"Actionable violation? What is that?" Paddy asked.

"A criminal act would be an actionable violation," Poindexter said.

"Well then, hell, we've got them, don't we?" Baldwin said. "I mean look at what happened the other night. They shot down two men in the street, then they hanged the third. There's no way on earth you could say that wasn't a criminal act."

"That was gratuitously malicious, an abuse of power, even an act of evil," Watermeyer said. "But within the strictest interpretation, it did not violate the law."

"Come on, Judge, how can you say that?" Cyrus asked. "They shot down two men in the street."

"The cowboys admitted that the deputies were attempting to arrest them. Well, the one who was still alive admitted it, anyway. And the cowboys resisted arrest by firing at them."

"What about the hanging?" Cyrus asked. "There was no way that was legal."

"In a bizarre way, it was legal," Judge Watermeyer replied. "The very fact that I pronounced them guilty and authorized the hanging makes it 'technically' legal."

"Judge, I was there," Baldwin said. "I seen the way they threatened you."

"I may have been coerced into conducting the trial," Watermeyer said. "But the trial was legal."

"How can you say that was legal? You can't hang a man for being drunk."

"He was not hung for being drunk," Watermeyer said. "He was hung for murder, which he committed by violently resisting arrest. In fact, he admitted that he was shooting at the deputies. If you kill a peace officer in the performance of his duty, then you are guilty of murder. There is no other way to interpret that, whether it was that mockery of the trial in the street or whether it was conducted in the finest courthouse in the land."

"The deputies were shooting at them!" Baldwin said. "What the hell were they supposed to do, just stand there and be shot?"

"No. They were supposed to acquiesce to the arresting authority. If they had done that, they would have spent the night in jail and gone back the next morning. None of this would have happened."

"All this because they had a few drinks in the Golden Calf," Baldwin said in disgust.

"Look, as the town council," the judge explained, "you are the ones who authorized the Regulators to enforce the laws and ordinances of this town. And as the town council, you are the ones who passed the ordinance against public drunkenness."

"Yes, but nowhere did we pass an ordinance that says you can shoot a man down in the street for drunkenness," Cyrus said. He held his hand out toward the judge. "And, before you correct me again, I know that when they resisted arrest it went beyond that. But in essence it was public drunkenness and that's all it was."

"What about the fire?" Castleberry asked. "Can't we get them for arson?"

"Can we prove that Culpepper or any of his people set the fire?" Judge Watermeyer asked.

"Come on, Judge, you know damn well they're the ones who did it," Paddy said.

"I agree with you," Judge Watermeyer said. "There is no doubt in my mind but that they are the ones who set the fire. But, I ask you again: Can we prove it? Do we have any physical evidence that points directly to them? Better yet, do we have any eyewitnesses?"

"No, no eyewitnesses," Cyrus said.

"Cyrus, you will forgive me for pointing this out, but several times you have left a lantern burning in your office all night long, have you not?"

"Yes, but that's never caused a problem."

"Who is to say that a gust of wind didn't blow open your front door and knock over the lantern?"

"I locked my front door when I left," Cyrus said. Then he added, "I think."

"All Culpepper's defense attorney would need is some other plausible explanation as to how the fire might have started," Judge Watermeyer said.

"Damn, Judge, he doesn't need a defense attorney as long as he has you," Heissler said.

"George!" Cyrus said sharply. "That was totally uncalled for! The judge is on our side, remember?"

"I'm sorry, Judge," Heissler said. "I'm just frustrated."

"Apology accepted," Judge Watermeyer replied.

"So basically what we are saying is, there's nothing we can do about it. The Regulators are here to stay," Heissler said bitterly.

"If there is nothing we can do about it, then what the hell are we holding this meeting for?" Baldwin asked.

"I didn't say there was nothing we could do about it," Cyrus said. "Maybe we can't fire them, but I think I know a way to make them quit of their own accord."

Cyrus's words got everyone's attention.

"Oh? And just how do you propose that we do that?" Castleberry asked.

"We could pass a resolution right now, repealing the enabling act," Cyrus said.

Heissler shook his head. "The enabling act?"

"You may recall that after we hired Culpepper, we passed the enabling act," Cyrus said. "The enabling act is what authorizes the Regulators to collect tax."

"But how are we going to do that without violating the contract?" Baldwin asked.

Cyrus held up his finger. "Ah, if you recall, gentlemen, the deputies are not under contract. Only Culpepper is. After the contract, he came back to us, seeking funds that would enable him to hire deputies. That's when we passed the enabling act. That authorized taxes to be raised to pay the deputies, but we did not enter into a contract with the deputies. They are Culpepper's responsibility, not ours. If we take away the tax, Culpepper won't be able to pay his men. And I doubt that they are such civic-minded and noble-spirited men that they will continue to work without pay."

The others laughed.

"You know, I think you may have something there, Cyrus," Poindexter said.

"Thank you, Abner."

"I move that we repeal the enabling act," Poindexter said.

"I second the motion," Baldwin said.

"All in favor say aye," Mayor Green said.

"Aye," the council said as one.

Cyrus smiled. "Gentleman, the enabling act is repealed. The Regulators can no longer collect their own, private tax."

"How are we going to let the merchants know that they no longer need to pay the tax?" Baldwin asked. "We no longer have a newspaper."

"We'll call a town meeting," Cyrus said. "Paddy, can we use the Golden Calf?"

"Absolutely," Paddy replied.

Culpepper didn't need to attend the town meeting. He learned of the town council's act within minutes of its passing. Not only did he know that they had repealed the tax, so did all of his deputies.

"If we ain't goin' to collect any taxes, how are we going to make any money?" Vox asked.

"Who says we aren't going to collect any taxes?" Culpepper asked.

"Why, the town council did," Vox said. "They passed a law about it."

"And tell me, Vox, just how are they going to enforce that law?" Culpepper asked. "We are the only law enforcement arm for the town of Salcedo. Are we going to enforce the law that says we can't collect taxes?"

Vox thought about it for a moment, then laughed. "You're

right," he said. "It don't make no difference what the town council says, does it?"

"Not as long as we control the town," Culpepper replied.

"You think we can control the town?" Vox asked. "I mean, if they all got together or something. There's only seven of us. There's got to be forty or fifty of them, if they all got together."

"We can control the town," Culpepper said easily.

Culpepper had not mentioned it to any of his deputies, but he had already made arrangements. When he got off the train in Marva, on the way back from Austin, he met with Emil Slaughter. Culpepper and Slaughter had ridden together in the Missouri Raiders, the guerrilla unit Culpepper had joined after leaving Lee's army following the defeat at Gettysburg.

His original idea for talking with Slaughter was to have him put together a group of men that he could use to replace the deputies he now had. But with the town throwing down the gauntlet, he had a change of plan. Instead of replacing his deputies, he was going to use Slaughter and his men to augment his deputies. That would bring his strength up to twelve.

He had seen it happen time and time again during the war. Twelve armed and ruthless men, ably led, could prevail over fifty men, if those fifty were not organized.

That evening every businessman in Salcedo gathered in the Golden Calf saloon to discuss the action of the town council.

Flaire came to the meeting, as did Violet McGee, who owned a business called Vi's Pies. Violet and Flaire were drawn together by the fact that they were businesswomen. In Vi's opinion, she and Flaire were the only businesswomen in town, but that was because Vi didn't count Darci.

In fact, though Flaire felt a little more kinship with Darci than she did with Violet McGee, it was Mrs. McGee who sat at the same table as Flaire. Darci stayed at the back of the room, by the piano, near Hawke, who was sitting quietly on the piano bench.

Hawke had decided to attend the meeting, though at first he had suggested that since he wasn't a businessman, he had no place here. But Paddy pointed out to him that, like Darci, he was a self-employed businessman since the tips he made from playing the piano were greater than his salary.

Hawke considered the comparison of what he did to what Darci did, then laughed.

"Sometimes the truth comes from the most unexpected sources," he said. "For, like Darci, I am a whore."

Paddy didn't understand the subtlety of the concept of prostitution of talent. But he didn't question it. He was just glad to have Hawke involved.

One of the businessmen who seldom visited the saloon was Ken Wright. He was back from his trip to the Bar-Z-Bar ranch, and he stood quietly at the back, watching as the other businessmen arrived. A few looked toward him and reacted, not in opposition to his being here, but in surprise at seeing him.

As the last of the businessmen arrived, including even Gene Welch, the undertaker, Mayor Green stood up and raised his hands.

"Could I have your attention please?" Cyrus called.

"Wait a minute, Mayor," Poindexter interrupted. "I know it's askin' a lot of a politician not to get into all this speechifyin'. But keep your remarks brief, will you? We don't want this here meetin' to last all night."

The others in the room laughed.

"I'll keep that in mind. I want to thank all of you for coming. I called you here to discuss the Regulators and the action we of the town council recently took to get rid of them."

"Yes, it's all over town what the council did," Beadle said.

Beadle owned the general store. "You repealed the Regulator tax."

"That's right," Cyrus said. "That means you don't have to pay the tax anymore. None of you do."

"That's all well and fine for you to say, Mayor. But this afternoon, even though the taxes have been repealed, Deputies Bates and Spellman come into my store to collect."

"Did you pay them?"

"You damn right I paid them," Beadle said. "You think I wanted to get beat up in my store, in front of my customers? Or maybe even worse? I mean, I shouldn't have to tell you, should I, Cyrus? Didn't they burn down your newspaper?"

"They probably did," Cyrus admitted. "But that's neither here nor there. The thing is, you shouldn't have paid them. And, after today, if they come around to see any of you, don't pay them."

"Well, I don't intend to pay them one more penny," Darci said.

There was a smattering of laughter from some of the more prudish businessmen, but many recognized Darci's position and admired her for her stand, even if quietly.

"I don't know about the rest of you folks," Ken said. "But I'd already made up my mind I wasn't going to pay them anymore. So, Mr. Mayor, you can count me in as one of the businesses that's goin' along with your plan."

"Thank you, Ken," Cyrus said. He looked out over the assembly. "Most, here, seem to be going along with it. Is there anyone who is opposed?"

No one spoke up.

"Ladies and gentlemen, I think it is fitting that we are taking our stand in the form of refusal to pay taxes, because like those patriots of old did when they threw the tea into Boston Harbor, our own revolution has begun."

"And, from now on, beers will be a nickel," Paddy said.

At the prospect of nickel beer, most of the men at the meeting cheered.

"Mr. Hawke, play us a ditty, will you?" Cyrus asked.

Smiling and nodding, Hawke turned toward the piano and began playing "Dixie."

Chapter 21

EVEN AS THE MEETING WAS GOING ON IN THE SA-
loon, Culpepper had most of his deputies gathered around
him in the Regulators' office.

Vox pointed toward the saloon. "It's just like I told you
they was goin' to do. They are down there, right now, orga-
nizing against us."

Culpepper looked up, then, to see Deputy Hooper coming
in. Earlier, he had sent Hooper down to hang out just outside
the saloon so he could listen in on the meeting.

"What are they talking about?" Culpepper asked.

"Just what you said they'd be talking about," Hooper answered. "They're sayin' they ain't goin' to be payin' no
taxes."

"They aren't planning an armed rebellion against us?"

"What? No, nothin' like that," Hooper replied.

Culpepper looked at Vox. "Still worried?" he asked.

"Well, I wasn't worried," Vox dissembled. "I mean, even
if they was to all get guns, I wasn't really worried."

"That's reassuring to hear," Culpepper said, though his
sarcasm was lost on Vox.

"So, what do we do now, Colonel?" Bates asked.

"I say we burn down the damn town hall," Deputy Spellman said.

"Yeah, like we did the newspaper office. And we ought to burn down the saloon too. That's the worst place of all," Vox said.

"Hold it, hold it," Culpepper said, holding up his hands and shaking his head. "We can't do any of that. The governor's not that far away from coming in here and declaring martial law as it is."

"Then what do we do? Just stand around and watch them make fools of us?" Bates asked.

Culpepper smiled. "No," he said. "We start enforcing the law."

"What do you mean? We've been enforcing the law, ain't we? Only now they say they ain't goin' to pay us," Hooper said.

"That's all right. We are going to show them what good citizens we are. We are going to enforce the law even if they don't pay us."

"What are you gettin' at, Colonel?" Bates asked.

"When I say we are going to enforce the law, I mean we are really going to enforce the law. Every paragraph of every ordinance," Culpepper said.

"Yeah," Bates said. "Yeah, I think I see what you mean."

"Let's get started."

Coming out of Beadle's general store with a bag of groceries, Lester Thomas walked over to the porch and spit out the wad of tobacco he had carried in his mouth for the whole time he was shopping.

As he stepped down from the porch and started to put his groceries in the buckboard, Deputy Cole came up behind him and hit him with the butt of his pistol. When Thomas came to in the jail a short time later, he was told he was under arrest for violation of the city ordinance against spitting on the sidewalk.

Arnold Fenton was arrested next, at gunpoint, for riding his horse faster than a man could walk.

By the end of the first day there were fifteen people in jail for everything from failure to pick up after their horse to not wearing a safety strap across the pistol in their holster.

It was late afternoon and when the door opened and Culpepper looked up from his desk, he expected to see another prisoner being brought in. Instead, he saw Hawke.

"Hawke," he said. "I didn't expect to see you here."

"What are you trying to do, Titus?" Hawke asked.

"What do you mean, what am I trying to do? I'm not trying to do anything other than what I am contracted to do, and that is enforce the law."

"You are going a little overboard with it, aren't you?"

"Well, let's just say that I want to show the town council that they made a mistake in taking away the tax. I want them to see what a good job I really can do."

"You've got no call to hold these people. Let them go."

"Are you threatening me, Hawke?"

"I'm not here to threaten you," Hawke said. "I'm just here to find out what's going on."

"You know, Hawke, we shouldn't be confronting each other like this. We grew up together, we've been friends for our entire lives. Hell, we've eaten from the same plate and drunk from the same cup. And yet here, so far from home, you are on one side of this issue and I am on the other. I don't understand. Did they pay you more than I offered?"

"You know better than that, Titus."

Culpepper chuckled and nodded. "I know. You always

have been one to do the right thing. Remember the sack of money that you found in front of the church that time?"

"Yes."

"How do you think it got there?"

"I don't know. I always supposed that the preacher must've dropped it."

Culpepper shook his head. "I stole it," he said. "I stole it, and I dropped it there. I knew that if I said I found it, everyone would believe I stole it, so I put it where I knew you would find it. I figured I could talk you into sharing it. If we had gotten caught, you would have told them we found it, and everyone would have believed you. But no, you turned the money back in."

"It seemed like the right thing to do," Hawke said.

"And you always were the one to do the right thing, weren't you?"

"That's right."

Culpepper drummed his fingers on the desk for a moment, then chuckled.

"All right, Hawke, I tell you what I'm going to do. I'm going to do the right thing this time and let everyone go. I won't even charge anyone a fine. This was just to show the town that we are serious about enforcing the law, even if we don't get paid. Why don't you go back and tell everyone that?"

"I appreciate that, Titus."

The smile left Culpepper's face and he pointed his finger at Hawke.

"But this squares us, Hawke," he said. "No more, we were kids together, no more we were in the army together, no more Chickamauga, no more Gettysburg. So you just go back and tell the town they had better watch their step. Because we will continue to enforce, with enthusiasm, every ordinance the town of Salcedo has ever passed."

"Don't step over the line, Titus," Hawke cautioned.

"Uh-huh. And just who decides where that line is?" Titus asked.

"I do," Hawke answered.

Darci was getting ready for work. Her skirt, filled with ruffles and trimmed in lace, ended just below her knees. The stockings were flesh-colored and skin tight. On her left leg, just above the knee, she wore a black garter with a tiny, red, artificial rosebud. She knew how to walk in such a way as to expose the garter without being obvious about it.

At the top she wore a blouse that was cut scandalously low, so low that one could see a generous spill of breasts. Another artificial flower that was tucked discreetly into her cleavage preserved a modicum of modesty, if not decorum.

She was about to tie up her hair with a red ribbon when the ribbon broke. She started looking for another ribbon, but couldn't find one. She let out a frustrated sigh. Although she could go to work without tying up her hair, she was always very particular about how she looked, so she really wanted to do her hair right. But that had been her last ribbon, which meant she would have to go get another one.

The problem was, she was dressed for work, so she couldn't go out into the street. She was showing too much cleavage and her dress was too short. There was a "decency of dress" ordinance that prohibited being seen on the street in clothes that were blatantly provocative. Darci would be disappointed if anyone thought what she was wearing wasn't provocative. She had chosen this outfit precisely because it was.

Walking over to her armoire, she started to take out a dress that would be more acceptable to wear in the street, but as she looked at it, with all the corsets, bows, and stays it would take to get into it, she realized that by the time she changed clothes twice, she would be late reporting to work.

Paddy probably wouldn't say anything. He was very good about that. But she didn't want to put him in that position.

Finally she decided to just run down the alley to the back of Flaire's dress shop. Going down the alley wasn't exactly the same as going out onto the street. In fact, she was often in the alley, when she was taking men to her crib, which was just across the alley from the back of the saloon.

Flaire would have some ribbon, she thought. She could buy what she needed from Flaire and run right back, all within a few minutes. And the chances were that if she kept to the alley, nobody would see her.

Stepping to the front door of her crib, she opened it, looked up and down the alley, and seeing no one, hurried down to Flaire's dress shop.

Reaching it, she raised her hand to knock on the door.

"Well, now, what do we have here?" a voice said.

Turning, Darci gasped in surprise and fear. Vox was standing in the shadows behind Flaire's dress shop. His obsidian eyes were shining in the dark.

"Vox!" she said.

"It's Deputy Vox to you, whore," Vox replied. He took out a pair of handcuffs. "I expect you had better come with me. You know better'n to be out on the street dressed like that."

"But I'm not in the street, I'm in the alley," she said.

"It's the same thing. You're outside," Vox said.

"Vox—I mean, Deputy Vox—please, I was just going to get some ribbon."

"I love it when pretty girls beg me," Vox said. "Now, turn around and put your hands behind your back.

Darci was tied to the bed in one of the jail cells. She was totally naked, and the clothes that had been ripped from her body were scattered on the floor around her. Deputy Gillis was over her, grunting out his need.

"Don't use her all up, Gillis," Cole said. "Save some for the rest of us."

With a few finishing barks, Gillis rolled off her, then got up and reached for his trousers.

"Put two dollars in the bowl," Culpepper ordered. He was sitting in a chair in the corner of the room, watching as, one by one, his deputies took their turn with Darci.

"What have we got to do that for?" Gillis asked. "I don't see no need in payin' for somethin' we can get for free."

"You can't get it for free," Culpepper said. "She's a whore and she charges two dollars. So put two dollars in the bowl."

Grumbling, Gillis paid the fee.

"All right, now get out," Culpepper said. "Cole, you have two dollars?"

"I've got it right here," Cole said, holding the money up.

"Then you're next."

It didn't take Cole very long. In fact, he finished before he started, and he complained that he should not have to pay since he didn't actually get to do anything.

"You will pay," Culpepper said.

With a disgusted snort, Cole put the money in the bowl, bringing the total to fourteen dollars. When Cole left, only Vox and Culpepper remained.

"All right, Vox, it's your turn," Culpepper said.

"You like this, don't you?" Vox said.

"I like what?"

"Watchin'," Vox said. "I've heard about you. You like watchin'. And I know it's true, 'cause I can see it in your face."

"Do you want your turn or not?" Culpepper asked.

"Hell yes, I want my turn."

"Then shut up and take it."

* * *

From the moment she was brought here, Darci had steeled herself to the ordeal. She was a whore and had been one since she was fifteen years old. She knew how to handle men, how to make them think she was enjoying it, and how to deaden her senses when it became too unpleasant.

That was what she had done tonight. She told herself that she was a log, with no sense of shame, or disgust, or pain. And holding that image in her mind allowed her to blur the men who climbed on and off her. She was barely aware of the change of men, and when Vox finished, it was almost as if he hadn't even started.

"Damn that was good," Vox said as he pulled on his trousers. "It's your turn now. And if you don't mind, I'm going to watch."

"Get out," Culpepper said.

"I won't be no trouble," Vox said. "You won't even know I'm here, I'll just sit over there—"

"I said get out," Culpepper said, more forcefully this time.

"All right, all right, whatever you say," Vox said as he packed his shirt into his trousers. "Hey, we goin' to keep her around for a few days? I'd kind of like to do this again tomorrow, maybe."

Culpepper said nothing, but his glare reemphasized his demand that Vox leave the room, so Vox did so.

With Vox gone, Culpepper went over to the bed and stared down at Darci.

Slowly, he unbuckled his belt, then unbuttoned his trousers and dropped them. His movements were so slow and studied, as opposed to the almost frenzied action of the others, that Darci couldn't help but watch.

Culpepper stared into Darci's face as he undressed, and there was something in his eyes, a melancholy that, despite her years of experience with men, she had never seen before.

Then, when he stood before her totally exposed from the waist down, she gasped.

There was nothing there!

Where there should have been a penis and testicles, there was a purple mound of misshapen flesh.

Darci looked up at him in surprise. "What . . . how?" she asked, so shocked that she was unable to formulate a complete question.

"It happened at Chickamauga," Culpepper replied. "I just wanted you to know why."

Culpepper pulled his clothes back up, then, almost gently, he began untying her.

"What are you doing?" she asked.

"What does it look like? I'm untying you," Culpepper said. "No hard feelings, I hope."

Darci sat up on the edge of the bed, gingerly rubbing her wrists. She stared at Culpepper suspiciously.

"No hard feelings? I was brought here against my will and raped by all of your deputies. Now you tell me I shouldn't have any hard feelings?"

"You weren't raped."

"What do you mean I wasn't raped? Of course I was raped."

"You are a whore," Culpepper said. "You charge men two dollars for your services, and I'm told that sometimes you let them do it for less than that. Every man who was with you tonight paid the full amount." He pointed to the bowl. "You have fourteen dollars there, minus the seven dollars that I intend to take out for taxes."

"The town council said we don't have to pay the tax anymore," Darci said.

"Is that a fact?"

"You know it is. Why do you think people have been resisting you for the last few days?"

"Right now you are in no condition to resist, are you?"

"I guess not."

"By the way, there is also a two dollar fine for indecent exposure," Culpepper said. "That was what got you arrested and brought here in the first place. That leaves you a total of five dollars."

Culpepper took the money out of the bowl, put nine dollars into his own pocket and gave her the rest.

"You are free to go," he said.

As Darci was leaving the Regulators' office, five men were just arriving on horseback. They dismounted, but all of them saw Darci and took particular notice of her.

Culpepper stepped into the doorway as the men were tying their horses to the hitching rail.

"Hello, Slaughter," he said. "I see you brought some men with you."

"Yeah," Slaughter replied. He looked at the others. "And they're good men too."

"Come on in," Culpepper invited.

The five men followed Culpepper inside, where they saw seven other men standing or sitting around the small room.

"Damn, looks to me like you're puttin' together a small army," Slaughter said.

"I am," Culpepper answered. "We're going to take over this town."

"Yeah, well, I remember the days when me 'n' you rode with the Missouri Raiders. We used to take over towns then too, but we was at war. What do we want to take over this town for?"

"I've got my own reasons," Culpepper said. "But I reckon we can come up with a reason for you."

"Only thing that would interest me would be money," Slaughter said.

"I think we can accommodate that interest," Culpepper said.

At that moment Cole and Spellman came into the office. An obviously angry Flaire was between them.

"Well now, who is this pretty little lady?" Slaughter asked.

"This is Miss Flaire Delaney," Culpepper said. "Hello, Miss Delaney."

"I demand to know the meaning of this!" Flaire said. "Why have I been arrested?"

"Why, for not paying your taxes, of course," Culpepper said.

"That's not a law anymore," Flaire said. "I don't have to pay them anymore."

"Well, we'll just see about that," Culpepper said.

"Want me to put her in one of the cells, Colonel?" Spellman asked.

Culpepper shook his head. "No, those cells are pretty nasty. Just put her in that chair over there."

"What if she tries to get away?"

"Handcuff her to the chair."

"Handcuff me?" Flaire replied in anger. "You are going to put me in irons?"

"That's what happens when people break the law," Culpepper said.

"But I haven't broken any law," Flaire protested.

"You've broken my law," Culpepper replied.

Still protesting verbally, though offering no physical resistance, Flaire was handcuffed to one of the chairs.

"Vox," Culpepper said. "I have a job for you."

Chapter 22

DARCI HAD NOT SEEN THE TWO DEPUTIES BRINGing in Flaire, so when she stepped into the saloon a few minutes later, she knew nothing of Flaire's plight. She stood for a moment just inside the front door, and though she showed no cuts or bruises, she looked disheveled rather than her normal, well-groomed appearance.

"Darci, where have you been?" Paddy asked. Then, seeing the way she looked, he asked, "Is something wrong? Are you all right?"

Darci didn't answer right away. Instead she went straight to the bar, where she poured herself a large drink.

It was a well-known fact that Darci did not drink, so everyone looked on in shock as she struggled with the first swallow.

"What is it, Darci? What has happened?"

"The deputies," Darci said.

"What about the deputies?"

"They . . . they . . . had their way with me." She took another swallow of the whiskey, then wiped her lips with the back of her hand before she spoke again.

"They paid me," she said. "Every one of them paid me."

She opened up her left hand and put five wadded one dollar bills on the bar. "See?"

"Five dollars? For all of them, they gave you five dollars?" Paddy asked.

"No, they gave me fourteen," Darci said. "But they took out taxes and a fine."

"Where did this happen?" Doc asked.

"Across the street, in a jail cell," Darci said. Though she had been in control of herself when she came into the saloon, she was crying now, and the tears slid down her cheeks as she continued. "They took me there, they tied me on the bed, and they . . . they . . ." She couldn't finish the sentence.

"Did Culpepper—" Doc started to ask, but Hawke interrupted Doc's question.

"No, he didn't. He couldn't," he said.

"The hell he couldn't," Doc said. "I know you and him go back a long ways, Hawke. But that man is pure evil."

"That's not the point, he couldn't have been one of the ones who had his way with Darci."

Darci looked at Hawke is surprise. "You . . . you know about him?"

"I know," Hawke replied.

"What the Sam Hill are you two talking about?" Doc asked.

Before either of them could answer, Vox came into the saloon. This time, Vox already had his gun drawn.

"You have some nerve coming in here now," Paddy said angrily. "Who do you think you are, taking this poor girl down there and . . . raping her?" he asked.

"We didn't do nothin' to that whore that don't happen to her ever' night," Vox said.

"What are you doing in here now?" Paddy asked. "And why are you holding a gun?"

Vox held up his gun. "I have my gun out because the last

two times I was in here I got tricked. First, this fancy-pants piano player took my pistol when I wasn't looking, then you throwed down on me with a shotgun. Well, I don't aim to be tricked again."

"What do you want, Vox?" Cyrus Green asked.

"It ain't what I want, it's what the colonel wants. He wants the town to round up two thousand dollars and deliver it to him by the end of the day."

"You are out of your mind," Paddy said. "After the way you've been bleeding this town, I doubt there is two thousand dollars among us. How are we supposed to come up with that kind of money?"

"Oh, the colonel don't much care how you come up with it. Just as long as you come up with it," Vox said.

"That's impossible. You can't get blood out of a turnip," Doc said.

Vox chuckled. "Funny you should mention that. Blood, I mean. You're right, you can't get blood out of a turnip, but you can sure get it out of a pretty girl."

"A pretty girl? What are you talking about?" Paddy asked. He glanced toward Darci.

"No, not her," Vox said. "She ain't the only pretty woman in town." He looked directly at Hawke. "Just so's you know, piano player. We're holding your friend Flaire Delaney until all the tax money is paid."

Hawke didn't say a word.

"Now, what message do I take back to Colonel Culpepper?" Vox asked. "Do I tell him you're going to pay? Or do I tell him to start cuttin' up on the woman?"

"You can tell him to go to hell," Paddy said angrily. "We ain't givin' him one red cent."

"That's easy enough for you to say, O'Neil," Vox said. "The colonel's not holding your girl." He looked at Hawke. "It's your girl he's holdin'. So, maybe you're the one I should be askin'. What message do you want me to take back to the colonel?"

"It doesn't matter," Hawke said.

"What do you mean, it doesn't matter?"

"You aren't going back," Hawke said.

"Now just why in the hell won't I be going back?"

"You aren't going back, because I'm going to kill you," Hawke said. The words were flat, cold, and expressionless.

Vox laughed. "Why, you dumb son of a bitch! I'm holding the gun on you and you say you are going to kill me? Mister, you're—"

Suddenly, and as quick as thought, Hawke's gun was in his hand. Shocked by the speed with which it happened, Vox stopped in mid-sentence and his thumb started to come back on the hammer.

Vox was too slow. Before he could react, Hawke's gun was already roaring. Vox went down with a hole in his neck, his carotid artery severed and spewing blood like a waterfall.

Hawke opened the cylinder of his pistol and pushed out the empty cartridge, then replaced it with a new one.

Culpepper looked up when he heard the gunshot.

"Sounds like Vox had to do a little persuading," Hooper said.

"Maybe," Culpepper said.

"Maybe? What do you mean, maybe?"

"It could be that Vox is dead."

"It can't be," Hooper said. "I was lookin' through the front window when he went inside. Vox already had his pistol out."

"This is Vox we are talking about, remember?" Culpepper said. "He has an amazing capacity to make mistakes."

"You know what I think?" Flaire said. "I think Mason

Hawke killed Vox. And I think he'll be coming after you now. All of you."

"I hope he does, Miss Delaney," Culpepper said. "Then you can watch him die, the way you watched your family die."

"What?" Flaire gasped. "What do you mean by that?"

"I think you can figure it out," Culpepper said. "I know you were only sixteen at the time, but what has amazed me is that, in all this time, you have never made the connection."

"The man sitting on the horse, the one who just watched. That was you?"

"Yes," Culpepper said.

Back in the Golden Calf, everyone was still in shock.

"How did you do that?" Paddy asked.

"How did I do what?" Hawke replied.

"You beat Vox in a gunfight while he was holding his gun on you! That is the damnedest thing I've ever seen! How did you do that?"

"It's a matter of reaction time. While I was drawing and firing, Vox was thinking about firing back. Translating your thought into action is the longest part of any draw. That gave me the advantage. I didn't beat him fair and square. I executed him."

"What now?" Doc Urban asked.

"Do you want your town back?" Hawke asked.

"Yes."

"Then you're going to have to take it back."

"Hawke," Darci said. "There are more of them."

"What do you mean, there are more of them?"

"As I was leaving the Regulators' office, five more men arrived."

"Damn!" Paddy said. "That gives Culpepper a small army."

"Then we'll put together our own army," Hawke said. "And like any army worth its salt, we have artillery."

"Artillery?" Cyrus said.

"You know what they say about artillery, don't you?" Hawke asked. He smiled. "Artillery lends dignity to what would otherwise be an uncouth brawl."

"Where are we going to get artillery?" Paddy asked.

"You let me worry about that. Paddy, get Baldwin, Poindexter, Castleberry, and anyone else you can round up, and bring them here."

"All right," Paddy said.

"What about us?" Cyrus asked, indicating Darci, himself, and Doc.

"Do you have a gun?" Hawke asked.

"Yes," Cyrus said. "Uh, no. I had one, but it got burned up in the fire."

"Here," Paddy said, taking his shotgun from under the bar and handing it to Cyrus. "You can use this."

"Thanks. This will be better than a pistol, anyway. I can't hit a bull in the ass with a pistol."

"Doc, when the shooting starts, we may need your services, so be ready."

"Sure thing. I'll go get my bag," Doc Urban said.

Hawke shook his head. "No, that's not a very good idea. Your office is right next door to the Regulators' office."

"How am I going to doctor without my bag?"

"You'll just have to do the best you can," Hawke said. "We'll meet back here in five minutes."

Leaving through the back door of the Golden Calf, Hawke headed east down the alley until he reached the blacksmith shop.

"Ken! Ken, are you in here?" he called.

"Yes, I'm here," Ken said.

"We're taking the town back."

"Good!" Ken said. "What do you want me to do?"

"Get your bow and several sticks of dynamite, then come with me," Hawke said.

Chapter 23

CULPEPPER WALKED TO THE FRONT DOOR OF THE
office and looked outside. The saloon was directly across the
street from him, but he didn't see anyone there. There was
nobody in front of the hotel either. In fact, there was nothing
moving . . . not one wagon, horse, or pedestrian.

"Something's wrong," he said.

"What's wrong?" Bates asked.

"I don't know," Culpepper answered. He shook his head
and stroked his chin as he stared up and down the street.

"This isn't Sunday, is it? Or some holiday?" he asked.

"No. It's just Thursday," Bates said. "Why, what is it?
What do you see?"

"I don't see anything."

"Then what's got you spooked?"

"The fact that I see nothing has got me spooked," Culpepper said. He continued to stare through the window, then saw
someone across the street, moving around on the roof of the
saloon.

"What the hell?" he said.

"What is it?" Slaughter asked.

"I thought I saw something, that's all."

Slaughter chuckled. "You ain't makin' a whole hell of a

lot of sense, Culpepper. First you was spooked because you wasn't seein' anything, and now you're spooked because you did see somethin'."

Culpepper stayed at the front door for a long moment, looking outside. Then he saw someone moving again, and this time he got a very good look at him. The man on the roof was Baldwin, and he was carrying a rifle. Suddenly it all came together and Culpepper knew exactly what was going on.

"Son of a bitch!" he said aloud. "Get ready, boys!" he shouted. "We're about to be attacked!"

"What are you talking about, attack?" Slaughter asked. "Who's attacking us? Indians?" He laughed.

"No, the town is," Culpepper said. "Hell, half the damn town is crawlin' around out there on roofs and behind the buildings. And they've all got rifles."

Slaughter walked over to the bat-wing doors to look outside. At that precise moment he saw someone with a rifle looking out one of the upstairs hotel rooms.

"Sonofabitch! He's right!" Slaughter yelled. He drew his pistol and shot toward the hotel. His bullet punched a hole in the glass window, but other than that, it did no damage.

"What did you shoot for, you dumb bastard?" Culpepper shouted.

"What are you talking about? I seen someone in the hotel window with a rifle pointed toward us," Slaughter answered.

"As long as they thought they had us in the dark, we had the advantage," Culpepper explained. "Now they know that we know."

"So what? There ain't nobody out there but a bunch of ribbon clerks and storekeeps," Slaughter replied. "Why don't we just go out there and . . . unnh!"

Slaughter's sentence was cut short by a bullet fired from somewhere across the street. It caught him high in the chest and spun him around. He had a surprised expression on his face.

"A ribbon clerk," he said. "Who would've thought?"

"Everybody out!" Culpepper shouted.

"What? What do you mean everybody out?" Hooper asked.

"We can't stay here all bunched up like this!" Culpepper shouted. "Get out! Take cover somewhere else and return fire!"

Cole started toward the front door.

"Not that door, idiot!" Culpepper said. "You'll be shot down the moment you step outside. The back door! Use the back door!"

Nodding, Cole started toward the back door, followed by the others. Within seconds no one was left in the Regulators' office but Culpepper and Flaire.

"Aren't you going to run too?" she asked.

Culpepper shook his head. "No," he said. "I'm staying with you." He smiled at her. "As long as they know you're in this building, they aren't likely to be shooting this way."

"You sent the others out to fight your battle for you?" Flaire asked accusingly.

"Damn right I did. If somebody's goin' to get killed, better them than me."

Baldwin was shot down as soon as he ran out the front door of the saloon. Doc Urban risked his own life to drag him back inside.

"How bad is he?" Darci asked.

"If I can get the bullet out before it starts to fester, he's got a good chance," Doc Urban said.

"Can you do it?"

"I can try," he said. He pointed toward the bar. "Get me a bottle of whiskey."

Darci hurried over to get the whiskey. By the time she got back, Doc had ripped open Baldwin's shirt and was staring at the bullet hole, red and bleeding.

"Here's the whiskey," she said.

"Pour it on the wound."

Hawke and Ken came in through the back door of the saloon. Hawke was carrying a bow and arrow, and Ken was carrying a heavy looking box.

Seeing Baldwin lying on one of the tables, Hawke asked, "How is he?"

"Too early to tell," Doc replied.

"Come on, Ken. Up here," Hawke said.

Ken followed Hawke upstairs, then they went up a second flight of stairs and through a hatch onto the roof. There, they saw Paddy and Cyrus, down behind the false front. Cyrus rose up and fired.

"Do you have them located?"

"Some of 'em, I'm not sure how many, ran into the livery," Cyrus said. "They're shootin' at us from the hay loft."

"The others went into the apothecary and the leather-goods store," Paddy said.

Before leaving the blacksmith shop, Ken had cut several small pieces of wire, and over the next couple of minutes he and Hawke were busy tying dynamite sticks onto arrows.

"What is that?" Cyrus asked.

"This, Mayor, is our artillery," Hawke replied.

When they had several arrows prepared, Hawke and Ken moved to the front of the roof. A bullet whizzed by their heads as they arrived, and looking across the street toward the livery, Hawke saw a little wisp of gun smoke drifting away from the open window up in the hayloft.

Hawke lit a cigar, then nodded at Ken. Ken drew back the bow, Hawke held the cigar to the fuse, and when it started sputtering, Ken released the arrow.

It fell short, landing in the water trough in front of the livery. After a second it went up with a window jarring blast, throwing out splinters and sending up a shower of water.

"Damn, can't you do better than that?" Hawke asked.

"I didn't take into account the extra weight on the arrow," Ken said. "Give me another chance."

Ken fit another arrow into the bow and Hawke lit it. This time the arrow sailed across the street in a high arc, sputtering and streaming behind a little trail of sparks and smoke. It went inside the great, black maw that was the opening to the hayloft of the livery barn. A second later there was a tremendous explosion. The front half of the roof blew off, while boards and splinters flew out from both sides and from the front of the building. It rained straw for the next several seconds.

"You got 'em," Paddy said. "It's Spellman and Cole, I can see 'em, lyin' there."

Ken fired another arrow into the livery, this time into the bottom, and again there was a roaring explosion, followed by a rain of pieces of shattered timber and straw.

From the smoke and dust at the bottom of the livery, two of Slaughter's men ran outside, firing as they emerged. They were cut down in a hail of gunfire from the armed citizens of the town.

Poindexter tried to improve his position by running across the street from the hotel to the leather-goods shop. He was shot down in the middle of the street.

Bullets whizzed and whistled through the town. In the civilian houses on both sides of the street, as the battle raged on around them, terrified citizens huddled under beds or hid behind iron stoves, awaiting the outcome of the fight.

Jarvis, who had taken a position on the roof of the hardware store, was hit and fell over the building's false front, landing on his back in the street below. Hawke took out

Hooper, while a blast from Paddy's shotgun opened up the belly of the last of Slaughter's men, spilling his guts as he died in the dirt.

For the first five minutes the shooting was so brisk that the shots were piled on top of each other, then the shooting eased until they came in twos and threes, then single shots, increasingly separated from each other like the last kernels of corn, popping in a pan.

Finally, all the shooting stilled.

There was a long moment of silence before Paddy called out.

"Looks like we got 'em all!" he said happily.

"Anybody see Culpepper?" Hawke asked.

"Maybe he's still in the Regulators' office," Cyrus suggested.

"I don't know, we weren't getting shot at from there," Paddy said. "I'll bet he was in the livery."

"I'm going to look for Flaire," Hawke said.

"Poindexter's still moving," Cyrus said. "We better get down there to look out for him."

The men hurried downstairs. Doc had just taken the bullet out of Baldwin when they reached the bottom floor.

"Poindexter's outside, hurt," Cyrus said.

Doc Urban followed them outside. He was just leaning over Poindexter when Bates stepped out of the apothecary with a pistol in his hand, which gave him an advantage over everyone else. Doc was unarmed, and Cyrus and Paddy had left their rifle and shotgun behind. Only Hawke was armed, and his pistol was in his holster.

"Well, now," Bates said. "You fellas had yourselves a grand old time, didn't you?"

"Where is Culpepper?" Hawke asked.

"Culpepper? I don't know," Bates said. "As far as I know, that cowardly son of a bitch is still in the office."

"I'm going after him," Hawke said, starting toward the Regulators' office.

"Uh-uh. No, you ain't," Bates said, brandishing his pistol. "Ain't none of you goin' nowhere." He looked up and down the street, now dotted with bodies.

"Damn if this don't look like a battlefield," he said. He shook his head. "None of this had to happen, you know. If you had just paid your taxes like you was supposed to, we'd all still be happy. Instead of dead. Now, who shall I kill first? I know. How about the mayor?"

Bates pulled the hammer back on his pistol and aimed carefully at Cyrus. Cyrus closed his eyes and grimaced but said nothing.

Suddenly, a little plume of smoke zipped down from the roof across the street, and an arrow buried itself deep into Bate's chest. Looking down, Bates saw not only the arrow in his chest, but the sputtering fuse of a stick of dynamite.

"Oh shit," he said.

"Get down!" Hawke shouted, and he, Doc, Cyrus, and Paddy dove for the ground just as the dynamite went off.

The explosion was so close that it caused Hawke's ears to ring and he felt the stinging blast of sand thrown up from the street. Looking up, he saw the grizzly sight of red chunks of what had been Bates.

"Anybody hurt down there?" Ken called from the roof of the saloon.

"I don't know. I'm all right," Doc said.

"Me too," Paddy added.

"Yeah," Cyrus said with a sense of relief. "Yeah, I'm all right."

Hawke got up, then looked up at Ken, who threw a little wave at him. Hawke waved back, then pulling his pistol, started toward the Regulators' office.

"Titus!" Hawke called. "Titus, come on outside. It's all over now, there's nothing left for you."

After a moment the front door opened and Culpepper came outside, holding a gun to Flair's head. Hawke pointed his pistol at Culpepper.

"No, no, no," Culpepper said in a singsong voice. "You don't want to do that, Hawke. Not unless you want the girl killed."

Hawke made no further aggressive action, but neither did he lower his pistol. For a long moment the two men were frozen in position, forming a dangerous tableau.

"Tell the man on the roof to throw his bow down onto the street," Culpepper said.

When his request wasn't complied with, Culpepper cocked his pistol. "Tell him," he said. "Throw down the bow now, or I will kill the girl."

Ken had been listening from up on the roof of the saloon.

"You don't need to do that," Ken called down to him. "Here's my bow." He tossed it over and it sailed down, then bounced a couple of times in the dirt of the street.

"Well, I'm glad to see that one of you, at least, is making sense," Culpepper said.

"It's over with, Titus," Hawke said. "Throw down your gun and surrender."

"Surrender?" Culpepper chuckled, a low, growling, evil-sounding chuckle. "Thanks to the town council, there is no longer any law in this town. So just who am I supposed to surrender to? You? The saloon keeper? The newspaper-man?"

"All of us," Hawke said.

Culpepper shook his head. "No," he said. "No, I don't think so. You won the battle, Hawke, but not the war. I don't intend to surrender."

"It doesn't look to me like you have any choice," Hawke said.

"As long as I have Miss Delaney, here, I have a choice. You folks can have your town back. I just want to get out of here alive. That's all I'm asking." Culpepper's voice became less belligerent and more pleading. "What do you say, Hawke? For old times' sake, just let me go."

"It's too late for that," Hawke said.

"Let me go, Hawke, and I'll let the girl go as soon as I'm out of here."

Hawke shook his head no, then aimed at Titus. "Looks to me like you've got yourself in a bind, Titus."

Culpepper laughed nervously. "Are you blind? I've got my gun pointed right at the lady's head."

"And I've got my gun pointed at you," Hawke said. Now, for the first time, he cocked his own pistol.

"I'm not bluffing, Hawke. I'm going to kill her."

"And I'm going to kill you."

This wasn't going the way Culpepper planned, and he licked his lips nervously. "I mean it, Hawke," he said. "I'm going to kill her!"

"And I'm going to kill you," Hawke said again. "And there is nothing you can do about it, because my gun is pointed at you . . . yours isn't pointed at me."

"You're . . . you're crazy!"

"Whatever you are going to do, Titus, do it," Hawke said calmly. "Kill her if you are going to, but I don't plan to stand out here in the hot sun all day."

Like a rat caught in a trap, Culpepper's eyes darted around the street, going from person to person. "Are you people just going to stand by and watch this?" he asked.

Nobody responded to Culpepper's cry.

Then, with a shout of defiance and resignation, he pushed Flaire away and turned his pistol toward Hawke. Hawke waited until Culpepper brought his gun to bear, waited until the fear left Culpepper's face, waited until Culpepper started to smile.

"I knew you couldn't do it," Culpepper said. "I knew you couldn't kill an old boyhood friend."

The smile turned evil.

"But I can," Hawke said, and he pulled the trigger.

The entry hole in Culpepper's forehead was small, but the hydrostatic action of the fluid in Culpepper's brain blew the back of his head off, and blood, bone detritus, and brain tissue sprayed out behind him as he fell back onto the front porch of what had been his office.

While the town was gathering up the dead, Hawke returned to his room over the saloon and packed his few things into his blanket roll and saddlebags. Then he walked down the alley to the livery, behind the blacksmith shop.

Only Ken Wright was there to tell him good-bye.

"You're leaving?"

"Yes."

"I wish you'd stay. Now that we've got our town back, I believe things are going to get real civilized around here. Wouldn't you like to be a part of it? I'm sure Miss Delaney would like to see you stay."

"I can't stay, Ken. I . . ."

"I know, Mr. Hawke. You got what the Indians call the wanderin' spirit, part wind, part buffalo. I seen that in you, first day you come here."

"You'll tell the others good-bye?"

"Yes, sir, I'll do that," Ken said. He watched as Hawke climbed into his saddle. "Mr. Hawke, if you ever get back this way, stop in and say hello," Ken said.

"I may just do that, Ken," Hawke said. "I may just do that."

Hawke didn't even look back at Salcedo until he was more than a mile away.

There was thunder in the distance and a smell of rain in the air. Hawke pulled out his slicker, turned down the brim of his hat, and settled in for a long ride. Somewhere, on the other side of the next range of hills, just over the horizon, there was another town, another saloon, another piano.